SUFFER
LITTLE CHILDREN

JOHN HARDY

BOOKS BY JOHN HARDY

MALAGA MYSTERIES
TWISTED TALES
ANDALUCÍAN MYSTERIES
MORE ANDALUCÍAN MYSTERIES
EAST SIDE STORIES
6.10 FROM DARLINGTON (SHORT STORY)
THE OTHONA VALEDICTION (3 SHORT STORIES)
DOUBLE JEOPARDY (SHORT STORY)
SEDELLA
THE QUEEN'S AGENT
DEATH IN THE SUN AND OTHER STORIES
DRIVEN BY CONFLICT
SUFFER THE LITTLE CHILDREN

WITH HEIKE VAGEN:
ANDALUSISCHE GESCHICHTEN

WITH ISABEL PÉREZ:
MISTERIOS DE ANDALUCÍA

WITH URSULA A. FEILER:
NOCH MEHR ANDALUSISCHE GESCHICHTEN

WITH DAVID LÓPEZ:
MÁS MISTERIOS ANDALUCES

ABOUT THE AUTHOR

John Hardy was born in 1934 in Marske-by-the-Sea in North Yorkshire, England. He worked for many years as a quantity surveyor, before becoming a lecturer in building construction. Later, he practised as a natural medicine practitioner in Essex and Cumbria, including homoeopathy, acupuncture and massage, specialising in allergies. Later, together his wife Wendy, he ran a wholefood vegetarian guesthouse on Alston Moor in the North Pennines.

For the last 23 years, he has lived in the Axarquía in Spain, a region to the north east of Málaga. He has published a wide range of material over the years, including articles on natural medicine, a book on civil engineering measurement, and various short stories.

Since living in Spain, he has written and published short stories of crime and mystery, the first one being *Andalucían Mysteries* in 2013, followed by *More Andalucían Mysteries*, *Twisted Tales* and *East Side Stories*. The first two of these have also been translated into Spanish and German. *Sedella - the story of a Spanish village*, about the village where he lives, was published in 2016, followed by *The Queen's Agent*, a historical spy novel, in 2017.

Death in the Sun and other stories is the 7th book, published in 2018, and is once more a collection of 18 short stories of crime and mystery. *Driven by Conflict,* the 8th book, is a collection of twenty short stories of people involved in conflicts, ranging from the domestic and parochial through to the international.

All are available as both paperbacks and EBooks.

ACKNOWLEDGEMENTS

First I would again like to thank my friend who lives in the village who has once more designed the cover. A friend who does not want to be named, despite his efforts on my behalf. For this cover he has taken a very old photo of the Ha'penny Bridge in Saltburn, modified it and shown it in a snowstorm to fit in with the story.

For anyone interested in finding out more about Saltburn, where much of the story is set, I can recommend the Facebook site 'Saltburn OneFifty Plus' where you will find lots of pictures and information on the town both in history and today.

Lastly of course I must thank Wendy for her typing, editing and patience.

PREFACE

This is a work of fiction. Although the area in which it is set is real, some of the locations are fictitious and none of the characters have any relationship to any real person living or dead, but are products of my imagination.

There is no St. Bede's grammar school for boys in Redcar, and any resemblance it has to Sir William Turner's grammar school, which used to exist in Coatham, are purely positional and architectural.

Howdale does not exist and those of you who know the area around Westerdale, Ralph's Cross and Farndale will know that I have manipulated and rearranged the lay of the land of that part of the world to fit it in. You have my apologies if this offends your sense of topography.

Saltburn Bridge, or 'The Ha'penny Bridge' as it was known locally, was built in 1868 by John Thomas Wharton of Skelton Castle. It was built to span Skelton Beck and connect the land he owned on Bank Top near Brotton with the new town of Saltburn on the opposite side. He charged half a penny for foot traffic across the bridge and then a graduated scale up to four pence for animals and horse and mule-drawn traffic. His hope was to encourage the sale of the leasehold land he owned at Bank Top for development, and to profit from the prosperity of Saltburn. This development never really took off but the bridge was extensively used to save several miles, as well as a steep hill down and up, on the route from Saltburn to Brotton and Skelton. As a teenager I crossed the bridge many times, sometimes managing to dodge paying the toll.

During the life of the bridge 79 people committed suicide by jumping off into the valley below, this combined with the 3 men killed during its construction brought the death toll to 83.

The end of the bridge came at 9.30 am on Tuesday 17th December 1974. In a series of explosions the bridge was blown up and plunged into the Glen some 150 feet below.

The winter of 1946/7 was noted for its impact on the United Kingdom. I remember it well as I was 12 at the time. It caused severe hardships in economic terms and living conditions, and there were massive disruptions of energy supply for homes, offices and factories. Animal herds froze or starved to death. People suffered from the persistent cold, and many businesses shut down temporarily. Roads and railways were blocked and power lines brought down all over the country. Conditions worsened even more from 21st of January 1947, when the UK experienced blizzards and several cold spells that disrupted the transportation of coal to the power stations, many of which had to be shut down. This brought severe restrictions to power consumption, including reducing domestic electricity to nineteen hours per day and cutting some industrial supplies completely. In addition, radio broadcasts were limited, television services were suspended, some magazines were ordered to stop publishing, and newspapers were reduced in size.

Although the blizzards were spread out over time, the worst one began on the 21st of January and spread nationwide. In the story, it hits the North Yorks area and Teesside in the early hours of the morning, bringing the whole area to a standstill.

PROLOGUE
BERLIN MID FEBRUARY 1945

The man known as El Conde Manuel Ortega was hurrying quickly through the streets of a western suburb in Berlin. As far as possible he was keeping close to the walls of buildings still standing and moving hastily across the gaps left by those destroyed by bombs. He was almost certain that he was not now being followed, having successfully left his two Gestapo tails outside the Officers' Club when he had slipped out by a side door. He was a regular visitor to the club and had many friends there. He had known therefore that going there wouldn't have raised any suspicions in the minds of his followers. They of course, not being army or SS officers, hadn't been able to follow him inside. He should, he thought, have at least an hour or even two before they became suspicious and made any move to find out if he was still inside or not. As he neared his tenement block the sirens started to sound, heralding another air raid. It was only four in the afternoon and, despite the cloud cover, not yet fully dark. Day time raids, he thought, were now becoming more common but this one was fortuitous for him. It would clear the streets of people and make anyone watching his flat more obvious. His suspicion that he was under surveillance had finally become unmistakable to him earlier that afternoon, and the need to run had then been essential.

For four years now he had lived in Berlin and been accepted as a Spanish nobleman sympathetic to the regime, and had made many friends in the higher ranks of the SS as well as the army. All this time he had been sending information back to London. Now, with the Russian army closing in on the city from the east and the British nearing the Rhine, he had come under suspicion and it was time for him to get out.

He approached his building from the rear and slipped inside the back entrance. When he reached his top floor flat, he saw that the two hairs that he had fixed with spittle between the door and the frame that morning were missing. There was probably, he decided, someone inside. It was possible but unlikely that both hairs had fallen or been blown off by a breeze. Occasionally in the past one of his markers had disappeared. But never before had both been missing on his return to the flat. Quietly he inserted his key in the lock and pushed the door open a crack. The hall was empty but he could hear faint sounds coming from the lounge, the door of which was part open. When he had first rented the apartment he had hung up a mirror on the wall opposite the door and he could see a figure looking through his desk clearly in it. He made a slight noise, and the man froze and then silently crossed the room and stood behind the door, taking a long knife out of his pocket. The intruder was unaware that Manuel could see his every move reflected in the mirror.

Manuel raised his foot and kicked the heavy wooden door hard, sending it crashing back on to the man behind it. He quickly went into the room and before the man could recover chopped him hard on the neck, killing him instantly.

It was now time to move fast. First he went to the window overlooking the main road, keeping in the shadow of the curtain. Outside it was quite dark by now but he could see a figure standing in a shop doorway opposite the main entrance, its presence outlined in the light from searchlights, flack and exploding bombs. The streets were otherwise empty as everyone else was in air raid shelters. The man was obviously a guard posted to watch for his return. He must have seen some movement in the window, for he looked up and down the road then raised his arm in a way obviously meant to provide reassurance to the searcher. Manuel gave a quick wave in reply and the guard settled back into his recess. All was well.

Manuel Ortega rolled back a section of carpet and prised up a length of floorboard. From the space between the floor joists he took several small boxes and removed their contents, putting them into a rucksack which was already packed with spare clothes. These cartons had contained two sets of identity documents, a revolver, a large wad of banknotes and his radio and code book. The last box he opened contained a bomb and detonator which he carried to the front door of the flat and fixed up a wire to the door handle, which would trigger the device when the door was opened. Then he took the jacket off the man he had killed and replaced it with one of his own, putting the papers identifying him as Manuel Ortega in the pocket. He forced a pair of his own shoes on to the man's feet, putting the ones he had removed into the rucksack to be got rid of later. He then made sure that the silver crucifix he always wore was on the lapel of the jacket he'd put on the man, and that his own wallet with his Spanish address and a few pictures of his alleged family were also in a pocket.

When all that was done, he dragged the dead man over to the door and placed his face next to the bomb. Then he put on the man's jacket, hat and long raincoat that had been lying on a chair. He now looked like the Gestapo agent from a distance and had his wallet and identity papers to prove it.

Just as he was about to leave the flat by way of a window that opened onto a narrow shared balcony and go into the next apartment which he knew was empty, he realised an error in his stage management. He quickly took off his own watch and swapped it for that of the agent. Reaching the ground floor, he made his way out of the rear door and then walked down the side of the building and stood where he could see the doorway where the watcher was concealed. He only had to wait five minutes before the man came out of hiding and walked to a telephone box a few yards away. Despite the sound of aeroplanes overhead and the explosions of both bombs and anti-aircraft guns, he thought he could hear the phone ringing in his flat, but that might just have been his imagination. He did see the man put the phone back down and then come out and gaze up to the flat. Then he went back into the box again and made another call.

Just seconds later a car swept round the corner, its headlights just thin beams from behind heavily covered headlamps. Three SS soldiers got out and went into a huddle with the Gestapo agent who had been watching the flat. They must have been waiting round the corner, Manuel realised, to get there so quickly. Then a jeep also came round the corner and more SS soldiers joined the small group by the telephone box. They were led by a man Ortega recognised, Oberführer Kurt Vogel. Vogel deployed his men outside the front door of the building and sent others down the side to cover the back entrance. Then he together with a sergeant, two soldiers and the watcher entered the front door.

Time then passed slowly for Ortega, but it could only have been a few minutes later that a huge explosion occurred and the flat window blew outwards with flames coming through the hole. All was confusion for quite a while then a fire engine and an ambulance arrived. They were on the scene very quickly and were obviously already on standby during the air raid. With any luck, Ortega thought, it would be put down to a bomb from one of the planes attacking the city. He turned and hurried off, keeping in the shadows at the side of the road. He would, he decided, go and seek refuge at Olga's.

Olga was a secular German Jewess who Manuel had met soon after his arrival in Berlin. She had until then successfully concealed her true origins from the SS. Then by some misfortune her Jewish identity had become known to the Nazis. By good fortune Manuel had been able to bring about her escape, give her a false identity and find her somewhere to live. Since then he had been able to use her apartment as a place to store some of his possessions, with of course her more than willing cooperation.

He reached her flat without too much difficulty and stayed there for the few remaining weeks of the war, until the British army liberated their part of the city.

PART ONE
CHAPTER 1

It was strange, he thought, coming back here after over nine years. Nine years spent first at Cambridge and then in wartime service. It had been a time of first tranquillity at college, followed by years of high danger during the war. Now he was once again retracing his boyhood steps to St Bede's Grammar School for boys, not as a pupil this time but as a master. As he got nearer to the school he saw that nothing much had changed, except that the wrought iron gates at the entrance were missing, with only the iron hooks from which they had once hung left projecting from the brick pillars. The gates had presumably gone, along with all the other scrap metal, to make spitfires, tanks, shell cases or whatever else the war effort had required. The boundary was not an iron fence but a wall, built of red brick and topped by a stone coping. And this was still as it had been the last time he'd walked alongside it.

He turned through the gap where the gates had been and there it was in front of him, St Bede's Grammar School. A three storey red brick building with tall stone faced windows, a blue slate roof and two irregular turrets, one at each end. Directly in front of him was the cloister around a square of grass that no boy was allowed to walk on. To the right of the cloister the school stretched for probably about twenty to thirty yards, whilst at its left was a building that ran down to the main road parallel to the path he was walking up. This housed the school hall and art room. It was quiet, no boys hurrying to school as there had always been when he was a pupil. This of course was to be expected as the term didn't start for a week yet. He was here to meet Mr Bartlett, the headmaster, get his timetable and visit his classroom. He turned right as he went into the cloister, followed it round to the left and then went into the main door of the school on its right hand side. The headmaster's study was on the top floor, and so he climbed the wide stone staircase quite slowly as he was a few minutes early and knew that Alistair Bartlett had always insisted on keeping to an exact to the minute promptness. Neither early nor late. He also wanted to look down the first floor corridor towards room 4B which was to be his domain.

He arrived outside the familiar door marked 'HEADMASTER' at exactly 10.28 for his 10.30 appointment, so he stood for just over a minute looking out of the window at the school playground below before rapping smartly on the door.

"Enter," came from the room beyond and he went in. "Ah, Sudbury, come in, come in. You had no trouble remembering where my room is? No, no, well come in and take a seat."

"Thank you, Headmaster," Lewis Sudbury replied, sitting on the opposite side of the desk to him.

"Good to see you again, Mr Sudbury," the head continued. He pushed over a thick file of papers. "Here's your teaching schedule, syllabi, book lists etc. You can see that as we discussed at the interview you are to take over all the Spanish lessons from Mr Allen who retired last year, and make up your hours by teaching geography. All as we agreed then. Plus as we also said you may have some German classes as well. Only at year one and two," he added hastily. "I know you said you weren't keen or too proficient at German...."

"I'm not qualified in it, Headmaster," Lewis interrupted. "It wasn't part of my degree."

"No, no, I appreciate that, but you have lived there, haven't you, and we are short of German teachers. The war, you know."

Lewis wondered sardonically if that was because they'd all been killed off or if it was just a rhetorical statement, but said nothing.

"We did discuss the possibility at interview," the headmaster went on. "And it will only be until I can find another full time German teacher. We are rather desperate and I would be indebted to you."

Lewis sighed and shrugged, then nodded. "As you wish then," he said. He could cope easily with first and second year German, he knew. He just didn't want to have anything to do with the language after his wartime experiences.

After about ten minutes during which the headmaster went through Lewis' schedule in some detail and answered his questions, the new master left Bartlett's room and went down to the first floor and into classroom 4B. It was a large room full of desks set out in lines of pairs and capable of seating about thirty six pupils, with a large desk on a raised dais at the front. Behind this desk a blackboard covered about half the wall. Lewis crossed the room and sat behind the desk and surveyed his new fiefdom. Then he opened the drawers of the desk one by one, discovering a box of chalk and a board duster in one of them. All the others were empty except for an empty sherry bottle. Appropriate for a Spanish teacher, he thought, whilst speculating how his predecessor had been able to buy genuine sherry in post-war Britain.

The door to the room opened and a tall scrawny figure in a brown dustcoat came in, paused when he saw Lewis, and then smiled. "You must be the new teacher then," he said, in a strong Teesside accent. "How do, I'm Barry Slingsby, the caretaker who looks after this room, amongst others mind. You can call me Barry." He was over six foot tall, thin and slightly stooped, with a narrow face and long grey unruly hair, probably in his late fifties.

"Hello," Lewis answered. "I'm Lewis Sudbury, the new form master of 4B."

"I know who you are, bonny lad. I remembers you from when you were here as a kid in the sixth form."

Lewis looked at him for a few moments but couldn't bring him to mind. Boys, he thought, paid no attention to caretakers. "Sorry, Barry, can't place you, but pleased to meet you. You can call me Lewis."

"Aye, but mebbe not when the boys are about eh, then you're Mr Sudbury. Gotta keep up appearances, good for discipline an' all, you knows. Now, staff room's not fitted up with milk and tea yet, but if you fancy a cuppa I've got the makings in my cubby hole."

Over the next half hour, Lewis learned more about the school and its masters from the caretaker than he had from the headmaster, but how much he could believe of the tales told by Slingsby was another matter. The man was a born gossip.

He made his way back to his home in Saltburn by bus and started to plan his first week of lessons which was due to start in just six days' time on the following Monday, September the fifteenth.

CHAPTER 2

Just over two months before he started at St Bede's, towards the end of June, Lewis Sudbury was finally demobbed from the army. He had spent several months after the war ended working in Germany, engaged with others in the task of hunting down as many SS officers as they could. During this time he also tried, as best he could, to rid himself of the memories of the events of the last few years. Memories that brought with them nightmares and sleepless nights, which in the end took a hold of his mind, and resulted in his being sent for treatment in a military hospital.

When at last he returned to some sort of normality he was discharged from both the hospital and the forces, and he returned to his home in Saltburn. It was here when he was deciding on his future plans that he saw an advert in the Northern Echo. It was from his old school that was looking for teachers. It had always been his intention to become a teacher, before the war had intervened, so he sent in an application the next day. Three weeks later he got a reply, requesting him to attend an interview. He was informed that because the school was undergoing a total redecoration this would take place in the Park Hotel on Granville Terrace in Redcar at 10 am in a few days' time.

He was met at the hotel by a Mr Willis who said he was the school secretary, and who also told him there were several others being interviewed that morning. He said that it would probably be about an hour before Lewis was called, but not to go away as the panel might change the order or be quicker than he, Mr Willis, expected. He advised Lewis to go into the lounge, where coffee was available, to wait to be called. He said he remembered Lewis as a student at St Bede's, but Lewis himself couldn't recollect the secretary.

As he'd been instructed, Lewis went into the lounge where a waitress brought him a cup of coffee and told him just to ring if he wanted another. There were two more men in the room also with cups beside them, sitting staring vacantly in front of them. Lewis thought they were probably also waiting to be interviewed, and said good morning to them before finding a vacant seat.

He'd not been sitting there long before another man came into the lounge. He was dressed smartly in a black three piece suit and was, like Lewis, wearing a St Bede's old boy's tie. He was about to say something when he closed his mouth and looked closely at Lewis, then smiled and said hesitantly, "Hello, you're Lewis Sudbury, aren't you?"

Looking at him, Lewis saw a small slight man with narrow features and piercing eyes topped with almost white blonde hair. He thought he looked familiar but couldn't place him. The man smiled again still uncertain and said, "Billy. Billy Roberts, everyone used to call me 'titch'."

"Titch Roberts, yes, now I remember you," said Lewis. "You were a year below me, I think. Are you here for a job as well?"

"Oh no. I work here in the Park. I'm the Assistant Manager. I've just come in to see if any of you want anything else whilst you wait." As he spoke, Mr Willis came in and took one of the two men waiting out of the room, leaving another behind as he went.

"Did you get a position?" the other man waiting asked the newcomer.

"No," the man replied, going to a coat peg on the wall and collecting a hat. "No, I wasn't what they were looking for, apparently. Well, good luck," he added as he left the room.

Lewis turned to Billy Roberts again. "You were a boarder, weren't you?"

Roberts grimaced. "Yes, in Blue Doors. But you were a day boy I think. Lucky you."

"Lucky?" queried Lewis. "Why lucky? I only lived in Saltburn so could travel here each day. Where was your home?"

"I lived in Farndale, so I couldn't get in each day, it was too far. So I had to board," Roberts said. "Farndale was where Mr Partridge the English teacher lived originally, before he moved to Redcar. When he first moved there, he stayed in Blue Doors before he got a place of his own. When he was there he became very friendly with Mr McIntyre, the master who's in charge of the place. He knew my parents and recommended St. Bede's to them. As he'd stayed in Blue Doors, and so knew it pretty well, he told my mum I'd be fine living there," Billy said, grimacing again. "He told her he'd make sure Mr McIntyre kept an eye on me for her."

"But why did you say I was lucky?" Lewis persisted.

"I hated boarding. And it wasn't very nice, Blue Doors I mean. I wouldn't let any child of mine stay there."

"So you're in the hotel trade then?" Lewis said, changing the subject.

"Yes, I didn't do well at St Bede's. I left after the fifth form, without a good enough School Certificate to go to university. But I did well in the war in the army catering corps. Then I came here, and now I'm the Assistant Manager. What did you do in the war, Lewis?"

"Oh, I was attached to the War Office. Nothing exciting," he said, not wanting to elaborate.

"So now you're going to teach at the old school," Billy said.

"If I get the post."

"Oh, as an Old Boy, you should have no trouble. But me, I'd not go near the place. I've not got pleasant memories of it at all. Oh well, good luck, if that's what you want. Now, I must get back to my duties if neither of you want anything else."

Sometime later Lewis was called into the interview room by Mr Willis. As they went down the corridor the secretary said to Lewis, "There's three of them on the panel. Mr Gregory Black, the Chairman of the County Council. We come under the County Council now since the recent Education Act so he has to be involved. Then the headmaster of course, Mr Bartlett, you'll remember him I expect." At Lewis' nod he went on, "And lastly, Sir Keith Dyke, one of our prominent governors. He's standing in for Arnold Bright-Wallace, the Chairman of the governors, who can't make it today. Well, here we are my boy. Good luck."

Once he'd sat down, Gregory Black said, "Lewis Sudbury." He looked at the papers in front of him and smiled. "I thought I knew the name. You were a friend of my son, who was in your form at school, I think. You came to our house a couple of times." He had quite a broad Yorkshire accent and Lewis suddenly realised who he was.

"Oh yes," he replied. "You're ...." he was about to say "Piggy Black's father." Just in time he stopped himself from using the boy's nickname. "Er, John's father."

"That's right, lad. I see you have a good war record, though it's not spelled out. Hush-hush I expect, and you speak Spanish and German, I see. Well Alistair here, Mr Bartlett, wants a language teacher, I believe. That's right, isn't it Headmaster?"

"Well, yes," Bartlett answered. "But the post was advertised as a teacher in Geography. That is your degree, isn't it Sudbury? Yes, I thought so. And Spanish too, and you speak German. Well, excellent."

"Yes, but I'm not qualified in German. And I'd prefer not to teach it if at all possible," Lewis told him.

"I see," said the headmaster, who didn't really. "Well, only if necessary then."

"Thank you, Head," Gregory Black said, who was impatient to get on with things. "Have you any questions, Sir Keith?"

"Nothing much, Chairman," said Dyke. "Just this. Are you willing to start in September at the salary advertised?"

"Of course," said Lewis, thinking why else would I be here? But not saying it out loud.

"Good, good. Well, that's settled I think," said Black. He looked across at Mr Willis who'd been taking notes. "You'll write a formal offer, Willis. That's it then. It was good to see you again, Lewis."

Taking this as the end of the interview, Lewis got up and left the room. Waiting outside was a large florid man who Lewis thought he recognised. As he passed him, the man said, "Is the meeting over? I'm waiting for Sir Keith Dyke."

"I think it's nearly over," Lewis told him. "I was the last to be interviewed, I think."

"Excellent," the man said. "Let's hope they hurry up."

As he went out of the hotel, Lewis remembered who the man was. It was Mr Fenn-Williams, who had been a science teacher at St Bede's when he was a pupil. If he was still there, he thought, then we'll be fellow teachers and not teacher and schoolboy as we once were. He remembered he'd not liked the man, and his attitude today showed that he hadn't changed much, if at all, over the years.

CHAPTER 3

The boy went to bed in his dormitory as usual that evening. His bed was the end one, next to the door, in Nightingale dormitory. As the boys in Nightingale were all fourth formers, they were in bed by nine and lights out was thirty minutes later. Boys in the first three years had already been in their beds for an hour, whilst the sixth formers wouldn't settle down until ten. Usually Miss Waverly, the matron, or Mr McIntyre, the master in charge of Blue Doors, (the building that housed the dormitories), came in at nine thirty to say goodnight and turn the lights off, and then one of them returned again at eleven to see that all the boarders had settled down. Just occasionally, if either of them were not available for any reason, then the assistant matron Tina Davis stood in for them. Tonight it was the matron who came both times.

The boy laid still and silent during all this time struggling to stay awake. Under the bedclothes he kept shining a torch on to his watch, counting off the hours. Twelve o'clock came and then one. He heard the nearby church strike its single chime and then carefully slipped out of bed. Putting on his dressing gown, he went silently out of the dorm and along the corridor to the toilets. All this was so far allowable and within the rules. When he had left his bed he had carefully put his spare pillow under the covers to simulate his body shape, which if not quite against the rules was certainly unusual.

What happened next was very definitely illicit. He took off his dressing gown revealing that he was fully dressed, having gone to bed without changing into his pyjamas. He then retrieved a rucksack from behind a cistern which was full of spare clothes, a bottle of water and some food that he had hoarded over the last few days.

Leaving the toilets, he went silently along the corridor and down the back stairs which led to the kitchens and staff rooms. This staircase was out of bounds to the boys, who used the main one at the front of the house. However he had reconnoitred them a few nights earlier, so knew where he was going. Near the bottom of the stairs was an outside door secured by two bolts and a solid old fashioned lock, the key of which was kept on a hook nearby. He knew where it was from his earlier visit. The door was to keep people out of Blue Doors not stop them leaving. Carefully and quietly, the boy fitted and turned the key and slid back the bolts, having oiled them first. On his previous visit he had made a mental note to bring a small tin of oil with him, so they would move silently and easily.

He stood for a while listening before, satisfied that no one had heard him, he opened the door and left the building closing it behind him. Then he put the key in the lock and relocked the door from the outside, and hid the key under a dustbin nearby. Going down the side of the house he reached the main road and turned to walk away, using his torch to see where he was going where there were no streetlights. Twice he had to conceal himself to avoid people still moving in the early hours, one of them a policeman on his rounds.

It was a cold windy night with clouds scudding across the sky, but fortunately it wasn't raining. It took him all night to leave Redcar behind and walk all the way via Guisborough to reach Lockwood Beck reservoir on the edge of the moors. Here he left the road and climbed the dry stone wall that surrounded the lake and went into the wood that was between the wall and the water. Once hidden from view, he had a spartan breakfast of bread and cheese washed down with water, and then settled down to sleep. He couldn't go on in daylight, and in any case he was tired after a night without sleep and his long walk. Despite the cold November day, with extra clothes on and in the shelter of the trees he was reasonably comfortable and he fell into a deep sleep.

In mid afternoon he woke up cold, stiff and hungry. Once more he ate bread and cheese washed down with water, and then jumped up and down to warm up and loosen his muscles. He was about half way on his journey and eager to get on, but knew he couldn't start walking until after dark. He hoped his sister would have some food with her when he met up with her in the morning.

CHAPTER 4

Thursday the 27th of November started just like any other for Lewis Sudbury. He got up at his usual time of seven and had his normal breakfast of porridge and toast. In 1947 Britain bacon was on ration and very scarce. So he only ate it at weekends and even then only if he was lucky enough to be able to buy some. He usually managed to be able to get half a dozen eggs a week but that morning he was out of them, which meant that it was only toast with a smear of butter on it for breakfast. He hated it when his butter ration ran out and he had to use margarine, it was a vivid yellow colour and hard. Some people said it was made from whale blubber. Whatever it was made from he didn't like the taste and it also reminded him of his years spent in Germany. So it was only a smear of butter that he put on his toast that and every other morning, to ensure that his ration lasted the week. After breakfast, he walked the short distance from his house in Albion terrace along Glenside to the stop in Station Street and caught the 8.20 bus. Station Street was both the bus and train terminus. It was quite convenient living in Saltburn as the United Bus Company ran a service from there regularly. The number 73 ran half hourly to Stockton which went through Redcar.

The bus he caught got to the clock tower in Redcar at twenty to nine. It was not far from there to St Bede's which he reached by a quarter to nine. After assembly he went into his classroom and then, when the boys were quiet, started to read the register. So far the morning hadn't varied from any of the ones of the previous five weeks that he had been at the school. It had become a familiar and settled routine.

It was then, though he didn't know it at the time, that his newly settled life started to become uncertain. It began at registration.

"Abbott."

"Here."

"Atkinson."

"Present, sir."

"Chapman."

"Here, sir."

And so on down to "Dyke." Silence. "Dyke. Robert Dyke."

"He's not here, sir." This from Simon Fletcher, followed by a chorus of others.

"Oh. Is he ill?" Lewis asked.

He knew that Dyke was a boarder in Blue Doors and wondered why the matron or Albert McIntyre, the master in charge, hadn't sent him a note.

"No, sir, haven't you heard?" Peter Lofthouse who was also a boarder called out. "He disappeared last night, sir." A chorus from the other boys confirmed this.

Lewis decided not to follow this up but to get on with the day's lessons. He was due in 1C for a geography lesson in a few minutes, and knew that Len Archer would shortly be arriving to take 4B for Latin.

"Settle down now. Mr Archer will be here in a minute. I'll see you all this afternoon for Spanish. I hope you've all done your homework." It was an arrangement that wouldn't be kept.

He had hardly been in with 1C for more than a few minutes when there was a knock on the classroom door and the headmaster entered. All the boys stood up, as they knew they had to when the head came into the room, to be waved back down by him.

"Sit down, sit down. I need to talk to Mr Sudbury. Get on with some reading or something or just sit quiet." He turned to Lewis. "Give them some work to be going on with; I need you to come to my office at once. I'll arrange for someone with a free period to sit with your class."

When they went into the headmaster's room, Lewis found it full of people. As well as Albert McIntyre and Miss Waverly from Blue Doors, and Willoughby Danbury the deputy head, there were two strangers there as well. The head went behind his desk and sat down. Everyone else but Miss Waverly was standing, she was sitting in one of the chairs for visitors but nobody else it appeared wanted to sit on the second empty one.

"This is Lewis Sudbury, the boy's form master," the head said, presumably for the benefit of the two strangers. "Lewis, this is Detective Inspector Fenwick and, er, Sergeant Vole?" he said hesitantly.

"Voyle, sir," said the elder of the two men, a heavy built tall man with iron grey hair. "Jack Voyle."

"Yes, yes, Voyle," said Bartlett, irritably. The head was an impatient man, often testy and prone to repeat words, especially at the start of sentences. Lewis had often wondered if this was a long standing habit or if it was nervousness brought on by insecurity. "The inspector wants to talk to you about Dyke. Mr McIntyre doesn't seem to know him well at all. You as his form teacher should be better informed."

This statement brought a response from Albert McIntyre that was cut short by the headmaster. "Yes, yes, McIntyre, no doubt you can't be expected to know all your boarders intimately." He turned to Lewis once more. "Er, the boy Dyke as you will know is the son of one of our governors. It is unfortunate and inconsiderate to say the least for him to run

27

off. I want you to talk to the inspector, Sudbury, and then go with him to see the family. Assure them that we are doing our very best to find him, and also try to discover what it's all about. Don't worry, I'll see all your classes are covered for the rest of the day. But it's inconvenient, disruptive, to say the least. Right, let's all get on with our duties, we've wasted too much time on this already this morning. Keep me informed, Lewis, if you would please."

The meeting broke up and Lewis took the two policemen down to the staffroom.

"Tea? Biscuits?" Lewis asked them as soon as they were seated. When they were all supplied with the refreshments, the inspector outlined what he knew of the boy's disappearance. Then he questioned the master about the boy. DI Fenwick was younger, shorter than his sergeant and not as thickset. He had a slim athletic body with a mop of rust coloured hair and an oval sunburned face. He spoke with a faint hint of a Birmingham or West Midlands accent. He told Lewis that the boy had apparently left Blue Doors by a rear door sometime during the night, locking it behind him and putting the key under a dustbin. Since then nothing had been seen or heard of him.

For his part Lewis described Robert Dyke as being a bright hardworking pupil who was quiet and not a good mixer. He was shy and almost withdrawn, Lewis told them, and didn't appear to have any close friends. He was good at sports and an outdoor type, and spent a lot of time when he went home walking on the moors. Or at least that was what the boy had told him. He described him as being tall for his age, fair haired and slim.

"Much as everyone else has said," agreed Fenwick. "His home is in Howdale, a small valley up past Castleton on the moors apparently. It's a sort of offshoot off Westerdale, I think."

Just then Mr Willis, the school secretary, came in. "Inspector," he said to the policeman. "Here's a picture of young Dyke. As you will appreciate we haven't many individual photographs of the boys, not with over 650 in the school. Only the annual ones of all the school together and he's only a face amongst all the rest of them on that. But this one was taken last year when he won the junior school marathon."

He handed over a photo showing a young boy in running gear to DI Fenwick who thanked him. "We'll get it copied and given to all our men who are searching for him," he told the school secretary.

Shortly after that Lewis and the two policemen left the school to go to Howdale.

CHAPTER 5

Inspector Thomas Fenwick had just been finishing his last cup of coffee when his phone had rung that morning. It was just after seven thirty and he was reading the paper prior to leaving for work. It was the desk sergeant on the phone.

"Tom, there's a lad gone missing from St Bede's, one of the boarders. Seems he took off sometime in the night from that place they board at, you know, Blue Doors it's called. Super wants you to go straight there as soon as you can."

Tom Fenwick grunted then said, "Ok, Dave, I'm on my way, send DS Voyle to meet me there, and a couple of PCs."

"Two of 'em are already there, Tom, they responded to the call at about six thirty. I'll let Jack Voyle know right off."

It only took Tom ten minutes to walk to Blue Doors, he had decided against going to the police station first and getting a car. It would be quicker and easier just to walk there. He got to Blue Doors well before his sergeant, who lived much further away and who came on his bike.

When he got to the house he found both the staff and the boys in a state of turmoil. The only person who appeared calm and was trying to bring order to the rest was the matron. She explained what they knew of the disappearance of the boy. Then, when the last of the boys had left for the school which was several hundred yards away, she and Mr McIntyre, the master in charge of Blue Doors, went with the two policemen to walk to St Bede's. Once there they went to see the headmaster, who called several other teachers to join them in his study.

Inspector Fenwick had only been in his present job for about a year, having been brought in to help revitalise the local CID at the end of the war. Most of the younger men in the police in 1939 had joined the armed forces, just as he had himself. At the outbreak of the war he had been a young constable of nineteen in Keighley. In 1940 he had volunteered and joined the army. By the end of hostilities he had been a major in the Special Investigation Branch of the Military Police. Then, on his demob, he had become a detective inspector. During the war many of the older men had stayed in the police force well past their normal retirement age to keep it viable. Then, after the war, they had all left the force and a new wave of young recruits together with some returning soldiers had taken their place. The CID was now made up of these, together with some of the older men who had served in the police force throughout the war but who hadn't yet reached retirement age. His sergeant, Jack Voyle, was one of these. The trouble with Voyle and some of the others was that during the war, serving under a regime of National Emergency, their powers had been almost unlimited. Now that the war was over, and these emergency powers revoked, they found it hard to readjust to a more normal situation.

Now, on the way to Howdale in the large Wolsey driven by a PC, the inspector questioned Lewis as to what he knew of Sir Keith Dyke, the father of the missing boy.

Lewis thought for a few minutes before answering. "Well, he's a governor of St Bede's and a magistrate and a County Councillor." This brought a snort of derision from the sergeant. Ignoring him, Lewis continued. "He's chairman of a shipping firm in Middlesbrough and I think a patron of several local charities."

"Have you met him?" the inspector asked.

"Once. He was on the panel that interviewed me for this job. He was on it along with the headmaster and the Chairman of the County Council, another man I knew. Or rather someone I had met a couple of times briefly when I was a kid. I was a friend of his son. At least, we were friends at school, but as I lived in Saltburn and him in Redcar, we didn't mix much out of school."

They travelled on in silence for quite a while. The car went through Skelton then Lingdale, before heading up past Lockwood Beck reservoir and out on to the moors. Several times it had to slow down to allow sheep who were grazing the unfenced moorland to cross the road in front of the car. The day was turning windy with cloud building up, and by the time they reached Castleton it was spitting with rain.

"Bloody kid will catch his death out there in this," Voyle said unsympathetically.

"Then we must do all we can to find him, Sergeant," Fenwick snapped, getting a grudging "Sir," in response.

They reached How End House, which as its name suggested was at the end of Howdale, by way of a narrow gated gravel track. The house was a large square stone built one, with thick stone tiles on the roof. It was symmetrical in nature with two square windows either side of the front door. Immediately above the windows and door were five more on the first floor. It had probably been built at the turn of the last century, somewhere about 1800 Lewis thought. Just a bit further up the track there were three much smaller houses, originally farm workers' cottages but now modernised and privately owned. As the car approached they could see several barns and sheds at the rear.

Sir Keith, a slightly corpulent man of about fifty with a balding head, showed them into the house. "Come in here, gentlemen," he said, ushering them into the first door on the left of the small entrance lobby where his wife was waiting. Unlike her suave confident husband, she was thin and a bit scraggy with long black hair and was clearly anxious.

To Sir Keith's impatient, "Well, man, what can you tell me?" the inspector told him all that they knew of his boy's escape from Blue Doors. Then he explained what the police were doing in their search for him. Lewis then said to Sir Keith that he was there to liaise between the school and him and his wife. All this was interrupted several times by Angela Dyke wringing her hands and saying, "Oh dear."

"Shut up, woman," Sir Keith told his wife brusquely after each interruption.

"Is that all?" Sir Keith said at the end. "Have you no news at all? I expected you'd have had some sightings of him or ideas as to where he's gone."

"We're doing all we can, sir," said the inspector, calmly stopping an angry response from his sergeant with a hard stare. "We take missing youngsters very seriously. You yourself can offer no explanation as to why he has run away or where he might have gone?" Then, when the baronet answered with an angry, "No," turned to his wife and said, "And you, Mrs Dyke, can you think of any reason for your son to go off like this?"

"Oh no," she said in a weak voice, giving her husband a despairing look.

"Lady," snapped Sir Keith.

"Beg pardon, sir?" asked the inspector, frowning.

"Lady, I said, not Mrs Dyke, Lady Dyke."

In the silence that followed, Lewis wondered what manner of man, with his son missing, could worry about such niceties.

"Quite, sir," said the inspector dryly at last. "Just so, Lady Dyke." And with that the three visitors left to drive back to St Bede's.

Lewis Sudbury wondered if it had been worth missing a day's teaching, just to prove the school was taking their prominent governor's concerns seriously.

CHAPTER 6

Shortly after the boy had woken up and finished his sparse meal, it started to spit with rain and the wind became stronger. At first, in the shelter of the belt of trees, neither of these things affected him too much. He pulled his blue school mac tightly around him and hoped that his sister Kitty would remember to bring his anorak with her in the morning. As the afternoon wore on he became colder and damper, but knew he couldn't move until it was fully dark. By five with the cloud down the November evening was growing quite gloomy, but there were still too many cars about and he knew he must wait a few more hours before setting out again.

It was nine when he finally ventured forth and he was cold, wet, hungry and low in spirits. He came out of the trees and made his way back to the road and turned to walk uphill. At the top where the road reached the ridge between two valleys it turned 90^0 to go to the left. At the side of the road here he knew there was a small spring that gurgled up through the ground. Here he drunk some of the water and then filled his bottle. The water tasted strongly of iron and peat and was icy cold. Refreshed, he started to walk along the road which kept to the ridge before descending into the valley on the right. At the bottom of the hill was a sign telling him he'd reached Castleton.

It was gone midnight when he carefully passed the railway station, the Eskdale Inn and the cricket ground, before going over the bridge that spanned the river Esk. He now had to make a decision as to whether to turn right and go along the valley bottom to Westerdale, or carry on up the hill and walk though Castleton village itself. In the end he decided to take the lower route and so avoid the village. It was late but there could still be people about and he was known here. In the early hours he

34

went unnoticed through the small village of Westerdale, and then once more walked uphill to the turn off to Howdale. At this point he went behind a dry stone wall and settled down to wait.

Kitty Dyke had been up early that morning, much to the surprise of her mother who usually had to almost pull her out of bed. She had come down today however before her mother had even called up to tell her the time. Then, to give her mother another surprise, she ate a huge breakfast. So large in fact that her mother wondered where she had put it all, as she said to her daughter who usually hardly ate anything in the mornings. Kitty could have told her that she had put much of it into a paper bag she was concealing under the table. But she didn't.

On most mornings of the week, when he was at home and not staying at his flat in Middlesbrough, Sir Keith, Kitty's father, drove her to school on his way to work. Where he got his petrol coupons to use his car so much often puzzled Angela, his wife, but his acquiring them on the black market never entered her head. She was in this, as in many other ways, naive, an innocent abroad. He stayed over in town when he was very busy at work, or at least that was what he told Angela. This could sometimes be as many as two or three times a week. She really didn't mind how often he stayed away overnight as their relationship was to say the least fraught, as it had been for many years now.

On Thursday mornings however, if Sir Keith was at home, he always left very early, far too early to take his daughter to school. He had several calls to make on his way into the office and so had to leave Howdale before 8 o'clock. So on the days he was away, and always on Thursdays, Kitty walked the mile or so into Westerdale to go on the bus with all the other children from the village. This was why she had arranged with her brother to meet him at the end of the lane on a Thursday.

To her mother's further surprise, Kitty was not only up early but she had her school bag already packed, ready to leave. It was only much later in the day that Angela discovered all her daughter's school books hidden under the bed, and much later again saw that a considerable quantity of her daughter's clothes were missing as well as some of Robert's.

After her mother had waved her off, Kitty waited until she had gone back indoors before going quickly to one of the old farm barns now used as a garden store and collected a carrier bag she had left there the previous day. A carrier bag full of food she had taken from the kitchen. This theft was also not discovered by her mother until much later that day.

When Kitty reached the main road her elder brother came out from behind a dry stone wall and joined her.

"Wotcha, Kit," Robert said. "You got everything?"

"Yes Bob, food, clothes, all you asked for. Are we going away as you said?" Kitty asked, a bit hesitantly.

Robert smiled grimly. "Yes. That is, if we are to keep us both safe. Come on, we've a long journey ahead of us and the first bit is on foot. How much money have you got?"

"Five pounds, four and six," his sister said. "All the money that was in my piggy bank."

"Good. Well, I've managed to save up quite a bit more than that. So we've got enough for the journey. Have you brought any food? I'm starving."

Soon they were walking along the road, with Robert sipping milk from the pint bottle Kitty had managed to steal from the kitchen and munching happily on a cold sausage and bacon sandwich. Despite rationing, the Dyke family never seemed to be short of meat.

Before they reached the village, they went down a cart track which led to a footpath over the moors to Kildale. They had planned, or rather Robert had, a route to Guisborough that would keep them off main roads. Once there, they could take a bus to Middlesbrough and then the train. With luck and by being careful they wouldn't be spotted or remembered when a search for them was begun.

But with any luck at all, Kitty's disappearance wouldn't be discovered until late afternoon, by which time they would be well on their way.

CHAPTER 7

Some weeks previously on a Sunday in October, a German national, Otto Kohistedt, crossed from Calais to Dover on the ferry. As he came through customs, he was met by a tall well groomed man in a neat three piece blue suit and shiny black shoes.

"Herr Kohistedt? Welcome to England." He had no trouble picking Otto out from the other passengers as he had a more than adequate description as well as a photo of him. The man he was waiting for had been described as five foot eight with greying brown hair, well built and with a scar running down his right cheek. It went on to say that the man always wore a black leather glove on his right hand which was a prosthesis, as was his right leg below the knee. He had been instructed to look after the man well and take him directly to the Home Office in London.

Otto looked at the man suspiciously, he was uneasy at being in England which until two years ago he had regarded as a deadly enemy. "Ja," he said cautiously. "Ja, that is me. And you are?"

"You can call me Jones," said the man. "I am here to see you are safely and quickly taken to London."

"You are in the security service, Ja?"

Mr Jones, if that was his name, looked around to see if anyone was paying them any attention. He had hard piercing eyes that missed nothing as they scanned the passengers rushing past them. When he was satisfied that nobody was taking any notice of them, he looked back at Otto and nodded. "Yes, but it's better if you don't say such things aloud." He had been told it was a straightforward babysitting mission with no danger to it, and that nobody was aware of Otto's arrival in

Dover. Or of who he actually was or why he was coming to England. But in Mr Jones' profession things were seldom what they seemed or as simple as they were said to be. All he knew of the German was that he was a so-called expert on the Soviet spy network in Europe. The Russians, who until now had been allies of Britain, were suddenly their enemies, whilst the Germans had become their allies. Mr Jones sighed and shepherded his new ally to the waiting car, keeping a sharp lookout for any trouble. But it was all quiet with no suspicious characters anywhere. Perhaps it was just a simple job of babysitting, he decided, without lowering his vigilance at all. They drove in silence from the port into central London. Why was the German being brought to England? Mr Jones pondered. He knew, but didn't approve, that many ex-Nazi scientists were being employed by both the British and the Americans, despite them in some cases having been rabid Nazis, who had worked in laboratories in concentration camps doing experiments on prisoners. But what, he wondered, could an ex-SS officer, which he was sure Otto Kohistedt was, offer to secure his freedom from prosecution and leave to come and live in England? It wasn't his business, he decided regretfully. So he delivered Otto to the door at the Home Office where his senior officers were waiting for the former SS man's arrival, and then left to continue with his own duties.

"Come in, Herr Kohistedt," said the man seated behind the desk as Otto entered the room. There were three British Intelligence Officers in the room but the only one who spoke during the short interview was the man behind the desk. "You speak fluent Russian, I believe?"

"Ja," Otto said curtly.

"And you have some knowledge of their security services, the NKGB and CHEKA and their agents working in Germany and perhaps also those here in Britain?"

"Ja." He was clearly a man of few words, the three man panel thought.

"And you are prepared to work with our service in return for immunity from prosecution and the right to live in this country?"

This time Otto allowed himself a small smile before answering again with the one word, "Ja."

"Right," the Chairman continued. "We will assign you to one of our agents who will work with you. We need you to decipher documents in Russian, debrief agents we have apprehended and to help us seek out more Russian agents. You are partly disabled, I believe?"

"Ja." This time the German elaborated. "I have lost a hand and part of my right leg."

"How did that happen?" the man asked, though he already knew the answer.

"In a bombing raid, one of your planes dropped a bomb near to me in Berlin towards the end of the war." That at least was what the German had believed for a long time, before finding out the true cause of the explosion. That had come about by a chance remark he had heard whilst in hospital when one of the nurses on duty had thought he was unconscious. He wasn't going to let these secret service men know that though. Just as they were not going to tell him they knew who he really was.

"Despite this, you are prepared to help us?" the man asked.

"Ja, of course. War is war and these things happen," Otto replied. He was more than willing to help his new employers, he thought to himself, if it allowed him to escape from prosecution and also to live here in England, at least for a time. He had his own reasons for wanting to come to Britain that he wasn't going to reveal to these men at all.

CHAPTER 8

It was déjà vu for DI Fenwick that Friday morning. He was drinking his last cup of coffee after breakfast when the phone rang and the desk sergeant told him of the absconding of a child called Dyke. Not, like yesterday, a boy called Dyke but that same boy's younger sister.

"She apparently left home yesterday morning, sir," the sergeant said. "On her way to school but never got there."

"Yesterday morning?" Tom Fenwick said sharply. "Why the hell am I only being told now?"

"Seems no one realised she was missing at first. Most mornings she didn't usually go on the school bus, only when her father wasn't at home and on Thursdays. He apparently always left home early on Thursdays. So she wasn't missed when she wasn't on the bus. Then her teachers thought she may be ill or something, because of her brother disappearing two days earlier, so it wasn't till tea time that anyone realised."

"So why wasn't I told last night?"

"As I understand it, sir, the family didn't call the local station till midnight last night, and since then the local bobby's been trying to get details and has carried out a search for her in the locality as best he could. Then he phoned it in and the super's just got here. He wants to see you before you go off to Howdale."

"The super's in already, at this time of the morning." It was a statement rather than a question.

"Yes, sir, he's in a right state," the sergeant replied.

"Right, I'm on my way," said Tom, gulping down the last of his coffee. "Get Sergeant Voyle in, will you?"

Sometime later, the inspector and his sergeant were given a briefing by the superintendent who finished by saying, "Now, careful how you handle this. Dyke is a big fish locally, magistrate, county councillor, on the police committee etcetera, etcetera, and I don't want to antagonise him. He is also engaged in some important contracts with the government and is highly regarded in Whitehall, I believe. But find out why the hell he didn't get on to us yesterday evening if you can. His two children go missing in two days, and not a word from him. What's he playing at? Anyway, I want 'em found and I want to know why they both, apparently, went off of their own accord. So kid gloves, but all the stops out, Ok?"

"Leave it to us, sir," Tom said grimly. "Come on, Jack." To which his sergeant just grunted.

When the two policemen reached How End House, they were met by an agitated Angela Dyke and the local policeman. To their astonishment, however, they were told that Sir Keith had gone in to work as normal.

"He's very busy," said Angela, who seemed even more nervous than she had been on their last visit.

"Right, tell me just what you know of what your daughter did yesterday," Tom asked the woman, who as well as being worried and nervous also seemed to be frightened. It was probably only fear for the fate of her two children, Tom thought, but then why had Sir Keith gone off to the office as usual? There was something not quite right here, he thought.

"Well," Lady Dyke began. "Kitty got up very early, she came down before I'd even called her."

"Was that unusual, ma'am?" Tom asked, as she broke off in her reply staring vacantly at a picture on the wall.

"What? What? Oh, yes. I usually have to call her several times and sometimes even go up and almost pull her out of bed. She's...." and she broke off again, fiddling with her wedding ring.

"Go on, ma'am, take your time." And slowly, with much prompting, the story came out.

Kitty had apparently eaten a huge breakfast and set out for school in good time to catch her bus. She had even, Angela said, apparently packed her school bag, ready to go. It wasn't until after she had failed to return home that afternoon that Angela had found out that all her daughter's school books were pushed under her bed, and that quite a lot of her clothes were missing. Angela said she had then discovered that some food was also missing from the larder.

"So it looks as if she'd planned to go off," DS Voyle interrupted brusquely at that point. It was the first time Angela had heard him speak and she looked at him in surprise, her tension seeming to mount.

The local PC then broke in and said that Kitty hadn't caught the school bus nor had she been seen all day at school. Her teachers had thought that she must have been in shock at her brother going missing and thought nothing of it. He also said that he had spent all that evening cycling round the local roads, but had found no trace of her. He hadn't got home until gone midnight, he told the inspector, and had returned to How End House at six that morning to find Lady Dyke up but that her husband had still been in bed. When he found that the girl hadn't returned, he had phoned the police station in Redcar and spoken to his inspector.

Inspector Fenwick spent the rest of the day ringing all the local hospitals and directing the search of the area. All possible places were searched and many people questioned, all to no avail. No trace of Kitty or her brother was to be found anywhere. Later that evening he returned to Redcar, having told Sir Keith after his return home from work that in the morning he intended to comb the local moors, woods and valleys to try and trace the missing youngsters.

"I'm not sure what to make of it, sir," he told the chief superintendent. "They both seem to have planned their disappearances with some thought. I'm sure they both will be somewhere where they can hide up for some time, perhaps quite a way from Howdale. But we can't take any chances; we must assume the worst and comb the area. I've arranged for several dog handlers and about twenty uniformed officers as well as one of my DC's to meet me at How End House in the morning to start a thorough search of the area. We'll start at the house and then spread out over a wider area. Thank God that the rain of the other day has stopped and the weather improved a bit. For October it's not too bad, but if they're outside though they could be in a bad way. Especially the boy, he's been out three nights now."

He got back to his home late that evening and picked up fish and chips on the way. He was tired and worried and in no mood to cook anything for his supper. As he walked through the streets eating his cod and chips he realised just how hungry he was and that he hadn't had anything to eat at all since his early breakfast.

He fell asleep in front of the gas fire with a glass of whisky beside him, and woke up at two in the morning cold and stiff with it still there beside him. The fire was out as the gas meter had run out of money and he'd been asleep so not noticed. He dragged himself upstairs and got into bed, envious of his fellow officers who had wives at home to cook for them and generally keep the house ticking over.

Just a few brief hours later his alarm clock went off, waking him. It was time to start another day. Sighing he got out of bed, it was Saturday and this was supposed to have been his weekend off. Fat chance of that, he thought, as he got dressed.

CHAPTER 9

Saturday morning in Saltburn also started early for Lewis Sudbury. But then they always did for him. He had no school so he used Saturdays to catch up on things like housework, shopping and gardening. He lived in Albion Terrace, in what used to be his parents' house, and which was now his since their deaths. Albion Terrace was a continuation of Glenside, both of which faced the Valley Gardens. It was a three bedroom semi, too large for him really, but he was loath to sell it having been born there and then lived in it up until he went to university at eighteen. This Saturday morning though he decided on a break to his normal routine. He would, he decided, drive up to Howdale to offer his support and that of St Bede's to the Dykes. Or that was what he told himself, whilst in reality the real reason was probably more to do with his feeling that something was amiss there, especially in the reaction of Sir Keith to the disappearance of his son. That and also the apparent nervousness of Sir Keith's wife Angela.

So after breakfast he put on a warm overcoat, blue scarf and a flat cap as it was a cold morning. He went out to the garage and drove off in his car, or rather the car that had, like the house, been his father's. It was a two-seater 1934 Austin Seven Opal. A black square box on wheels, as he always thought of it. It was quite economical on fuel though, and as he didn't use it much he had enough of his meagre allowance of petrol coupons for the trip.

As he drove up into the moors the weather, which had not been too bad for a couple of days, began to worsen and the wind got stronger, and by the time he neared Castleton it was raining. Looking around him at the bleak scenery, he hoped that

Robert Dyke wasn't out there somewhere, cold and wet and probably hungry.

He turned into the narrow road leading to How End House, opening and closing the gate at its entrance. He had to park on the verge some way off from the small group of houses as the space in front of them, which had at one time been the farmyard, was full of people and vehicles. He pulled in behind the last of the others already parked along the edge of the road and walked the last bit of the way. Most of the crowd already there were uniformed policemen. There was a small group in civilian clothes just outside the front door of How End House, amongst who were DI Fenwick, DS Voyle and Lady Angela Dyke. Standing next to Angela was a younger woman that he didn't recognise. There was no sign of Sir Keith at all.

As he got near to the group, the DI turned and said with a smile, "Mr Sudbury. What are you doing here?"

"I might ask the same of you, Inspector," Lewis replied. "I've come to see if there is anything I or St Bede's can do to help Lady Dyke, and her husband as well of course. Where is he, by the way?"

"Well, we're here to start a search of the area for Robert and his sister," answered the DI.

"His sister?" Lewis said, frowning.

"Yes. Kitty. Didn't you know she's gone AWOL too?" and when Lewis shook his head brought him up to date on the developments of the past two days.

"Good God," said Lewis, looking round. "So what, you're going to comb the moors? Do you really think they're out there?"

"No, or at least I hope not. They were both too organised for it just to have been a ...." he paused, thinking. "A spontaneous last minute thing. They had obviously thought things out. But you never know and I can't afford to just dismiss the possibility. If they are out there and I hadn't looked for them, well there'd be hell to pay. So yes, we're going to comb as much of the area as we can. Hill, dale, moor and woodland, without exception."

"So where is Sir Keith?" Lewis asked again.

"Playing bloody golf," broke in Sergeant Voyle angrily.

"Golf?" echoed Lewis in disbelief, getting a yes from the DI who also glared at his sergeant.

"Oh dear," said Angela nervously, in distress. "He values his Saturday morning golf after a long hard week at work." She turned to the younger woman by her side who had snorted at this. "You know he does, Beryl. Oh, it's all too much," and she broke out crying.

To Lewis' raised eyebrows, Tom Fenwick said, "You haven't met Beryl Cooper, have you sir? Beryl, this is Mr Sudbury, he's Robert's form master. Lewis, this is Miss Cooper, Lady Dyke's sister."

Sister? thought Lewis, she only looked in her mid twenties, whilst Angela was he knew forty six, though she looked at least sixty today, due no doubt to her worry and anxiety over the children.

"Half sister, Mr Sudbury," said Beryl, holding out a hand. "Our father, Mr James Cooper, married again when his first wife, Angela's mother, died."

Lewis looked at her, she was nothing like her sister he decided, medium height with as far as he could see dark brown hair and eyes and a slim body, but muffled against the cold and rain in a woolly hat, scarf and raincoat it was hard to be sure.

Beryl, looking at Lewis, saw a man of just over medium height of athletic build and with a pleasant face, with darkish almost black hair and eyes. His eyes were too far apart and his nose a bit too big for him to be described as being handsome, but it was a pleasant face she thought, and kind.

"Right, Sergeant," the inspector said, breaking into her thoughts. "Off you go and get the search underway."

"We need to search that place first," DS Voyle said almost angrily, pointing to one of the small ex-farm labourers' cottages.

"I've told you once, Sergeant," the DI said in a cold voice. "We've no search warrant and no cause to ask for one...."

"Pair of poofters," the sergeant said angrily. "We didn't need no warrant a couple of year ago. But I say they're fairies and most likely to have harmed the kids...."

"Sergeant, listen. It was different in the war, you had emergency powers then, now you need a warrant. And homosexuals, if that is what they are and not cousins as they say they are, are not the same as paedophiles. They are no danger to children. And yes, it may be against the law but you have no evidence that that is what they are. And lastly, we aren't here to hound homosexuals, we are here to look for two vulnerable children. Now, get the men formed up in a line and get them started. You'll go up the hill on that side of the valley, through the wood and up on to the moors. It's about a couple of miles to the top of the ridge along which a small road runs. At least that's what's marked on the map. When you get to it you can regroup, and then go on down the other side to another road in the next valley. I'll get the transport there waiting for you in, say, three hours' time, it's about five miles in all. Don't rush but do a thorough search." As the sergeant made to argue some more, he waved him away angrily. "Get off now, man, as you're ordered."

The two women, Lewis and Tom Fenwick, and the small group from the three cottages, stood and watched as the line of police, two dog handlers amongst them, began to walk up the grassy hillside and then disappear into the belt of trees that covered the side of the valley.

"Come inside and have a warm drink," Beryl said to the two men. She seemed to have taken control of things, her sister Angela being too distraught to cope with the situation.

Once inside in the warm when they had all taken off their outdoor clothes, Lewis saw that he had been right about Beryl. Her hair was a dark chestnut colour and her body was almost boyish with small but firm breasts, and her legs were long and shapely. She was nothing like her elder taller scrawny sister with her straggly grey hair. But then Lady Angela was under a lot of stress, and seemingly almost deserted by a husband who had abandoned her to go and play golf, despite the family crisis.

"Now, Lady Angela," the DI said. "Can you show me the children's bedrooms? I'd like to search them to see if I can find any clues as to where they might have gone."

"Of course, Inspector," Angela replied. She seemed glad to have something positive to do to aid the search for her children.

When they were left alone, Lewis said, "Do you live locally, Miss Cooper?"

"Beryl, please call me Beryl," she answered with a grin. "No, not really, well I suppose not too far away. Redcar. Do you know it or are you new to the area, Mr Sudbury?"

"Lewis. Oh yes, I know Redcar, I was born and bred in Saltburn, and of course I teach there now. I went to school there as well. St Bede's, where I'm now a master, was where I went to school as a boy. Where in Redcar do you live?"

"Oh," she replied. "Somewhere between the clock tower and the pier. And you, where do you live now?"

"Saltburn," Lewis told her. "In Albion Terrace opposite the Valley Gardens, not far from the Ha'penny Bridge."

They chatted together for quite a while before the other two came back downstairs, the DI shaking his head to Lewis' questioning glance. "No, nothing," he said. "Nothing to indicate where they might have gone, that is." Looking at the schoolteacher and Beryl, he thought they looked very friendly after such a brief acquaintance.

Shortly after that, they heard two long whistle blasts come faintly from the wood opposite the house.

"They've found something," the DI said. "Stay here," he said to the two women. "Will you come with me Lewis, please?" He wanted the schoolmaster there in case they'd found Robert Dyke.

"Sure," said Lewis, and the two men put their coats back on and went out together, walked up the slope and entered the wood.

CHAPTER 10

Otto Kohistedt had been working for MI5 now for a few weeks, and was beginning to relax and believe that he was now accepted by the organisation. He had worked hard translating various documents from Russian into English, and had sat in at two interviews of Soviet citizens who Five, as the internal security service liked to call itself, thought may be spies. He believed that not only was he now fully established as a member of the debriefing team, but also that his true identity was not known to them.

He wouldn't have been quite so blasé if he had been party to a meeting going on at that very moment in the office of his head of section. The senior officer had thanked his subordinate for his report on Kohistedt. Then he summed it up. "Well," he said. "You are very happy with his work and believe he is trying his very best on our behalf. That he is not holding anything back."

"Yes sir, as I reported we have had a second Russian speaker beside him all the time without his knowledge, and his translation has been accurate."

"Yes. So now we all agree he can be left unsupervised to carry on this work?" This brought nods from the men gathered round his desk. "And you are absolutely sure he has no knowledge that we know his true identity? Good, well I think we can leave it at that for now, gentlemen. I'm sorry to have brought you all in here on a Saturday morning, those of you not on duty that is. But now we can all get back to our weekend." And the meeting broke up as they all left.

Otto, who was blithely unaware of all of this, was sitting reading the Saturday papers in the flat where he was living near Liverpool Street station. Several of them had reports about two missing children in North Yorkshire, a brother and sister. All the papers had their own take on the story, ranging from them being runaways to their being the victims of kidnapping. Most of them carried pictures of the children and their parents, and some also had a photo of the police officer in charge of the hunt for them. In one paper there was also a photo of their house, with a group of people stood outside. The caption read 'Rural home of Sir Keith Dyke, father to the two abducted children'.

Otto, who for years had only known a state controlled press, was fascinated by the way that the differing papers were apparently allowed to report whatever they wished. What, he wondered, was the truth of it, had the children run away or been kidnapped or killed or what? All the papers, it appeared, had their own view and theories on the matter. This would never have been allowed to happen in the Third Reich, he thought, they would all have been told to report the same story, the one that suited the party. He sighed, knowing it would take quite a time for him to come to terms with his new life.

He was putting the papers in a neat pile on his table when he looked once more at the shot of the house with the group of men outside. One of the men in it looked somewhat familiar. He was wearing a dark brown overcoat and a blue scarf and holding a cap in his hand. What was it about him, he pondered, was it the way he was standing, the shape of his body or his facial features? No, he couldn't place it and of course it couldn't be true. He knew no one in England, except those he worked with and the man he was seeking. He would almost certainly be in or near London and not in a rural part of the north of England. Where was it exactly? Somewhere called Howdale in the North York Moors, he read. Wherever it was, he had never heard of it and had certainly never been there. Shaking his head, he put the paper on to the top of the pile.

CHAPTER 11

Lewis Sudbury and Tom Fenwick set off across the meadow, walking towards the wooded hillside in the direction taken by the policemen just over an hour ago. From time to time, as they went uphill through the trees, they heard a single long whistle blast, blown by a PC to guide their steps.

"Odd, isn't it, that Dyke has gone off playing golf when his two kids are missing," the DI said. "What's that all about, is he just insensitive?"

"It could be he's worried but doesn't know how to show emotion," replied Lewis, thinking of the confident looking man on his interview panel. "Or perhaps he has an idea of where they've gone and so isn't worried. Or maybe he thinks they're capable of being out for a few days, they did take food and clothes with them and presumably some money as well. Or perhaps he just doesn't like children, his own included. Also of course it's possible they may have been kidnapped, and he's received a note warning him not to involve the police. I don't know, you're the policeman, not me."

Tom smiled grimly. "You seem to have more theories than me, Lewis. I'll have to give them all some thought." Just then another whistle blast sounded, much closer to them this time. "That way I think," he added, pointing slightly off to their right. "They can't have found them this close to the house, surely. Well, we'll soon know."

Shortly after that they reached a group of men standing at the side of a small beck that ran through the wood. The water had carved out a gully in the soft peaty earth about four feet across and three feet deep. Where the men stood the stream went down a step in the hillside, and part of the side of the gully had recently fallen away. Sticking out of the newly

56

exposed earth face was an almost skeletal hand, and beside it a boy's black cap with blue stripes around the edge. The hat was soiled and crumpled with the lining torn and hanging loose.

"The dog found this, sir, and dug down a bit," said the dog handler who was standing by the spot.

"We waited until you got here, boss," Sergeant Voyle added. "Before doing anything else or to dig up the rest, like. Didn't want to disturb what may well be a crime scene."

That's a first, Voyle waiting for me, thought Tom. "Right, first things first. Jacobs, you go back down to How End House and tell Mrs Dyke that we've found a body, but that it's not either of her two children. Then phone the station and get them to organise a doctor and ambulance as quick as they can. And I want someone with a camera up here as well, oh and a couple of men with spades."

"Right sir," said the young PC, and set off at a jog back down the hill.

The DI turned to Lewis. "What do you make of the cap then? It's one of St Bede's, isn't it?"

"Yes, it's one of a School House student, that's the house young Bob Dyke's in. But it's not his obviously; it's too old and has probably been buried for a long time by the look of it. He's also in School House, but it must be just a coincidence, surely?"

"How come you know it's a, what did you say, a School House one?" Sergeant Voyle asked.

"Right, see the blue markings on it? That says it's School House. Gregory's House have red ones, Nelson's green and Moore's purple ones. All boarders are in School House, so this boy, or at least this cap, and young Robert Dyke, they all belong to School House."

"Clear as mud," muttered the DS.

Fenwick ignored his sergeant and knelt down to examine the hand protruding from the earth face. "This looks like a boy's or at least a child's hand by its size and has obviously been here for some time." He got up and stretched. "Well, we'll just have to wait for the quack to turn up before we know any more. Right, Sergeant, get the line moving again. I'll stay here and wait for him."

The unhappy Sergeant Voyle, who clearly wanted to stay and wait for the doctor, reluctantly gave the orders and went off with his men to continue combing the area.

It was quiet in the wood when all the police had moved off, with just the sound of the small beck gurgling beside them and some distant birdsong. The November weather which had been variable for days had once more changed, this time for the better, and the sun broke through the thin cloud cover. The two men stood in silence for a while and then Tom said, "So, what exactly did you do in the war, Lewis?" It was the classic question of the time. But one Lewis was not free to answer.

"You were in the Military Police yourself, weren't you?" he temporised.

"Sure, you know all about that. I told you my story on the drive here the other day. But you, what did you do?"

There was a long silence before Lewis spoke. "Me? Oh, I was not in the services as such. More of a back room boy, really. How long do you think the doctor will be?"

Tom recognised an evading move, a sidestepping of the question, when he heard one. He was probably in one of those hush-hush units he thought. One of the funny sods, an intelligence agent of some sort. He smiled slightly and said, "Oh, an hour or so probably. If you can't or won't tell me your part in the war, give me your opinion on Sir Keith."

Lewis thought for a bit then said, "I've only met him once, before the other day that is. He was on the panel at my interview for the job, along with the headmaster and the Chairman of the County Council, Gregory Black, as I told you yesterday. He didn't have much to say for himself and only asked one question as I remember it. Asked if I was married or when I could start at the school, I think, but I may be wrong. It was a long time ago. But I know he's a magistrate and something big in Teesside docks, shipping I think. The head is somewhat in awe of him I reckon, but apart from that, nothing much really."

"Humph. Not much more than I know then," said the DI. "But there's something odd about his attitude to his children."

"Could just be a problem with showing emotion, or a lack of empathy, a rift or something in the family. I don't think his sister-in-law Miss Cooper likes him though, and she's a good judge of character, I'd say."

Tom grinned. "I thought you were getting on well with Beryl. Thick as thieves you were, when Lady Dyke and me got back from looking through the kids' rooms. She's a good looking girl that one."

"Bit more than a girl," said Lewis evenly. "She's all of twenty four or five."

"Twenty four," Tom said, grinning even wider. "I established that when I questioned her before you showed up. She was in the Wrens in the war, lives in Redcar and works in a library, if I'm remembering it right."

"Questioned her? Why?"

"Oh, routine. I have to establish a picture of all friends and family of the Dykes. Nothing more than that. Tell you what, let's have a scout round whilst we're waiting, just to see if we come up with anything. You never know."

Sometime later, their search having drawn a blank, they heard the sounds of people approaching.

The first ones to appear were PC Jacobs and three civilians, the doctor and two ambulance men carrying a stretcher. "The photographer and diggers should be here shortly, sir," Jacobs reported. "I'll just go back to How End and bring them up, see they don't get lost like."

"Thank you, Constable," Tom said. "Afternoon, Silas." This to Dr Silas Messenger, who he knew well.

"Tom," said the doctor. "PC Jacobs told me you're found a body up here. A boy, he says. Let's have a look then." He stooped down and examined the hand protruding from the earth. "Well, he's dead, has been for some years, I'd say. Was buried about three feet down beside the stream, and the water has widened the gully over time and last week's rain must have brought about the collapse of the side of the grave. Not much there you haven't worked out already for yourself, I expect. I can't do much more till your men with spades get here." The doctor was a short dumpy bald headed man, wearing an expensive looking camel haired overcoat. He took off his glasses and wiped the sweat off them with an immaculate white handkerchief then lit up a cigarette. "Quite a pull up here, isn't it, hard to get a body here, I'd say. Even if it's only that of a boy."

"There's a road a short way further up the hill," answered the DI. "No doubt that's the way they brought him."

"Why wasn't I told that? I could have come that way," the doctor complained.

"Ask the station," Tom smiled at him. "They sent you the directions, not me. Anyway, the climb will have done you good."

"They just said How End House in Howdale. Where does this road up there go to anyway?" the doctor asked.

"From Ralph's cross on the top of the moor to Farndale, I think," said the inspector. "That's what it showed on my map anyway."

"Oh well, it would have been quite a long detour to get..." began the doctor, when he was interrupted by the arrival of Jacobs with three uniformed men. "Ah, here come your men. Let's get on with it then."

Careful not to cause any more earth to fall into the gully, the two policemen started to dig, whilst the photographer took a picture of the exposed side and the protruding hand with the cap lying near it, it having been put back in position by the DI. When the body was uncovered, they could see it was that of a partly decomposed naked boy.

"I'd say he was about thirteen or fourteen, something like that, and that his neck's broken and the back of his head stove in. What killed him I won't know till I've got him back to the mortuary," the doctor told them.

In a decomposing heap near the body was a pile of clothes. The inspector gave instructions for the cap and what was left of the clothes to be taken back to the station and the body removed. Then he walked back to How End House with Lewis.

CHAPTER 12

"A boy, a boy, probably from St Bede's, about fourteen or thereabouts you say, found buried up near Sir Keith's house? Are you sure, man?" Alistair Bartlett sounded disbelieving on the other end of the phone.

When he had got back to How End House, the first thing Lewis had done was to borrow the phone to ring the headmaster at his home. The head had been dozing in an armchair after his lunch. Once Mr Bartlett was fully awake, Lewis had told him about the discovery of the body.

"Not much doubt at all, sir," Lewis answered. "And probably he's from School House. A jacket, tie and school cap found near the body were all from School."

"A boarder then, eh, you reckon, like young Dyke?"

"Well maybe, sir, but he could have been a day boy, as you know not all School House boys are boarders." This brought a grunt of agreement from the headmaster. "He's probably been in the ground for three, four years." Lewis went on. "Something like that the doctor thinks anyway at first glance."

"1944 or 45 then," the head mused. "End of the war or thereabouts. Well within my time here. But I don't know of any boy who went missing at that time from School House or any other."

"No, sir," Lewis said, but there must have been by the look of it, he thought.

"Lewis," said the head after a few minutes thought. "Would you come back to St Bede's this afternoon? I'll get Mr Willis, the school secretary, to meet us there to see if we can find out who he might be."

"Yes, Head, I'll do that. But I may be some time. I think DI Fenwick might want me to hang on here for a bit."

"No problem, Lewis. I have to find Mr Willis and spoil his weekend and bring him in to school. That may take some time and if we get there before you, we'll make a start."

Lewis put the phone down and went to find DI Fenwick to tell him what he'd arranged with the headmaster.

"Good," the DI said. "Now, can I ask you a favour too?"

"Ask away."

The DI continued. "As I think I explained to you the other day in the car coming over here, I am a fairly new appointment as are most of my DC's. All the older men who stayed on through the war, past their retirement age, have now left the force. I have a few like DS Voyle who are now nearing retirement age. In total, my section is well below strength and only just able to cope. Of my two sergeants one, a new appointment, is fully occupied with a series of serious break-ins in the area to the west of Redcar where we border the Middlesbrough force. We are co-operating with them on these robberies and so he is fully engaged there. My other sergeant, Voyle, will now have to lead the search for the two missing children as I must concentrate on the murder, with only the help of one DC. What this long preamble is all about is leading up to me asking if you could return here tomorrow with your findings on possible candidates for the murdered boy, and perhaps help me talking to the family."

"Well I would be glad to but ....." Lewis began.

"Don't worry about petrol," the DI cut in. "I know you won't have much, but I can let you have some coupons, courtesy of the police, as you'll be on our business."

Shortly after that, Fenwick left to meet up with his DS and brief him on taking over the hunt for the two children. He was confident that Voyle, despite all his faults, could do this job well. It was straightforward policing and he was good at that.

That done, he intended to go back to Redcar and attend the post mortem which Dr Messenger had promised to do later that day. With the ambulance also gone, Lewis was left alone with the two women, Sir Keith not yet having returned from his game of golf.

"How are you getting home?" he asked Beryl. "I could give you a lift."

"Thanks," she said, "but no thanks; I'm going to stay over with Angela. So if you're coming back here tomorrow, I'll see you then and I might well take you up on your offer then. If it's still open, that is."

When Lewis got to St Bede's some time later, he went up to the school secretary's room to find the headmaster and Mr Willis looking through a pile of files and folders.

"Ah, Lewis, come in, come in. We're looking through the records for pupils aged between 11 and 15 between the years 1943 to 46. We thought we'd allow a good range beyond what you said, as you also said it was only an estimate of the time and age of the boy."

"Have you found any likely boys?" Lewis asked.

"Not really," answered Mr Willis. "In fact we have no reports at all of any boy missing in that time."

"Now you're here, you can help," added the head.

They worked through the files for another two hours without any luck. There were a few 'loose ends' as Alistair Bartlett called them. Boys that had gone home at the end of a term or a year who had been expected to return but had failed to do so. There was always a reason, in most cases satisfactory. They were left with two possibles. One of them was from 1943 of a fifteen year old who had gone home to Newcastle in July and not come back in September.

"I think he's too old and the date's probably too early," Lewis said. "But I'll take his details to give to DI Fenwick tomorrow. I think he might have been killed in an air raid."

The second boy was nearer to the age and time that the doctor had given. His name was Percy Kerridge and he was just fourteen when, in the June of 1944, he had gone back to his foster parents' home in Middlesbrough and hadn't come back to school in the September to start another year.

"You have to understand, Lewis," said the school secretary. "It was wartime. We had quite a few boys go missing, as you've seen for yourself from the files. Most of them were accounted for one way or another. They'd usually moved with their parents to a safer area, or to be near their father in his barracks. Or in a few cases they had been killed by bombs. But it was a confused time and all loose ends were not always tied up. However, of all these, the two from School House who are nearest in age and time are these. And young Percy Kerridge is the most likely. I remember him well, as I do most of our boys. He was a lively intelligent youngster. I always assumed he'd been caught up in a bombing raid or something. The docks, steelworks and chemical plants on Teesside took quite a pasting, you know. But often bodies were not found or easily identified, and records often went astray or were destroyed in bombing raids. Poor lad, if it's him I wonder what happened for him to end up buried up on the moors."

It was late afternoon when Tom Fenwick got to the mortuary, where he found the short bulky Dr Messenger hunched over the dissecting table. The DI didn't like attending post mortems and was glad that this one was nearly over when he got there. Sometime later the doctor stood up straight, stretching his cramped limbs, and gave him a nod. He was usually cheery and flippant at these times, but even he was affected when it was a young child.

"See you in my office in a few minutes, Tom," he said as he took off his coverall and went to scrub himself down.

He entered the office shortly after, drawing heavily on a cigarette. Grimacing, he said, "Don't really like these things, Tom. Coffin nails, my wife calls them, but they take away the smell and taste of that place," and he nodded towards the operating room.

"What can you tell me, doc?" asked the DI.

"Ah. Don't rush me. I need to do a few more tests, you know."

"Well, preliminary thoughts," the DI pressed him.

Dr Messenger sighed. "Oh, all right. Probably, and I mean probably, the boy was fourteen, give or take a month or so, and he'd been in the ground for roughly three years, I'd say."

"1943 or 44 then," Tom said. "So what did he die of?"

"Well, as I said at the grave, he had a broken neck and the back of his head was stove in. Either could have killed him, but don't ask me to choose. At this point, I can tell you no more," sighed the doctor then he added, "I may not be able to add much to that at all after all this time. But I'll let you know if I find anything else."

And with that the DI had to be satisfied. He thanked the doctor and went wearily home.

CHAPTER 13

Lewis Sudbury may only have been living at his parents' house The Laurels in Albion Terrace for a few weeks since his return from the army, but already he had got into a routine. On Sunday mornings he got up quite late, had his breakfast and then walked to the Ha'penny Bridge, went across it and then turned right to walk up to Brotton, a village not too far away. Then he would usually go past it and carry on up onto the moors, and not return for several hours. It was his way of clearing his head of all the disturbing memories of his time in Germany during the war that still haunted him. These memories still gave him sleepless nights or nightmares from time to time. He was therefore totally disorientated when the alarm went off at 7.30 that morning. At first, he thought it must be a weekday and time to get up and get ready to go to school. What lessons did he have to give today? was his first thought, before remembering that it was Sunday. And that today he had agreed to return once more to Howdale to help Tom Fenwick with his enquiries. The only good thing, he thought as he rolled out of bed, was that he'd be seeing Beryl Cooper again, and with any luck bringing her back with him in his old Austin. She had, he admitted to himself, made quite an impression on him.

The fine weather of yesterday was still holding, with clear skies and a promise of a sunny day, but it was much colder and there had been a touch of frost in the night which had resulted in a coating of ice on the inside of his bedroom window. When he went outside he saw that there was white on the grass and the garden fence. Then, when he tried to start the car, it refused to fire and he had to get out and use the crank handle before it hiccupped and then finally started. Knowing from experience that the heating system of the car was extremely inefficient, he put on a thick coat, gloves, scarf and hat before setting out.

Despite the cold it was a pleasant drive up to Howdale. The heather on the moors was coated with frost which glistened in the bright sunshine and the sheep, which the previous day had been huddled together with their backs to the wind, were now all grazing peacefully, and several times he had to swerve as some of them ambled across the road in front of the car. Peewits and lapwings wheeled overhead and he could hear their cries over the sound of the car's engine.

When he reached How End House, he found the large black police Wolsey used by DI Fenwick in the yard plus two other vehicles, one a white van that he recognised as being the one used by the dog handlers. As he pulled up, Beryl Cooper came out to meet him. She smiled and said, "The inspector asked me to come and tell you that he's in the study with Keith and Angela."

"Oh, Sir Keith's here today, is he?"

She grimaced and said, "Yes, but he's not in a good mood. The inspector caught him as he was about to go out and stopped him."

When they got to the study, Fenwick said, "Good morning, Lewis. Did you have any luck with your search for possible candidates for our body?" Then, when the schoolmaster nodded and held up the files he'd brought, said, "Good. I'll read those in a bit. First, just to bring you up to date, I've sent my DC out with PC Jacobs and a dog handler to search around the grave. You never know, they might find something of interest, even after all this time. When I asked Sir Keith and his wife here about relatives where the children might have gone, they came up with three.

"The first is an elder brother of Sir Keith's, who lives in London."

"They wouldn't go there," broke in Sir Keith. "I've told you that already, they've never met him. I never got on with him, and we've had no contact for years."

"Nevertheless," Tom Fenwick said firmly. "We've got to check him out. I've asked the Met to go and see him," he told Lewis. "Next is an aunt of Lady Dyke who lives in Leeds, she also seems unlikely as she's not a healthy lady and the children hardly know her either. The third one is another sister of Lady Dyke who lives in Teesdale, way out past Barnard Castle, and was a favourite of them both. She's Kitty's godmother and they went to visit her with Lady Dyke a few times over the past few years, despite the war, but she's never visited them here."

"No," said Beryl. "Gloria never came here if she could help it. She didn't get on with Keith." Just as I don't, she finished silently to herself.

This brought a snort from Keith Dyke and he muttered, "She was an interfering old biddy."

There was a long silence and then Tom said, "So I've asked all the local boys to go and see if there's any sign of the children at these various places."

At that moment there came a loud hammering on the door.

"Who on earth is that?" asked Sir Keith irritably, whilst Beryl with a look of almost contempt at him went to find out. She came back with an out of breath PC Jacobs. "Sir," he began, to be hushed into silence by the DI.

"If you've got a report for me, come outside and tell me in private." He turned to the others. "Excuse me a moment. Lewis, I'd like you to come with me and bring those files with you please." Then he went to the door, pushing Jacobs out of the room in front of him. Once out in the yard he said, "Now,

Constable, what's the matter? What brought you back here in all of a rush?"

"Sir," Jacobs said, his breathing almost back to normal. "Sir, I think we've found another grave."

"Good God, are you sure Jacobs?"

"Almost, sir. You can see a definite patch with, well, sort of differing plants, grass and such like. And the dog, she won't leave it and wants to dig. But George, that's her handler, sir, he won't let her, like."

Fenwick thought for a few moments then said, "Right, go and get those two spades from the tool shed whilst I get the doctor up here again. He's going to love this, breaking into his Sunday." He went back into the house to use the telephone, leaving Lewis standing alone in the yard.

An hour later PC Jacobs and DC Edward Metcalf had uncovered the skeleton of another youngster. It had obviously been in the ground for longer than that of the young boy discovered the day before as now all that was left were bones. There were a few shreds of cloth still around them, but most of the clothes had rotted away. All that remained that might have been any use in identifying the body was a leather belt with a metal fastener that looked to be shaped like a snake.

During the time the two constables were digging, Tom had read the two files. He agreed with Lewis that Percival Kerridge was in all probability the identity of the first body. "So now who can this be? And is it another student of St Bede's?" He looked around the tree covered slope, shaking his head. "And is there any more of them buried up here? I'll have to organise a full search."

Just then Doctor Messenger arrived, puffing up the hill. "This is too much, Tom," he said. "I was just doing a bit of gardening." But there was a gleam in his eye, and Tom and Lewis suspected he wasn't displeased to have been taken away from his labours. He squatted down beside the open grave. "Well, there's not much I can do or tell you here, except you can see the skull has been hit with a heavy object. I need to get the skeleton back to the morgue. Even then, there's not much to go on. I can say it's been here longer than yesterday's offering. At least six or seven years, I'd say, but maybe even longer than that. To be really accurate you'll need an expert on bones, and even then they mightn't be able to tell you much more." He stood up. "I've got the mortuary van coming with two attendants, so we'll do the rest. Just leave me young Jacobs here to fill in the hole when I'm done. Oh, I can tell you one thing right now though."

"What?" said Tom impatiently as the doctor paused. "Spit it out, man. I've not got all day."

Silas grinned at him. "It's not one of St Bede's students this time, Tom."

"How the hell can you tell that, man?" Tom snapped.

"Because it's a girl," said the doctor. "Look at the pelvic bones, they...."

"Alright, alright, I'll take your word for it," Tom said irritably. "A girl, eh. How old, any idea?"

"By the size of her, I'd say about in the same age range as the boy. Say between twelve and sixteen."

"Right, let's get on with it," Tom said. "Constable, make sure that belt is taken off carefully, so that it doesn't fall to pieces. Then put it in a bag and I'll take it with me, it may help in identifying who she was."

"Yes sir, I'll see to it," answered DC Metcalf.

CHAPTER 14

Lewis went back to How End House, leaving DI Fenwick at the site where the bodies had been found. On arriving at the house he told Sir Keith, Angela Dyke and Beryl Cooper of the discovery of another body in the woods.

"It's not....." Angela began.

"No, it's not your son or daughter," he reassured her.

"Is it another boy from St Bede's?" Beryl asked.

"No. In fact it's that of a young girl of about the same age," he replied. "And she's been buried up there for longer than young Percival Kerridge, if that's who the boy is. She's been there for probably at least two years more than him, according to the doctor."

"Who's this Percy Kerridge?" asked Beryl.

Lewis realised they didn't know what was in the files he'd brought the DI, and told them what they had contained.

"She must have died sometime in the war then," Sir Keith cut in, ignoring his explanation. "She could have been killed in an air raid or something."

"The doctor thinks she had her head caved in, just like the boy, so it's not likely to have been a bomb," Lewis replied. "And anyway, how did she then come to be buried up there if it was? No, the two deaths are in all likelihood linked. DI Fenwick certainly thinks so and is intending to carry out a further search up there tomorrow, to see if there are yet more bodies."

"Oh dear, surely not," said Angela.

Lewis then went into the study with Sir Keith and Lady Angela, leaving Beryl in the kitchen making tea for them all. Once alone, he brought them up to date with what the inspector had told him of the search for their missing children. This wasn't much as no sightings of them had been reported.

He also said that Mr Bartlett, the headmaster, had asked him to assure them that the school were helping the police in their search for their children and that he, Lewis, had been asked to help them in any way he could.

Whilst they were in the study, Lewis watched them both to gauge their reactions to all his comments. He noted that Sir Keith seemed detached and almost uninterested, just as he had been every time Lewis had met him over the past few days. He also thought that Sir Keith resented not being able to go wherever he had been meaning to before the inspector had arrived. He didn't appear to be at all concerned for the safety of his children. He also noted a change in the attitude of Lady Angela. In the beginning, when first her son and then her daughter had gone missing, she had been pale and anxious and at times almost hysterical and near to despair. Now she was much calmer and almost relaxed. He wondered if the doctor had given her some powerful medication to calm her nerves and suppress her emotions. It was the most likely explanation, he decided, and he could think of no other.

Soon after that Beryl came in with tea for them all, and Lewis asked if he could use their phone to ring the headmaster to bring him up to date on the morning's events.

"Another body, another one, but not one of our boys," Alistair Bartlett said, on hearing the news. "A young girl you say, and probably buried a few years before young Kerridge. Hmm, well thank you for letting me know. Do you think you could get into school early in the morning? I'm ringing round as many masters who were teaching here in the war, asking them to come to a staff meeting and I'd like you there too. You know more of this than anyone else. Say eight o'clock, if you can make it?"

"Fine, sir, I'll be there."

By mid afternoon, Lewis and Beryl found themselves alone together and at a loose end. The DI had returned from the murder site and gone off to find his sergeant, to see how the search for the two children was going and to make plans for a thorough search of the area to see if there were any more bodies buried in the wood.

Before Fenwick left, he had a chat with Lewis who said to the DI, "I think Dyke's behaviour is very strange." This was a sentiment Tom shared and couldn't argue with at all. Lewis then went on saying, "Do you think he is somehow responsible, Tom?"

"I've no idea, Lewis, but I'll keep the idea in mind and get one of my DC's to check him out. It wouldn't be the first time a father harmed or killed his children. But if so he's a cool one."

After the DI had left, Lady Dyke went up for a lay down and Sir Keith was busy in his study. He had also made it clear to Beryl that he wasn't amenable to her staying at How End House any longer.

"He's a horrible man," she said to Lewis. "I only came here to support Angela, I can't stand him at all. But in any case, I've got to go home today as I need to go to work tomorrow. I had to take a day's holiday to come up here yesterday as it was, as I usually work on Saturdays."

"I'll drive you. It'll take you ages to get back by bus on a Sunday afternoon, even if it's possible at all. Perhaps we could stop for a meal on the way."

"I don't know where you think will be open on a Sunday afternoon in November up here." She grinned at him. "It's not London, you know. But yes, I'd like a lift. Thanks."

"I'm not a Londoner, I'm Saltburn born and bred, but you're right, there won't be much chance of a meal. Tell you what, I've a few eggs at home. I could make egg and chips."

"No. I can probably do better than that," she answered. "That is, if you'll come all the way to Redcar. But I'll have no fresh milk or bread in the house as I've been here for two days. But I've tins, so I can do better than eggs."

In the end Lewis won, as he trumped Beryl's tins with a promise of fresh bread and milk. What sealed it was his offer of a glass of whisky for after the meal.

They drove back down off the moors in the gathering gloom of the November evening. By the time they reached Skelton and neared the sea, a thick mist was forming and Lewis had to drive the last couple of miles at a snail's pace. Once at The Laurels he lit the fire he'd left laid in the hearth and started making the meal.

Beryl stood and watched him sipping a whisky that they'd decided to have before eating to help warm up. "You can cook as well, can you?" she asked.

"As well as what?" he asked her.

"Oh," she said vaguely. "You know, teach, and help policemen. I was just talking."

"Yeah, I can cook as well. I've had to look after myself since I left home to go to university, and then in the war. You know," he said, waving the spatula around in the air.

"I see," she said. "And the war, what did you do in the war?"

"Oh, you know, all sorts," he said vaguely.

"No, I don't know. Were you in the army, the navy or what? I was in the Wrens."

"Something called the SOE," he said at last. "But I can't tell you more than that. Now let's eat."

But she stood for a while looking at him and frowning. "SOE, Special Operative Executive? Means something like that, doesn't it? Bit of a dark horse, eh? Ok, I'll not ask any more at present." And she downed the last of her whisky at one go and grinned. "Now, what was that about eating?"

Later that evening they sat side by side on his settee, drinking some more of his scotch. Drowsily he said, "Well, that was nice, but time to go, it'll be a pig of a drive in this mist and I've got to be in school early in the morning. The head's called a staff meeting."

"I could always get a bus home. There's a regular service from here, even on a Sunday."

"No, I'll not hear of it," he said, turning to look at her beside him. She turned at the same time and they gazed at each other. Then they kissed.

It was minutes later when they finally drew apart. The suddenness of it had taken them both by surprise, though each had been attracted to the other since they first met. For some time they sat in silence, then she said, "Have you any.....you know, attachments?"

"No. Have you?"

"Not for a long while. Whilst I was in the Wrens, but that was over a long time ago. What about you, you can't have got to your age without something."

"Not since I was living in Germany in the war. A time that I can't really tell you about. And she, well, she lives in Israel now. And it was a sort of mutual protection, something I shouldn't really mention." He broke off in confusion.

"Ok. I'll not pry." And she leaned in and kissed him again.

After a while he put a hand inside her blouse and fondled her breast, whilst she stroked the bulge in his trousers.

"Of course, I could stay the night," she said dreamily. "So you wouldn't have to drive nor I go on a cold bus."

"That sounds like a good idea," Lewis said. "Then we can both go to Redcar on the 73 bus in the morning and I'll not waste any more petrol. That way I save on fuel coupons, and I can take you for a drive next weekend."

And on that satisfactory note they went upstairs.

CHAPTER 15

The next morning started early for Lewis and Beryl. Normally Lewis had to leave on the eight twenty bus to get to school for about quarter to nine, or the one at seven fifty if he wanted to get there early to do some last minute prep. This morning he had to catch the seven twenty bus to get there in time for the eight o'clock staff meeting. Beryl, who could have left on a later one, decided to catch the same bus as him and go home before going into work. So they both got up at half past six when the alarm went off. It was still dark outside and the mist of the night before had been replaced by driving rain. The wind was a blustery northeaster and they could hear the sound of the waves pounding the beach.

There was little food in the house as they had eaten what there had been the previous evening. There was porridge however, there always was porridge, Lewis told Beryl, and the milkman came to the door shortly after they'd come downstairs. Lewis was able to rouse the fire which he had banked up the previous night before they went to bed, so they ate a reasonable meal in the warmth. The bus stop was only a few hundred yards away and near it there was a large glass canopy in front of a line of shops, creating a covered area over the pavement under which they could wait until the bus arrived.

Reaching St Bede's, Lewis went straight to the headmaster's study where the meeting was to be held. It was only a quarter to eight when he got there but he wasn't the first to arrive. Already in the room with the head were Mr Willis, the school secretary, Elizabeth Waverly and Albert McIntyre, the matron and the master in charge of Blue Doors. On his way to the study, Lewis had been stopped by a grinning Barry Slingsby. The caretaker had told him with some relish that there was a right barney going on in the headmaster's room. When he walked in, however, they all stopped talking and watched him enter in silence.

"Ah Lewis, there you are." Lewis, who thought this self evident, said nothing and Alistair Bartlett went on, "Nice and early, that's good. The others will be here shortly, I expect." To which Lewis simply nodded in reply.

Soon the others trickled in in ones and twos until the room was crowded. In all, another nine masters came in and the headmaster said, "I'm sorry it's so crowded, gentlemen, but I didn't want to use the staff room where anyone else could overhear. I think all the masters who were at the school in the war are here, bar three. That's Mr Gilmore, Mr Charlie Olley and Mr Pemberton. They for one reason or another can't make it. So we'll begin, I think. I have asked Mr Sudbury here to bring us up to date on all that's going on. I should explain to all of you that Lewis has been liaising with both Sir Keith Dyke and the police on our behalf. Lewis?" He gestured for him to continue.

Lewis spoke for a while, outlining the events of the last few days. He finished by saying, "So, I can confirm that when I left Howdale yesterday, Sir Keith was aware of our concern both over his missing children and of our offer of help, if needed." A murmur of approval went up at this. "As far as the police are concerned," he continued, "DI Fenwick is extending his search of the area for Robert Dyke and his sister Kitty. He is also reasonably sure that the body found in the woods near How End House is that of a Percival Kerridge, late of School House and Blue Doors." Here William Plinney, the housemaster of School House, and Albert McIntyre looked at each other uncomfortably. "The inspector is also sure that the boy was probably murdered and buried in the woods, almost certainly sometime in 1944, most likely in the July after the end of the summer term." He paused and cleared his throat before going on. "Lastly, and some of you may not know of this latest development which may or may not have any connection with this school, is the discovery yesterday of a further body."

At this announcement, the room broke up into a babble of conversation. The head called them all back to order and Lewis went on. "It was the body, or perhaps I should say the bones, of a young girl of about the same age as Kerridge. She had been in the ground for probably two to three years longer than him, which dates her death at about 1941 or 42. Her grave was found just a few feet away from the boy's. The inspector believes both of them had been murdered. This all means, in his opinion at any rate, that the two deaths are connected. It is, he believes, too much of a coincidence to think otherwise. He is also carrying out a further search of the area around the two graves, to make sure there are no others. I don't think I can tell you any more about it," he finished and sat down.

"Now, I know we will all want to thank Lewis for his work on our behalf, and it goes without saying that you will all help the police in their investigations if they question you," the head said. "It is in the interest of all of us and the school that things are brought to a speedy and satisfactory conclusion. We do not want this, and the negative publicity it will bring, hanging over St Bede's. So if any of you think you may have some information of import, you must speak to the police at once." To murmurs of agreement, he brought the meeting to a close.

All the masters went into the staff room to get a cup of tea before assembly, and several of them came up to Lewis to question him and air their opinions.

Later that day in the evening he went to the police station, at the inspector's request, to update him on the meeting and give his impressions of the reactions of the masters.

"There are a few things that struck me," he told the DI, "but nothing definite. When I got there the head, McIntyre, Mr Plinney and the matron were in an argument. From what I heard and what the caretaker, Barry Slingsby, said he overheard, I think they may have been discussing the identity of the dead girl. But I'm really not sure about that. As for the rest of them, I am pretty certain that to most of them the discovery of the girl came as a surprise. But two, Mr Jones who is a maths teacher, and Mr Partridge, who teaches English, didn't seem at all surprised by the discovery. And Sylvester Partridge, who's also the housemaster of Gregory's, worries me a bit."

"Gregory's?"

"Sorry, Gregory House. That's the red house, just as School is blue. Then there's Nelson's that's green and Moore's which is purple. The school has four houses, all with their differing colours, and the boys all belong to one or the other. I think I explained this the other day, or at least some of it."

"I see, or at least I think so," said Fenwick, who had just been to a local elementary school not a grammar school. That of course hadn't had houses or any divisions at all. "So what makes you uneasy about him?"

"Well, nothing I can put my finger on precisely, but he seems sly in some way. And always pops up in places, listening in to conversations, getting digs in at other masters. You know, not a nice man at all."

"I see. It's just a hunch, a feeling you have then?"

"Yeah, something like that. So how did you get on?"

"Well, no real progress," the inspector said. "I've put Jack Voyle in charge of the search for the two youngsters, and I'm going to handle the murder enquiry myself. We've had no luck as yet in our search for the identity of the girl, but I'll feed your remarks about the altercations between the headmaster and the others about it into the equation. I'd like, if you'll agree, for you to be a conduit between the school and me, and give me any help you can."

"That's no problem, Tom," Lewis told him. "As the head has asked me to keep in touch with your enquiries and give you any help I can."

"Thanks," the DI said. "Oh, and by the way, I drove down that little lane that runs past where the bodies were. I went with that local PC, Jacobs. He took me down from How End to the gate, and then we turned right, away from Westerdale, and then up the hill. It meets the road from Castleton near Ralph's Cross."

"Yes, I'm with you so far," Lewis replied. "I've been up there many times."

"Well, we turned right and shortly came to the lane." Tom told him. "It's a narrow unpaved one which in the end brought us to Farndale. We stopped just above the site of the graves, they're only about 100 yards or so off the lane. We didn't find anything useful of course, it was all too long ago. But if they weren't carried up from the house, then those two kids could easily have been brought that way. It seems the more likely of the two to me.

"Got time for a drink before you go home?" the DI finished.

"Just a quick one then, as I've got a ..... a meeting arranged for a bit later," Lewis said. He had in fact arranged to meet Beryl.

"Right. Come on then," Fenwick said, hiding a grin, he had a very good idea of what was going on in that quarter.

PART TWO
CHAPTER 16

On Wednesday 4th of December at eight thirty, DI Fenwick called his team together with the exception of his sergeant and two detective constables, who were still working with the Middlesbrough force on the robberies around Teesside. That investigation looked as if it would last for quite a while yet. He had some good news for them, which he gave at the start of the meeting.

"I'm pleased to say that we now have a new detective sergeant in post who will be joining us on Monday next, DS Rutter," he told them. "He's newly promoted and comes to us from the Northumberland force. This is just one more step in the county's post-war rebuilding of CID," he announced and then continued, "I'll take him into my team looking into the two murders, along with Teddy here," he said, turning to Edward Metcalf, "and DC Gregory Lince. Sergeant Voyle and DC Hubbert will continue the search for the two missing children, with the assistance of the uniformed officers already helping them. It's important that we find them as soon as possible, as the boy has been missing now for almost a week and winter is fast approaching. If they are out in the open we must fear for their survival. But I have every confidence in Jack here." And he had. He entirely trusted Jack Voyle to organise a search for the missing children, whereas he didn't want him as part of his murder squad with his outdated views and draconian tactics. Jack didn't know whether to be pleased or annoyed. On the one hand he wanted to be part of the team investigating the murders, but then again he enjoyed being in charge of the search and not just a shadow behind his superior officer, who he knew regarded him as a bit of a dinosaur.

"Now," the DI went on. "It may well be that if what he discovers is the bodies of the runaways, and then the two enquiries will converge. But let's hope not. Now, to give everyone the facts and bring you all up to date. No sign of either Robert Dyke or his sister have so far been found, but they must be somewhere. Their father shows little sign of concern, but that of course may just be his way of coping with the situation. Their mother, who was at first distraught, has calmed down but this may be because she is under sedation. Our contact with the family and the school is Mr Sudbury, a teacher at St Bede's, who has been most helpful. He told me last night that Lady Dyke is going tomorrow to stay with her sister who lives in Teesdale. This sister lives on a fairly remote farm, and Lady Dyke's doctor has recommended her to stay there to keep her away from the public and press. Sir Keith and Lady Dyke have two relatives living in London as well as her sister in Teesdale and they have all been visited by the local police, but they have found no trace of the children at any of the addresses. We have a few other likely people to question about the two murdered children, or at least the boy Percy Kerridge. Oh, and here I must also say that part of our enquiry must concentrate on the time he went missing, in 1944 I think it was. It's not at all clear what happened then. I will put the new sergeant on to that when he arrives. And then there's the identity of the girl, which as yet is unknown. But to get back to the several hints given to me by Lewis Sudbury about the murders. He says that the attitude of Mr McIntyre and Mr Plinney are both, in his opinion, slightly suspicious. Mr McIntyre is in charge of Blue Doors where the boarders live, and Mr Plinney is the housemaster of School House, which both Robert Dyke and Percy Kerridge belonged to. However, he cannot be more definite then to say 'suspicious' and that they both gave slightly differing accounts of their relationships with the boys. He knows that the two men are friends and often visit Blue Doors, but then as he says a lot of the schoolmasters do. The person who seems most concerned about both the boys and what happened to them is the matron of Blue Doors, Miss Waverly. But that is no surprise as they were both in her charge. Then there is a Tina Davis who is her deputy and a younger woman, I think she wasn't there when the girl was killed. But she had just been appointed when the boy disappeared." He paused and looked at his team, who were all listening and taking notes.

"And don't forget those two perverts living next door to the Dyke's in How End," put in DS Jack Voyle.

There was a stir of interest in the room at that and the DI said drily, "Sergeant Voyle seems to think that the two men are not cousins but a homosexual couple, and also that that makes them child molesters."

"It does," insisted the sergeant. "And lawbreakers."

"Not in my book," said Fenwick firmly, "and we are investigating murder here, not other types of law breaking. Now, one last thing. Lewis Sudbury is also suspicious of two other masters, a Mr Jones and a Mr Partridge, who he thinks may know something of the murdered girl's identity. Partridge is also very friendly with Mr McIntyre, the Blue Doors master. It's all a bit vague but comes out of a staff meeting and some comments he thought they made. And also from some things a school caretaker told him.

"Well, that's all for now. We have enough to keep us busy. So let's get on with it, shall we?"

When Sergeant Voyle and his constable had left, he deployed his own men. Ted Metcalf was to try to discover who the girl was, by going back over old records from the 1940's to see if he could find any likely missing person reports. That, he knew, would be difficult as it had been during the war and lots of people, including children, had just disappeared. Greg Lince was given the job of interviewing the teachers that Lewis had indicated as being perhaps involved in the boy's disappearance and murder. He himself would help in this, as well as look at Mr Fenn-Williams, a science teacher who Lewis had described as somewhat sinister and unwholesome in his attitude to the boys in his class. He had also told the inspector that Fenn-Williams was a close friend of Sir Keith, and that he had a memory of him waiting for the baronet at his interview for his job. The DI hadn't passed this information on to the rest of his squad as he thought it a very vague assumption. But Lewis had backed up his own aversion to the man by saying that the caretaker at the school, Barry Slingsby, who had been there for years and knew all the gossip, thought so too. According to Lewis, Slingsby had said to him, "Keep well away from that one, bonny lad, he's na' good at all. Makes me flesh creep, he does. Shouldna' be around young lads at all. He's also pally with Sir Keith and often visits him at home." It's wasn't much to go on, any of it, but it was all they had at present.

CHAPTER 17

During the week Lewis had seen Beryl several times after school, and had stayed one night in her cramped flat in one of the small streets between the clock tower on the High Street and the pier. It had been a good week in many ways, he thought. His teaching was going well especially the Spanish classes. He had about twenty boys who had chosen it to be one of their School Certificate examination subjects. They were new to Spanish, as the boys in their first three years all did Latin and French and a few of them German, but Spanish only became an option in the fourth form. Now, with the term about half over, they were all learning the basics to his satisfaction. The boys in year five, who would take the Certificate in June and had had a year already with Mr Allen, should be ready easily by then, he thought. The sixth formers, who had passed the School Certificate last year and who were working for their Highers, though fewer in number, were also doing well. He thought Mr Allen must have been a competent teacher.

Barry Slingsby, who had taken to bringing in cups of tea when he had a free period and was working in his classroom, and who was a born gossip, filled him in with all the school scandals, as well as relating humorous anecdotes about all the other teachers. From him he learned that Mr Danbury, the deputy headmaster, was having an affair with Mrs Fenn-Williams, the wife of one of the science masters.

"Mind you," Barry had said. "Fenn-Williams' a fat old bastard and she's quite a bit younger and a looker. I dunna know why she got together wi' him in the first place like. Willoughby Danbury now, he's a much younger and fitter bloke altogether. No wonder the lass fancies him, even if he has a daft name like that." His views on the masters Jones and Partridge had also been equally irreverent. "Them two, sly buggers, both of them. Mark my words, they know more about that young lass buried up at Howdale than they're letting on. I thinks they knows who she is."

How much of all this was true, and how much invention on the caretaker's part, Lewis didn't know but he passed it all on to DI Fenwick anyway.

Also of course the week had seen his relationship with Beryl develop and flourish. So by Friday he was in a good mood when he got back to Saltburn and home. He spent Saturday shopping, tidying the house and doing odds and ends in the garden. Not that he could do much gardening, as the days were short and the weather becoming quite cold and frosty. That night it was almost as bright as day as the moon was almost full and the sky was cloudless. Just the sort of night that a few years ago the Luftwaffe would have loved, he thought, standing outside looking up into the sky. Or the RAF as well, he said to himself, shivering at the memory of the raids on Berlin he had witnessed whilst he was living there. He went indoors, impatient for the morning when Beryl was coming over to spend the day with him.

He woke early the following morning, and after a wash and shave had a cup of tea before going out to meet the ten past eight bus which Beryl had said she would be on. It was still dark, and though the sky was clear with a host of stars shining brightly the moon, which was now low in the sky, was just a white globe on the horizon obscured by a thick mist. He reached the bus stop just as the red double-decker was pulling up and Beryl got off.

"Have you had breakfast?" he asked her.

"Just a cup of tea and a piece of toast," she said.

"Good. I've got some powdered egg and we can have an omelette. I've even got some real butter, so that's even better."

"I don't want to use up all your rations," she protested.

"Oh, that's ok. But I'm afraid the coffee isn't the real thing, only that chicory stuff you get in a bottle, Camp it's called," he said, with a grimace.

It was getting light when they left the house to go for a walk, and the day was still fine with just a coolish wind blowing off the sea. They walked the few yards to the Ha'penny Bridge and went across it, stopping halfway to look down at the valley 150 feet below. Directly under them was a small stream and the path that led through the gardens below. The bridge was a long spindly metal framed structure over 600 feet long and now only used by pedestrians, cyclists and the odd pony and trap. It had been built generations ago to cater for animals and horse drawn carriages, and wasn't strong enough to carry motor cars. Beryl leaned over the parapet looking down and shivered, not just at the cold. "Lots of people have committed suicide by jumping off here, you know," she said.

"Yes," Lewis answered. He had been brought up in the house in Albion Terrace which was only a few hundred yards away and so knew all about that.

"Come on, let's get on," she said and then, when they had crossed the bridge and turned right towards Brotton, added, "So tell me something about you. What exactly did you do in the war?" Then when he hesitated she laughed and said, "Ok, ok, if you can't or don't want to, tell me about you."

"Well, I was born in 1920, in the house we've just had breakfast in and I lived there till I went to Cambridge. My father worked for the steelworks, Dorman Long. He was an engineer and often went abroad or to other parts of Britain to help design or supervise some of their projects. That's how he met my mother, who was Spanish. He went to Málaga once and there she was, a secretary or some such thing, I think. She came originally from a small rural village, a pueblo in the nearby sierras. As a child I spent quite a few holidays there. That's how I came to speak the language." He stopped talking and they walked on in silence for quite a while. It was full light now and a pale sun was shining down from the blue December sky, but there were ominous clouds with red streaks on the horizon. The morning was quiet, only broken by some birdsong, blackbirds and sparrows, Lewis thought, and the mewing of gulls.

"So then you came back here and got a job at St Bede's teaching Spanish," she said. It was a statement rather than a question.

"Well, not exactly," he replied.

"How not exactly?"

"It's complicated," he hedged.

"I can do complicated," she said firmly. "Tell me."

"Ok. It's like this. All grammar schools teach modern languages as well as Latin. Always French and some of them German as well. Now, St Bede's had a reputation as a good school for languages and Mr Bartlett, the headmaster, is very keen to keep Spanish on the curriculum. When the school was fee paying, this brought in lots of students, some from quite a way away. Now, since the Education Act of last year, we're funded by the government, but he still wants to attract boarders from all over, they pay good fees for boarding. And our reputation for languages is well known. The school had a teacher who ran the Spanish lessons, Mr Allen, who left last year, and the head wants them to continue as I said. French and German are taught from year one, but Spanish is only offered from year four. So it's not a full time teaching post. And of course if we don't attract enough students, it will cease to be taught altogether. So I was appointed as a geography teacher who would also teach German and Spanish. So it's up to me to keep the subject on the syllabus. If I do, then I will also keep my job as a Spanish teacher. If I don't, then I'll have to just teach geography and German. There, does that make sense?"

"Yup," said Beryl. "So you speak German too?"

"Well, my degree is in geography and Spanish, but yes, I can cope with German as well. I just don't want to."

"Is that because of your experiences in the war?"

Lewis grimaced. "Ok, yes. I'll tell you a bit about it. There's not much point in secrecy now, even though I'm not supposed to talk about it. It's old history and it would seem that Russia is the enemy now. I've nothing against the German language or most of its people. It's just that I lived there for a bit in the war, undercover stuff, you know," he said vaguely. "And I had to mix with some unsavoury characters and pretend to be one of them."

"I see," Beryl said. "That can't have been very nice."

"Far from it," Lewis replied, pulling a face.

They walked on as far as Lingdale, and she told him something of her life in Redcar and the Wrens. She finished by saying, "So now I live in that little flat you came to. My parents still live on Redcar Road, but I couldn't go back home after all those years away. And I work in the library."

In Lingdale they went into a pub and he had a pint of John Smith's beer whilst she had a cider. They had planned to go on and up on to the moors then to Guisborough and return home that way, but when they came out the weather was deteriorating and some clouds were building up.

"We'd best just go back the way we came, it's all downhill so won't take as long as it did getting here," Lewis said. So they started to retrace their steps. They soon discovered that they were walking into a cold wind which was strengthening all the time. By the time they reached Brotton, though it was only mid afternoon it was already becoming dark and a few spots of sleety rain were being driven into their faces.

Sometime later they reached the Ha'penny Bridge, went across to Glenside and turned left towards his home. The sleet was now turning to snow and they were glad that for the last few hundred yards they had the wind behind them. Lewis quickly got the fire going with some sticks and logs before putting on a few pieces of his meagre supply of coal.

Later that evening after they had eaten Beryl said, "Oh. I never said, my sister Angela has gone to stay with Gloria in Teesdale for a few days. She went on Friday. I think the change will do her good. There's no news on her children, I suppose? From your inspector friend, I mean?"

"Not that's he told me." Fenwick however had already told him of Angela going to Teesdale but all he said was, "I believe they've widened the search out and have contacted a lot of other police forces to look out for them."

"I wonder where they've gone," Beryl sighed. "I hope they're all right. Ah well, let's not let it spoil our evening."

CHAPTER 18

Otto Kohistedt was having a clear out of his flat that Sunday. He had been in England now for several weeks and had accumulated a lot of clutter. He was more relaxed at living here now, and believed his new identity had been accepted by his MI5 masters and that he was doing a good job. He might not have been quite so complacent if he could have heard the comments made about him by some of the senior men he worked for.

So, all in all, Otto was getting used to his new life, both at work and also in his free time away from the office. His flat was small and fairly cramped and nothing like the one he'd had in Berlin, but then again it was far better than where he had lived after the Third Reich and infinitely better than his time in the internment camp. When he'd been discharged from hospital he had first lived for a few weeks in a home for wounded soldiers, before being sent to the camp. It was when he was there that he had managed to swap identities with an inmate who had died of a wound he'd suffered fighting on the Russian Front. Then he'd had the good fortune to be recruited by the Intelligence Service and brought to England. He believed that he was proving to be useful to them, and that as long as that was so he would be safe. He was also becoming used to living in London and was friendly with several of his neighbours, but still found much there that he didn't understand and more that he actively disliked.

For a start, his immediate superior officer was a Jew. After years of actively persecuting Jews, he found working with one very hard to stomach. Another thing was that most of the British agents were university graduates whilst he, before the war, had been a shopkeeper. He had spent years in the SS ordering intellectuals around and found his new colleagues condescending. He also suspected that they constantly made fun of him, but couldn't understand their humour. If that were not enough, he also believed that some of them were homosexuals, another scourge that along with Judaism he'd striven to destroy. Although he knew that homosexuality was illegal in Britain, he daren't do anything to denounce them for fear of reprisals and, in any case, who could he report it to as everyone in the department seemed to be aware of it and just treated it as being normal. The police weren't an option either, in case they discovered his true identity. No, he had decided, he must just live with it.

Pushing these thoughts aside, Otto got on with his clearing up of the flat. He neatly piled up all the scattered magazines and newspapers. That was another thing that he found disconcerting about living in Britain, how free the press appeared to be. They constantly criticised the government, something that just wouldn't have been tolerated in Germany. What was it that Goring had always said about controlling the flow of news? Of how propaganda was the key to control? He sighed, ah well, Goring was gone along with all the rest of them now. They were all dead, imprisoned or on the run like him. He would just have to get on with his new life and come to terms with it.

A picture in one of the papers caught his eye as he put it on to the top of the growing pile. He remembered seeing it weeks ago now, and thinking someone in one of the photos was familiar. But it couldn't be, could it? He stared at it for a while and then went over to the table and found a pencil.

Afterwards he wasn't sure why he had had done it, what had brought the idea into his mind. He drew a small pointed beard on the face, then added a moustache with curled up ends.

Finally, he drew straight lines over the mop of hair over the face. Yes, he thought, I do know the man. Staring at him was El Conde Manuel Ortega, his nemesis. It was a face he wasn't likely to forget, a face that belonged to the man who was responsible for the loss of his hand and half a leg. Was it El Conde? Or was it just someone with a startling likeness to him? But it couldn't be could it, he told himself, Ortega was dead wasn't he? His body had been found at the scene of the explosion, the one that had caused his own injuries. He knew he must find out, one way or another. He read the article that the photo was attached to.

The man was a schoolteacher, he discovered, and the photo had been taken at a place called Howdale in the North Yorkshire Moors. He wasn't confident of his knowledge of English geography, but thought that Yorkshire was in the north of the country. Not as far north as that fool Hess had gone, that was Scotland, but somewhere in between here in London and there. Tomorrow, Monday, he must look at a map, there were several in the office, and see just where this Howdale was. And then what, what could he do about it?

He sat thinking for a long time. So long that the gas meter ran out of money and the fire went out without his knowledge. When he at last stirred, the room was icy and he became aware of how cold he was. He looked out of the window and saw that snow was falling, and such traffic as there was on the road had their lights on. He got up stiffly and searched for a sixpence or shilling to put in the meter, but as was always the case in such situations he couldn't find one. Shivering, he put on an overcoat and went outside and walked to Liverpool Street station which was only a short distance away. It was Sunday afternoon but he found a man still there selling papers and bought the News of the World, giving the man a ten shilling note and asking for as much of the change as the man would give him to be in sixpenny or shilling coins.

Back in his flat he fed coins into the meter and re-lit the fire, and then he put the kettle on. There wasn't much of interest in the paper, certainly no pictures or even news of the bodies found in Howdale or the missing children, they seemed to have dropped off the radar altogether. The paper was full of the looming coal shortage, exposés of several purported black marketeers and one story of a clergyman suspected of bigamy. He threw the paper on to the floor then remembered he was clearing things up, retrieved it and put it on the top of the pile. Then he poured another cup of tea and sat brooding again.

The first thing to do, he decided, was to find out if this schoolteacher really was Ortega. To do this, he'd have to visit this Howdale place himself. That wouldn't be easy as he was kept busy all week and he daren't just not turn up for work. Perhaps he could do it one weekend, say the one after next. That would give him time to find out just where the place was, if it was Ortega and make plans.

What sort of plans was the next question? There were two opposing priorities, he decided. The first was to make sure that Ortega, in his present guise, didn't pose any problems for him and that he would never be in a position to reveal to the world his true identity. This was imperative. The second was his need for revenge against the man who had betrayed him and caused his injuries. But were the two at odds with each other? If he were to find and kill the man, without bringing suspicion on himself, then wouldn't that serve to achieve both ends? But it would take time and organisation to bring it about. Organisation he could manage, but time was a different matter. He must somehow manage to get some time off from the section. Well, first things first. He must go up to North Yorkshire and find out if the schoolteacher and Ortega were one and the same. If he was, he decided, then revenge must come before anything else. If necessary, he could always escape from England and go to South America or somewhere else safe.

The room was warmer now with the fire turned fully up, but when he looked out of the window he saw it was now completely dark and that the snow was still falling. It was time to make some supper, and then perhaps listen to some music on the gramophone he'd just bought. Not that he had many records to put on it. Alternatively, there might be something worth listening to on the Home Service. He never listened to the Light Programme as he didn't understand British humour.

He got up and went to look in the larder to see what he had in there to cook for his supper.

CHAPTER 19

Over the past few weeks, Lewis' life had taken on a regular pattern. On Tuesday and Thursday evenings he met up with Beryl after school. They usually went to the pictures or just spent the evening together at her flat. On one of these evenings, normally the Tuesday, he stayed the night there. She in her turn came to Saltburn on Sunday mornings and stayed over until the Monday, going back with him to Redcar on the number 73 bus at eight twenty on Monday morning. The early snow of the first weekend they had spent together had cleared, but the weather had turned very cold and frosty. Despite this, and some further short spells of snow showers, they usually managed to fit in a walk during the Sunday, either on the beach or going by bus to the nearby moors.

On Friday evenings he met up with DI Fenwick for a chat and a drink. They were becoming quite friendly as time passed. With not much movement on either the whereabouts of the runaways or any progress on the murders, the DI had become more and more reluctant to talk about the two cases, and their conversations widened to other topics.

The Friday evening of the 20th December was no exception. The two men met up in the Park Hotel near the bus station in Redcar at six o'clock, and sat chatting over a couple of pints. Outside a bitter wind was blowing and their talk turned to the likelihood of a serious fuel shortage. Since October there had been warnings of the coal stocks running out with Manny Shinwell, the Minister of Fuel and Power, trying to convince the country that there were sufficient stocks to last the winter.

"I have a gas fire in my flat, if you can call the few rooms I live in a flat," the DI said. "How do you keep your house warm, Lewis?"

"Mainly with a fire that I try to keep in all day and night if I can," the teacher replied. "It has a back burner, so I always have hot water. I also have an electric fire, a two bar one, which I can move to wherever there's a plug."

"Can you get enough coal then?" Fenwick asked. "I'd heard stocks were low and a sort of rationing was being implemented by most of the coal merchants."

"Well, I have some and also a stack of logs. I also use sea coal too, that's very good for banking the fire up to keep it in overnight and all day when I'm at school."

"What the hell's sea coal?" The DI, who was from Birmingham and not a local, had never heard of it.

"Well," Lewis said. "If you go down on to the beach at low tide, anywhere between here and Saltburn, you'll see black patches on the sand. They are sheets of fine coal that have been washed up by the tide. If you scrape the surface carefully, you can collect it up. You burn it by putting it in paper bags or you can just put it on top of a fire, but as it consists of very small particles it can put the fire out. But it's excellent for banking up a fire to keep it in."

"Well I never," said the inspector. "Where does it come from?"

"I think some of it is washed out of the mines that go under the sea in Durham and Northumberland," Lewis replied. "That and perhaps some that is lost overboard from ships."

Then they chatted about football. Fenwick had always been a Wolves supporter but since coming to Redcar he had taken to watching Middlesbrough.

"The Boro had a good win last week at Blackpool, four-nil. Micky Fenton put one of them in, he's scored more goals than anyone this season so far. Do you ever go to watch, Lewis?"

"Sometimes," Lewis said. "I'm thinking of going next week, on Boxing Day, to see them play Leeds. I'll be on my own at Christmas. But then I always have been since my parents died. How about you, Tom, are you going home to Birmingham?"

"Just for Christmas Eve and Christmas Day, I can't afford any more time off. If you like I'll come with you on Boxing Day if it's quiet at the station. But what about Beryl, isn't she around?"

"Oh, she's going to spend some time with her parents. She asked if I wanted to join them on Christmas Day, but I think I'll give it a miss," Lewis told him. "We've only been together a few weeks. It's a bit soon to be getting.... well, too close."

Fenwick grinned at him. "She's a bonny lass," he said.

Lewis thought it was time to change the subject; he didn't want to talk about his relationship with Beryl. So he said, "So how is the investigation going, Tom?"

Tom sighed. "Nowhere, really," he said reluctantly. "In the case of the two Dyke children, we've searched all the surrounding areas. I've had my DC's and a lot of PC's combing the moors around Howdale, and there's been a lot of the public helping as well. But there's no sign of them at all. Of course there's miles of open country and we can't be sure, but I don't think they're out there. I think they had this all planned out before they ran off, and they're tucked up cosy somewhere. Or I hope so at least given the weather, but they must have had help from someone. Beats me who, though.

"I've checked Sir Keith's brother in London and his wife's aunt in Leeds, but they're not there. And Lady Dyke is still in Teesdale. I went up there myself last week, and she showed no sign of wanting to return home. I don't think she and Sir Keith get on very well. One odd thing though is that she seems not at all worried about her kids. I think she, like me, believes they're holed up somewhere safe."

He stopped talking and Lewis went to the bar to buy two more pints. When he came back the DI continued. "I've looked at that master you mentioned, Fenn-Williams, but found nothing really except that he appears to be a friend of Sir Keith. I've even checked out those two men again, the ones that DS Voyle thinks are responsible, but have drawn a blank. They are cousins of a sort, or their parents were, so that makes them half cousins or something like that.

"I've looked at the other two cottages at How End as well. One of them is occupied by a middle-aged widow, she's very independent, has to be to live out there on her own, but there's nothing suspicious about her. She was a favourite of both the kids apparently. She's very lively for her age and well turned out.

"The third cottage is odd to say the least, but not connected to the runaways, I'd say."

"How's that?" asked Lewis.

"Well, it's owned by a Wilfred Lawrence, but he's away a lot of the time. He hasn't been there for a couple of months now, so he wasn't around when they went missing. He too was a favourite with the kids and, when he was at home, saw a lot of them and they called him Uncle apparently, a sort of honorary title. He works in London, in the Foreign Office, but I can't get anywhere with them. All they'll say is he's abroad or not available, depending who I talk to." He grinned at Lewis. "I think he's one of your lot."

"If he works for the Foreign Office then he's MI6, if he is one of the funny squad as you call them," said the teacher. "I was never in Six, or Five for that matter."

"What were you exactly?" Fenwick asked.

Lewis looked at him, considering. There was no real reason for secrecy, he thought, and Fenwick was a policeman. "I was SOE," he said, "But don't broadcast it."

"Special Operations Executive," murmured the DI. "Dangerous work, I expect."

Lewis shrugged. "I just want to forget it now."

"Well, anyway," the inspector went on, after a pause. "This Lawrence character is away a lot. But when he's at How End, he's very friendly with Mrs or I should say Lady Dyke and the kids. Sir Keith doesn't like him one bit though. That much I do know about him, if not much else."

They sat silent for several minutes then Tom said, "Another pint?"

"Thanks. Just one more though then I'll have to go," Lewis said with a grin. "Else my fire'll be out when I get home."

"Ha-ha," said Tom sardonically. "You'll just have to put your electric fire on. Do you know, the Coal Board is blaming the rise in sales in electric fires for the extra demand for electricity and therefore for coal? So the shortage is all your fault." With that parting shot, he went to the bar.

When he got back, Lewis asked, "And what about the two bodies?"

"Nothing more there either," the DI said. "I looked at those two masters you mentioned, Jones and Partridge, but got nowhere. My lads have produced a list of six possibles for the girl so far, but it's a long time ago and we've little to go on. And it was wartime. 'The fog of war' is what my superintendent keeps saying. As for the boy, it was almost certainly Percy Kerridge, but we've found no trace of his foster parents. They may well have died in the bombing of Middlesbrough, but we've got no record of it. It's another case of the fog of war, I'm afraid. But we'll keep on, even though the Super has said we mustn't spend too much of our time on it, as we've got a lot on our plate. And he's right there.

"Well, I'll let you know about the Leeds match next week, as soon as I know if I can get there. In the meantime, have a good Christmas."

"And you, Tom," said Lewis, leaving to go and catch a bus to Saltburn.

CHAPTER 20

Earlier on that same Friday, Beryl Cooper had travelled by train to Darlington to do her Christmas shopping. She had had that day off from work as she always worked in the library on a Saturday, and therefore had a day off in lieu sometime in the week. It was because she worked on Saturdays that she only stayed at Saltburn with Lewis on Sundays and not the whole weekend. She had discovered Darlington as a good place to shop when she had gone to visit her half sister in Teesdale. She had visited Gloria shortly after she had moved there and then several times since, and she had often combined these visits with shopping trips. Before that she had always gone to Middlesbrough or Stockton, as most other people she knew in Redcar did. To get to Teesdale to visit Gloria she had gone to Darlington by train and then caught a bus, discovering the town on her way. She liked the permanent market hall and the shops that surrounded it.

She didn't really know either of her half sisters all that well, as Angela had been over twenty when she was born and already married, and Gloria only a few years younger. Neither had had much time for a small baby by a stepmother, but they had always been kind and sent her presents at birthdays and Christmas. That was why she had felt the need to go to Howdale to support Angela when her children had run off.

She was now very concerned as Angela had gone to Gloria's house in Teesdale, and had remained there and hadn't returned home yet. She knew that Gloria didn't like Sir Keith, Angela's husband, just as she didn't herself, but she now believed that Angela herself also disliked him. She thought that perhaps Angela had only stayed with him for the sake of providing a stable home for her two children. There was also something else strange that was worrying her. When she had written to Angela in Teesdale, she had appeared to be not at all worried as to where Bob and Kitty were. Her reply had been almost cheerful, rather than anxious. Another disturbing thing was that Angela had asked her not to come to the farm in Teesdale to visit her until after Christmas. Not, in fact, until the New Year and only then if she wrote again to say she was coming. Because Gloria didn't have a phone, she couldn't ring to talk to Angela directly at the farm. She had told Lewis all this, but he had said he couldn't understand it either. Lewis told her that the DI now believed the children were probably holed up somewhere, as he put it. Perhaps, he added, Angela might think the same, and even have some idea of where that could be.

This of course brought another problem into her mind as she went round the shops looking for Christmas presents. That problem was Lewis himself, and not just what to buy him for Christmas. She wasn't at all sure as to what their relationship was. She had, in some trepidation, asked him to spend Christmas day with her at her parents' home. It had been a bit of a relief when he'd turned down the offer, both because she hadn't actually asked her parents' permission and also because she had been worried that they would be unsure of each other on the day.

Despite having two half sisters, because of the age gap she had grown up almost as an only child. She had been very shy and her parents fairly strict, and so she hadn't had many close friends. Her parents were also quite religious and made her go to Sunday school every week and become a member of the church choir. She was sixteen when the war started, and had left school earlier that year and gone to work in the library. She had always been a loner and very inexperienced when it came to boys. At school she was always on the fringe of the groups of girls who giggled as they talked about the boys they had been out with. She had heard phrases such as, 'I told him he couldn't go inside my bra', or 'I said no higher than my stocking top', without really understanding them. She had always been frightened to go out with boys because of things her mother said to her. Such things as, 'If you get pregnant, you'll have to marry him', and 'That's your life over, my girl'. In the summer she'd mainly stayed at home when the population of Redcar nearly doubled, both with people on holiday and at weekends when people from Teesside came for a day at the seaside. Many of these were youngsters looking for a bit of fun, especially with girls. She'd only really met boys of her own age at the church youth club, where she learned to dance. But they had been quiet, well brought up boys who were a bit like herself.

Then, when she was eighteen, things had suddenly changed as she was called upon to do some work to help the war effort. She could, she'd been told, go and work in a factory or become a land girl amongst other things. But she had chosen to join the Wrens, the Women's Royal Naval Service, and so suddenly within just a few weeks of her birthday she had found herself in Plymouth. After several weeks of basic training, she'd become one of the Wrens in the chart room plotting the position of shipping in the channel.

Here in the barracks she'd met girls from all over England, and the talk had gone from the giggling innocence of schoolgirls to the more knowing gossip of her new companions. She now knew that when her fellow Wrens said, 'We did it,' it was not bragging and the probably untrue boasts of schoolgirls, but the real thing. She learnt just what French letters were, as the Wrens shared them out when someone was short of them. But through all of this, she remained as usual on the fringe and not involved. Then one day she met Duncan and it all changed.

Duncan was a second lieutenant, handsome and just a couple of years older than her. He came from north London, from a middle class background similar to hers. He was in charge of an armed fishing boat that was based in Plymouth harbour, from which he and two RN ratings went out most days with the civilian crew. Their job was to protect the boat from the enemy when it was fishing, but also to pick up any pilot who had been shot down. Who had ended up 'in the drink' as Duncan put it. His ambition when he became a first lieutenant was to be put in charge of one of the MTB's, Motor Torpedo Boats, some of which were also berthed in Plymouth. These MTB's were sleek 60 foot long boats, armed with two torpedo tubes and a machine gun. The boat was capable of an astonishing speed of 40 knots. Or so at least Duncan told her. As well as also picking up pilots who had ended up in the drink, they kept a lookout for U-boats and German ships and sometimes carried out raids on enemy ports.

Shortly after they met, they fell in love and Beryl soon found out what 'doing it' was all about. It was wartime and there was danger everywhere, and after a few months they were seriously talking about marriage. Despite some of her fellow Wrens warning her not to rush into things, she paid them no heed. All they both wanted was first for him to meet her parents and she his, before they went ahead with the wedding. That only required both of them to have a few days' leave at the same time. When that happened they would go together first to London and then on to Redcar. Unfortunately this never occurred, and one day Duncan's armed fishing boat was sunk by an E-Boat, with the loss of all hands. An E-Boat was the German equivalent to the British MTB.

Beryl was heartbroken and although she had one or two brief dalliances with other naval officers wouldn't countenance during the war any other long standing relationship. Now, however, with memories of Duncan well in the past, she wasn't sure if it had really been love at all or just an intense wartime romance. Then she had met Lewis and had been instantly drawn to him, as he apparently had been to her. But she couldn't decide if it was more than just a mutual attraction or something deeper. It certainly wasn't as immediate or passionate as her affair with Duncan had been, but then she couldn't expect that as the situations were not comparable. She couldn't decide if this was really love or not, and in any case she didn't know what his feelings for her were.

As she bought presents for her friends and family, a tie for her father, some perfume for her mother and toys for some of her friends' children, all these worries flooded into her mind. These included the disappearance of her sister's children, the refusal of Angela to go back to Sir Keith and her own and Gloria's dislike and distrust of him. All of this, plus Angela's apparently relaxed concern over the children and refusal to let her visit her in Teesdale, pushed the problem of Lewis into the back of her mind. So her only concern as far as he was concerned now was what to get him for Christmas.

CHAPTER 21

On the Saturday morning, Lewis decided to go to Middlesbrough to do some Christmas shopping. It was already the 21st of December and although he didn't have many presents to buy, as yet he hadn't bought any of them. Usually of course on a Saturday he caught up with his domestic tasks, but this week as St Bede's had broken up for the Christmas holidays he had done these already, as well as going on to the beach to collect more sea coal. So he could put off the problem of Christmas shopping no longer. He usually bought presents for an aunt who lived close by, the sister of his late father, and also for his immediate neighbours who had been lifelong friends. Getting something for them would be no problem at all, but buying one for Beryl was his real concern.

His main worry was just what sort of present it should be, something special or just the usual token between friends? He couldn't decide just what their relationship was, or what indeed he wanted it to be. How serious was it between them? Did he, or indeed did Beryl, want it to be long term? Since his escape from Germany at the end of the war, and the two years since, he had had no relationships with women at all. For over a year, until his discharge from the SOE with the nominal rank of brigadier, he had been in no fit state for relationships of any kind. During this time, he had struggled to come to terms with his time in Germany as a supposed supporter of their aims and methods. He'd had recurrent nightmares in which SS officers committed horrendous acts of torture on innocent civilians. Now he was almost back to normal, and ready to resume his life again. Would this be with or without Beryl as a permanent feature in it? This was the problem he was wrestling with. Just what did they both want from each other? He suspected from her reactions to him that she too had issues about commitment rooted in her past, just as he did.

The second problem, even if he was able to find an answer to that one, was just what he should look for. Clothes were out of the question, as first he had no idea of her size and secondly he hadn't any clothing coupons to spare. Boxes of chocolates were also not an option because of rationing not to mention their availability. Silk stockings were really only available on the black market, and in any case he thought they might be seen by her as too suggestive.

In the end, he came to the conclusion that it probably came down to a book or a piece of jewellery. He had left his house, walked to the station, decided to go to Middlesbrough by train rather than by bus and settled in a carriage before he had reached this conclusion. As he settled back in satisfaction, the train pulled out of the station. It was the usual LNER shuttle between Saltburn and Darlington, and was made up of carriages divided into individual compartments with no linking corridor, and he had chosen a no smoking one near the front. When they reached Redcar he lowered the window and looked out on to the platform, watching as packages were loaded into the guard's van at the rear of the train. He wasn't paying any attention to the passengers on the platform, and so didn't notice the man who had just come down the steps of the bridge. The man, after a casual glance in his direction, had stopped for a moment then stared more closely at him and then boarded the train a few compartments away.

As he got out at Middlesbrough, Lewis thought of even more problems about choosing a present for Beryl. First, as to buying her a book which he had thought such a good idea, just what book should he get her? He knew she was an avid reader and worked in a library, so he had no idea what she had already read, or even what particular type of book she would like. As he handed in his ticket he'd already decided against looking in bookshops, so that left jewellery. Then the next problem began to form in his mind about the sort of thing to buy, as too cheap would be to give her just a trinket and be not at all suitable, whilst to buy her something too expensive might suggest he was looking for a more permanent relationship. This brought him in a full circle to the question of just what their relationship was or what they wanted it to be. It was at this point, as he went out into the street, that all his thoughts of present buying left his head.

He had been trained on joining the SOE to be aware of when he was under surveillance, and for years had lived in Germany using this skill. It had been what had ultimately saved him from arrest, and certain torture and death. Even now, a few years on in England in peacetime, his antenna was still working and he became convinced he was under surveillance. He immediately started to find out if he was being followed, and if so by whom. He entered a shop, then immediately turned and went out again, then stopped and looked for a long time into a shop window. His follower wasn't experienced in the art of tailing people, and Lewis had little trouble at all in isolating him. The man was easy to spot as he wore a Tyrolean hat that was quite distinctive. It was russet brown with a curled brim, and had a brown band with a grey feather in it. He could see the hat clearly over the heads of the crowd even when he couldn't see the man himself.

He hadn't left Saltburn until mid morning and it was now just after twelve, but the streets were crowded. This would be, he reasoned, because of the nearness of Christmas. Even in these days of austerity everyone was out, just as he was himself, buying last minute presents. He saw some people wearing the same coloured scarves of red, white and black, and remembered that Middlesbrough were at home to Brentford today. He went into a pub and pushed his way to the crowded bar. He bought a pint of Cameron's bitter and then went and stood leaning on the wall opposite the door. The room was full of men with either red and white hats and scarves, or red, white and black ones, the colours of the two teams.

He had been in the bar for over fifteen minutes before the man who had been following him came in, looking around to see if he could spot Lewis. Lewis looked away, but out of the corner of his eye saw the man nod to himself and then cross to the bar and buy himself a drink. Once he saw the man pay and then pick up his glass, Lewis drained his own and left, watching as the man hastily put his drink down and rushed to follow him out. Smiling to himself, Lewis thought that the man was an amateur at this game and proceeded to lead him a merry dance all over the town as he went from shop to shop.

It took Lewis quite a while to recognise who he was. He had aged quite a bit over the two years or so since he had last seen him, and developed a pronounced limp. Lewis deduced from the stiffness of the man's right leg that it was probably a false one, and obviously causing him pain and slowing down his movements. But it was, he decided at last, Kurt Vogel, the SS man he had last seen going into the tenement all those years ago in Berlin. The man he had thought had been killed in the explosion. 'What is he doing here in Middlesbrough following me?' Lewis asked himself. Whatever the reason, he was obviously up to no good and he knew he'd have to be very cautious. The man he'd thought was dead was probably out for revenge.

By a quarter to three, the streets were full to overflowing. It was just half an hour away from kick off and a stream of supporters were walking towards Ayresome Park. In the crush it was no problem for Lewis to slip his follower and then fall in behind him. The hunter had become the hunted.

Lewis followed the German for over half an hour, as the man tried to find his quarry again as the streets emptied of the football crowd and returned to their still crowded state full of Christmas shoppers. Following the man at a distance was made quite easy, as all he had to do was keep his hat in view. At last, the man gave up and went back to the station and caught the Saltburn train. Lewis did the same, and watched as Vogel got off at Redcar. He waited until he was handing his ticket in at the barrier, and then got off and went after him. From the station Lewis followed Vogel until he reached a B and B in the town and went inside, and then Lewis went back into the town centre. Vogel, he thought, didn't know where he, Lewis, lived but he knew he'd have to be on the alert in the future. The German was obviously up to no good.

It was now nearly half past five and he hadn't bought Beryl's present, and she was due at his home at about seven that evening to stay over until Monday morning. In desperation, he went into H Samuel's the jewellers on the High Street and looked at their display of jewellery. He saw a nice set of gold and diamond earrings with a matching necklace. It was quite expensive but well within his means, and without further thought he bought it for her. The manager also offered to wrap it up for him and supplied a tag for him to write on and attach to the package.

All thoughts of what such an expensive present would say about their relationship had gone from his mind, because of the disturbing discovery of Kurt Vogel looking for him. His only thoughts were that he had only been just in time to buy it before the shop closed at six o'clock, and that he hoped Beryl would like it.

As he went back out on to the street after leaving the shop, to catch a bus to Saltburn, the newspaper men were out selling the first edition of the Evening Gazette's 'Pink 'Un' and shouting the result of the match. "Middlesbrough two, Brentford nil. Read all about it." He bought a paper and stood at the bus stop reading it.

CHAPTER 22

Otto Kohistedt hadn't been able to get enough time off from work on the weekend he'd planned to go up to North Yorkshire to try and find El Conde Manuel Ortega, or Lewis Sudbury, which he thought was what he was called now. He had had to postpone it to the one before Christmas. So it was on the Friday night, the one when Lewis had been sitting in the pub in Redcar talking to DI Fenwick, that he had caught a train to Darlington.

He had left his flat near Liverpool Street station and taken the tube to King's Cross. Here he caught the overnight train which left London a few minutes before midnight, and reached Darlington just over five hours later. The train hadn't been all that full and he'd been able to get some sleep and even stretch out on his seat, rather than having to sit up straight all night. Once there he had gone to Redcar on the small shuttle, arriving there very early in the morning, far too early to do anything but wait a couple of hours until the town came to life. It was bitterly cold and he was glad the waiting room was open to shelter in. He sat in there, thinking of what his next moves could be. The school of course would be shut, both because it was a Saturday and also because of the Christmas holidays, so he wouldn't be able to wait outside to follow Manuel, or Lewis as he must now think of him, when he went home. But that was true of any Saturday, he mused, and Saturdays and Sundays were the only days he could come up here. That is without losing his job and thereby threatening his safety.

At nine o'clock he postponed any decision, and went to find somewhere reasonably cheap to spend the night. A porter at the station he questioned sent him to a B and B in a road just behind the bus station. Mrs Overton was only too glad of a booking, not many people came to Redcar looking for digs outside the holiday season. He went up to his room, and after a wash and change of clothes to freshen up after a night spent kipping in a railway carriage, decided to take a stroll around the town to get an idea of its layout.

It was whilst he was walking around that he thought he had an amazing stroke of good luck. Up ahead of him was a man wearing a dark brown overcoat and a blue scarf, whose walk he thought looked familiar. Or at least he imagined it was, though in truth he hadn't seen Manuel Ortega for many a year. But from the back, even though he couldn't see his face, he was sure the man looked just like the one he'd seen in the photo in the paper, the one named Lewis Sudbury, who'd been standing in the yard at How End House. The one he'd thought was Manuel. It was too good an opportunity to miss, and he followed the man down the street.

His quarry reached the railway station and went in. After allowing a short time to elapse so that the man had time to buy a ticket, he went in after hm. There was a train at the platform on the far track, and he could hear the stationmaster shouting, "Darlington train". He was in time to see a brown overcoat going over the bridge, so he went up to the window and bought a ticket to Darlington. Once through the barrier, he sprinted over the bridge as quickly as he could with his false leg, but slowed down as he realised the train was being loaded with parcels and not about to leave immediately. He looked up and down the platform, but couldn't see a sign of a brown overcoat anywhere. Then he saw a man standing looking out of one of the windows of the train. He was wearing a brown overcoat and had a blue scarf around his neck; he must have just got on and was closing the door, the German thought. In his excitement, he didn't notice that it wasn't the same shade of blue as the scarf the man he had been following had been wearing. But it wouldn't have mattered if he had, for he was sure the man at the window was Ortega. He quickly got into an adjoining compartment. Manuel or Lewis got out of the train at Middlesbrough with Kurt or Otto behind him.

For quite a long while Otto followed Lewis, as he went from one shop to another seemingly at random. Otto watched him buy some pipe tobacco at one and then perfume at another, before looking around a large department store called Binns. In here he added a scarf, a pair of woollen gloves and a couple of children's toys to his purchases. He was Christmas shopping, Otto decided. The streets were full of people shopping and also a growing number of others were joining them, mainly men wearing coloured scarves and hats, and chanting and singing. There must be a football match in the town, the German decided. He was quite used to the streets of London filling up with football supporters on Saturdays. With all the people milling about, he had no trouble following Lewis without being noticed. Or at least that was what he believed. In Germany in the war he had been the man in charge, not one of the field agents. As such he had always believed that his men, who had continually claimed that following suspects was difficult, were exaggerating. He'd always thought it was easy, and now he told himself he'd been right. It wasn't difficult at all.

Around lunchtime Lewis went into a pub, but Otto remained outside for quite a while letting a steady stream of customers enter and leave before going inside himself. When he entered, he spotted Lewis leaning on a wall. Keeping well away from him, Otto went up to the bar.

"Yes, ducks, what can I get you?" the blousy barmaid with red hair and vivid lipstick asked him around her cigarette.

Whore, Otto thought, wishing for the days when, in his black uniform with the silver flashes on the collar, he would have evoked fear and respect from women like her.

"Yes, love, what it is?" she asked again, impatiently.

"I'll have a pint of beer, please," he said.

"What sort of beer, dearie?" she asked almost rudely. "We've got John Smith's, Cameron's, and Scottish and Newcastle."

"That one," he said shortly, offended by her attitude, pointing to the nearest pump. He'd scarcely paid and taken a sip when he saw Lewis drain his glass, put it down on a nearby table and go out of the door. Cursing, he put his glass down and hurried out after him, conscious of the malicious smile the barmaid gave him.

Outside the crowds had grown denser than when he had gone into the bar, and he had trouble keeping his quarry in sight, and shortly after that he just seemed to vanish. Hell, where is he, he thought, pushing his way through the mass of people. A group of men chanting and whirling rattles pushed him to one side as they streamed past. "Idiots," he muttered to himself, struggling to get past them.

He searched for over half an hour but caught no sight of Lewis, and in the end had to stop searching and return to the station to catch a train and go back to Redcar. He was now no further on in his search, except that he thought Lewis must live in Redcar as he'd caught the train from there that morning. All he could do was to return to London tomorrow, hope that his employers didn't know of his journey, and work out a way to discover where the schoolmaster lived in the town. Then he would also have to decide how to kill him without suspicion falling on himself. He was determined he would have his revenge.

CHAPTER 23

In Howdale, Christmas Day started cold and frosty but with clear skies and little or no wind. In How End House, Sir Keith Dyke woke up alone. It was the first Christmas he had been on his own since his marriage and the house was quiet and empty. He had given the two local women who came to help Angela with the housework the day off to be with their families, so he would be alone all day. Because Angela had been away for a few weeks now, and the children missing even longer, he hadn't bothered to put up any decorations or buy a tree. He was woken at eight by the phone ringing downstairs and he got out of bed, put on his dressing gown and went down to answer it. The hall was cold and slightly damp, and even in his slippers his feet were cold.

"Yes?" he croaked into the phone. "Who's that?"

"Keith," a voice said. "It's Edgar. How are you, old man? No news from that bitch of a wife, I suppose?"

"Oh morning, Fenn," Keith smiled into the empty hallway. "No. Not a peep from her. I suppose she's still up at that farm. But I'm actually better off on my own." He paused for a moment then went on. "Except for the appearance of it, of course. I don't want to make people think there's a problem between us. That wouldn't do at all."

On the other end of the phone Edgar Fenn-Williams sighed. "No," the science master said. "I suppose not. Not just now anyway, not until all this business with the police poking around is over. Look, the buses will be running tomorrow, can I come up and see you? I could stay for a few days and we can talk over our options."

"Yes, that would be good," Keith replied. "It's a pity you couldn't have come today. I could have driven down to get you."

"I have to visit my nephew, you know we always do at Christmas, and we have to keep everything looking as normal as possible. Even if my wife has left me alone to go off with Willoughby Danbury for the holidays. So I'll just have to go by myself and make excuses for her not being there. I think she's planning to ask me for a divorce. I hope so anyway, then we'll both be free, that is if Angela doesn't come back to you. Oh, and Happy Christmas, Keith."

"Yes, I suppose we will be, free I mean. But I must keep everything looking normal for as long as possible, at least on the surface. A scandal wouldn't be good for business. Anyway, Happy Christmas to you too, Edgar, see you tomorrow."

They rang off and Sir Keith went upstairs to dress and face the day alone.

Across the yard, the two cousins and the widow were beginning their preparations for Christmas. They had all got together to celebrate the day for several years now. They had a roaring log fire in the hearth, and she was putting the goose she had plucked and stuffed yesterday in the oven. It was one of the geese she kept behind her cottage. At the same time the men were preparing the vegetables they had grown, potatoes, cabbage, parsnips and Brussels sprouts. On the sideboard were bottles of elderflower, bramble and red currant wine they had all made the previous year. As well as these, there was a half empty bottle of dandelion wine on the table alongside three almost empty glasses. Austerity didn't touch these three, as they were self sufficient in most things. It would be Christmas as usual as far as they were concerned, and the celebrations had already started.

They were all concerned about the family next door though and it had dominated their thoughts for weeks now. The consensus they had reached, however, was that Lady Dyke and the children were best off without Sir Keith. They also hoped that the bairns were safe and well somewhere. They picked up and emptied their glasses on that thought.

In Redcar police station DC Greg Lince, who had drawn the short straw to be on duty on Christmas Day, was sitting with his feet up on the desk, smoking a cigar his wife had given him for Christmas and reading yesterday's Daily Chronicle. It was quiet here in the station, as it usually was on Christmas morning, and he was bored and thinking of his delayed Christmas dinner that he would have when he got home that evening.

Far away in Birmingham, his inspector was waking up to face a day with his parents, his brother and his wife and their three children aged from three to eleven. He had been away from home for years now and had little in common with any of them, and in any case didn't particularly like children or they him. He had had a day of them all already and was looking forward to five o'clock when, lunch and the King's Speech over, he could set off back to his small cold flat in Redcar. It was mid morning before he finally got up, unable to put it off any more and went downstairs into what he thought was a minor riot, but which in fact was just his two nephews and one niece playing with their new toys. His entry into the room brought a fresh outburst of noise as he handed them their presents from him. Sometime later, as he helped his sister-in-law peel the potatoes, the thought of the two Dyke children came into his mind and he hoped that they were also enjoying their Christmas, wherever they were.

In Saltburn, Lewis got up late and went down to make his solitary breakfast. Yesterday he had seen Beryl after she had finished her work at the library, but only for a short while as she was going to her parents later to stay over until Boxing Day. They had swapped Christmas presents with strictures on both their parts not to open them until Christmas Day. He looked out of the window as he waited for the kettle to boil, and saw that a pale sun was shining from a washed out sky and that there had been a frost again. It had been a cold winter so far and the long range forecasts, if you could rely on them, were for it to continue and get even worse. The last time the coalman had called, according to his neighbours who took it in for him, the man had only had about a dozen bags on his cart. Certainly, when Lewis got home, he found that the coalman had only left him two bags. He remembered that he must go next door to give them their Christmas presents and those for their grandchildren. That thought in turn reminded him to open Beryl's present. While the tea brewed, he went to get it off the hallstand where he'd left it the night before.

Opening the parcel, he found she had given him a sweater. It was blue and had a red pattern on it. She had obviously knitted it herself and he knew it must have taken quite a lot of time to knit and also that the wool would have required a lot of clothing coupons. He thought that showed that she was quite committed to their relationship, and eased his worries that she might consider his present a bit over the top.

That afternoon Beryl rang him. He wasn't expecting her to, as he knew her parents didn't have a phone, but as he heard the pennies fall into the box realised she must have gone out to a phone box.

"Lewis," she burst out excitedly. "First, thank you very much for the jewellery, love, I'll not ask how much you spent." There was a catch in her voice, and then she went on, "It's lovely. Oh, I do miss you, you know, on this of all days."

"I miss you, Beryl, and thanks...."

"Shh! Listen, I haven't long, I've come out whilst the King is on the radio and haven't any more change for the phone. I didn't tell you yesterday as I wasn't sure.... well, never mind that now. I didn't tell you that because I volunteered to work yesterday, Christmas Eve, as the library was open and nobody wanted to work, well..."

She didn't tell me because she wasn't sure of our relationship, Lewis thought, as she paused for breath, just as I wasn't sure either. But now she is. And she's nervous and babbling on, which isn't like her at all.

Breath back, she continued. "Well, I've got Friday, Monday and Tuesday off, and Wednesday is New Year's Day so the library isn't open then. So I could come over and stay with you for six whole days." She broke off again then went on doubtfully, "That is, if you want me to."

Hearing the uncertainty in her voice, he suddenly realised that he did want that. Very much indeed. "Yes, of course I do, love," he said. "And thanks for the sweater, it's...." He was going to say fine, but knew that wasn't strong enough. "Lovely, really nice. It must have taken you ages."

"It helps to pass the time when I'm behind the desk in the library," she laughed. "If you're sure about the long weekend, we'll have to think of something to do, to pass the time."

"There's always bed," he answered.

"Yes, that," she said, "But not all the time. I'll think of something. Well, I must get back to my duty. We had chicken for dinner, and Christmas pud. I hope you managed something nice."

"Sure," he said. "But next weekend will be nicer. I'll see what I can get in for us to eat, so that we needn't go out." He had in fact had corned beef sandwiches with a sweet pickle that his next door neighbour had made, followed by a baked apple off the tree in his garden. He'd been saving up his coupons so that he could buy something a bit special for her next visit. He was very glad he had, as now the visit would be a long one.

Giggling, she said, "Bye, love. Oh, I forgot, Happy Christmas."

"Happy Christmas." He hesitated and then added, "Darling," before putting the phone down. Well, I think I'm committed now, he thought, as he went back into his living room and switched the wireless on to get the football results. Middlesbrough had been playing away at Leeds today, and tomorrow on Boxing Day Leeds would be at Ayresome Park playing them. That was the match that he and DI Fenwick were going to see, if the inspector could get away from the station. He waited impatiently until the results came on and the reporter read out the scores, at last getting to the Leeds match.

"Leeds United three, Middlesbrough three." Lewis heard the score almost in disbelief and wished that he'd been there. It must have been quite a match, he thought. I should have gone, he told himself but knew it was impossible on Christmas Day to have got to Leeds on the train, and he didn't have enough petrol to get there and back. And he needed what petrol he had for next weekend, so that he and Beryl could go out somewhere nice. Perhaps tomorrow's match would be as good, he thought to himself in consolation.

Later that night, Lewis found an old Evening Gazette from Monday, and looked at the adverts for the cinemas in Redcar and Saltburn, thinking that perhaps he and Beryl could go to one on the Friday or Saturday evenings. He saw that the Regent at Redcar had a new Hitchcock film called 'Notorious' on the Saturday, whilst the Saltburn cinema was showing a musical, 'London Town' with Petula Clark in it on Friday, and a film with both Eric Portman and Dulcie Grey on the bill on Saturday, called 'Wanted for Murder'. All three of them sounded like their sort of films, he thought.

All the excitement caused by Beryl's call and the football result had driven all thoughts of Kurt Vogel and the danger he might pose completely out of his mind, and it wasn't until he was in bed that it came back to him. That night he had one of his nightmares about the war which he thought had gone for good. It had been over six months now since the last one.

CHAPTER 24

Lewis woke on Boxing Day unrefreshed and with a headache after his disturbed night. After a lethargic wash, he swallowed two Aspro's and made a pot of tea but didn't feel like any breakfast. He had thought that his nightmares and disturbed sleep were a thing of the past, but the appearance of Kurt Vogel had brought them back.

Shortly after ten o'clock the phone rang and such was his mood his first thought was that it would be Beryl ringing to cancel their time together. His pessimism was unfounded, as when he answered he heard the voice of DI Fenwick.

"Morning, Lewis," the inspector began. "How was your day? Mine was as bad as I expected."

"Oh," said Lewis listlessly. "It was quiet, but then I didn't expect anything else."

"Well, I'm ringing with good news." In contrast to the teacher, the detective was sounding positive. "The station is quiet and my two DC's on duty can easily be left for the afternoon, so I'll be with you for the Leeds match this afternoon."

"Good," Lewis said, his mood lightening somewhat, as he'd forgotten about the day's arrangements with Fenwick altogether.

"Did you see the score yesterday?" the inspector said. "Three-three in the end. Micky Fenton got one of the Boro's goals and Johnny Spuhler the other two."

Lewis, who hadn't known who had scored, just grunted into the phone and Tom Fenwick said, "So, I'll see you as arranged at half past two. Don't be late," he said cheerily and rang off.

Feeling slightly more cheerful after the call, Lewis thought he would go out for a short walk to clear his head. He was just putting his overcoat on when the phone rang again. He stared at it beside him on the hall table and almost didn't pick it up, fearful that this time it would be Beryl cancelling their few days together. Then he shrugged and grimaced, even if he didn't answer it, it wouldn't change anything, he knew. So he lifted the phone and said, "Yes," curtly into it.

"Lewis," said a suave voice in his ear. "How are you, old man? Happy Christmas, by the way." He couldn't have been more startled if the handset had bit his ear. It was the well-known voice of his ex-boss in SOE that he hadn't thought to ever hear again.

"Sir," he managed to blurt out at last. "To what do I owe this ...?" He baulked at the word pleasure, paused and then started again. "Why are you ringing me, what do you want?"

"Mr Merton, not sir," the general said. "Just as I didn't call you Brigadier. We're both just civilians now."

Lewis doubted that General Merton was, or ever would be, just a civilian. He repeated, "So what do you want?" One good thing was that he was now wide awake and alert with his headache gone. Whether this was the result of the pills, the inspector's call or his being on his guard against the general, he didn't know, but only that he was.

"Come come, Lewis old chap. I'm just ringing to see how the new job is working out and to wish you a merry Christmas. Which I note you haven't returned." The general sounded cheerful and as usual well in control of himself and the situation. "Why should I want anything?"

After a pause, Lewis said, "Ok. Happy Christmas to you, sir. I'm quite well, thank you, and the job is just what I thought it would be. So goodbye."

Lewis waited, not putting the phone down and the general went on urbanely and not at all put out. "Well, Brigadier, there's just one little thing you might do for me." He stopped speaking when Lewis said, "Hah," in reply then continued smoothly on. "Well, not for me directly, but for someone who works with me."

"SOE?" said Lewis bewildered. "I thought that was disbanded."

"No, not SOE. I work for the Foreign Office now."

"Six, then?" Lewis asked.

"You always were melodramatic, Lewis. It's just a favour for a friend I work with. He wants to talk to you."

"Me? Are you sure you've got the right man? I'm just a schoolmaster now. What does he want, to get his kid into St Bede's?" Lewis was almost mocking.

"Now, now, my boy," said the general sharply. "I understand that you are helping the local constabulary in the form of a certain Inspector Fenwick, in the cases of two missing children and two more who appear to have been murdered. Isn't that so?"

How the hell does he know all that? Lewis wondered, but answered his own question. Because MI6 and MI5 had agents all over the place. He should know that better than most.

"So, what if I am helping Tom Fenwick?"

"Well," the general began, choosing his words carefully. "This, er, colleague of mine might have some information to offer on the case, but neither he nor I want any direct involvement with the police. He, we, thought you might act as a conduit, a liaison man, between them and us. What about it, Lewis? He would be available on Saturday to talk to you. You could travel here tomorrow and stay the weekend. You've no school as it's the Christmas holidays. All expenses on us, of course. We've booked you a room in a very nice hotel in Bayswater. You could take in a show or something up here.

128

He'd only want to take up a couple of hours of your time, and he lives quite close to the hotel. What do you say?"

Lewis said, glad of an excuse, "Can't do this Saturday, sir. I've got a rather important er, liaison of my own, you could say, starting tomorrow then lasting for a few more days."

There was a long pause before the general said slowly, "Is this anything to do with, I believe she's called Miss Cooper?" How the devil does he know about Beryl as well, Lewis thought. Then once again he answered himself by acknowledging that Six had agents everywhere. The general was carrying on speaking and Lewis had missed the first few words. "....with you. We could pay for her fare as well, and we'll change the booking to either a double or two single rooms. Just as you wish. How long was that 'few days' by the way?"

"We have plans from tomorrow until the second of January," said Lewis, stretching it by a day. If the secret service wanted him to come to London that much, then they could pay for him and Beryl to spend their time together there. At the other end of the phone, Lewis heard the general sigh.

"All right, Brigadier," he said. "You always could drive a hard bargain. Just travel up tomorrow and I'll arrange all the rest. Now, here's where the hotel is and where to go to meet our man on Saturday." And he proceeded to give Lewis all the details.

Later that day, Lewis met up with the DI and they walked to Ayresome Park from Middlesbrough station together. Tom told the schoolteacher all about his Christmas in Birmingham, whilst Lewis walked beside him deep in thought. They bought their tickets and went into the ground, with Fenwick acknowledging greetings from some of the constables on duty who he knew. As they took their seats in the New Stand, Tom said, "You've not really been listening, have you Lewis?" getting a denial of this from him. "Tell me what you've been up to then," the inspector demanded.

"Not much, very quiet time really," Lewis said. "But I hope to go away for a few days tomorrow."

The DI looked at him. "Alone, or with Beryl by any chance?"

"With her, I hope," Lewis said. "But if she isn't keen I'll probably not go and just spend it at home with her."

Fenwick couldn't really make head or tail of this answer, but before he could reply or ask Lewis to expand on it, the teams started to come out of the tunnel opposite where they were sitting. The noise of the crowd drowned out any more conversation.

Soon the match was underway and the inspector's attention was fully on the game. Leeds United, who were in their usual away strip of white shirts and black shorts, were playing from left to right. The Boro in red shirts and white shorts were soon in control of the game and their goalkeeper, Dave Cummings, had little to do. It was an exciting match, and although the two teams had played each other only yesterday they both seemed full of energy. Lewis was lost in thought all through the match and hardly noticed what was happening on the pitch. His thoughts were full of the appearance of Kurt Vogel in Redcar and any danger he may pose; the phone call from his ex-boss General Merton and just what that might herald; and his hope that Beryl would agree to come to London with him and if she could wangle an extra day off from her work at the library. He barely registered the fact when the Boro centre forward, Micky Fenton, scored the first goal. Or when he then got a second and the outside left, Geoff Walker, also scored one to end the match three-nil in Middlesbrough's favour.

Fenwick had been aware of his friend's preoccupation, but whatever he said he couldn't break into his thoughts and they travelled back to Redcar in silence.

"See you after your break," he said, as he left the train. "So as I'll not see you for a bit, I'll wish you a Happy New Year now."

"What?" answered Lewis, becoming aware of where he was. "Oh, yes. Right, and to you too, Tom. All the best for 1947."

The train reached Saltburn and he got out and walked back to the Laurels in Albion Terrace. Once there he revived the fire, as the weather was still very cold and snow was once more forecast. Beryl was due later that evening to stay for the next few days as they had arranged. She was going back to her flat from her parent's home, to collect some clothes and catch the bus that would get to Saltburn at eight forty. Once he had got the house warm, he went into the garage and got his car out. He would drive to Redcar to tell her of what he had arranged with the general, he had decided. Then, if she agreed to come to London with him, she could pack a suitcase for the trip.

Lewis reached Beryl's flat before she did and sat outside waiting for her, watching as the first few snowflakes fell from the sky, glistening in the streetlights. When she appeared, he got out to meet her.

"What are you doing here, Lewis? I was going to catch the bus."

"Let's go inside out of the cold and I'll tell you," he answered.

It didn't take long to explain and to his relief she was delighted. "Oh yes, I'd love a few days in London. We can go to Piccadilly Circus to see the New Year in, I've heard that's the place to be. I wonder what this general of yours wants, have you no idea?"

"No, not a clue."

"Well, I'll ring the library on Monday and say I'm taking a day's leave, so that won't be a problem. It's really quiet at this time of year. Oh, and on the way to yours tonight, we'll have to call in at my parents' house to let them know where I'm going. It's a chance for you to meet them. You do want to, don't you?" She stopped talking breathless and looked at him anxiously. She was almost sure that he wanted their relationship to be long term. Surely he wouldn't have bought her such an expensive present if not. When he smiled and nodded, she relaxed and then smiled slyly at him. "You did ask for a double room, didn't you?"

"Of course, love. Now come on then, get packed."

As it was late by the time they left her parents' house, they stopped at Marske on the way to Saltburn and bought fish and chips for their supper. Once at her parent's house he'd been introduced and then given a slice of her mother's Christmas cake, with a piece of white Wensleydale cheese and a glass of whisky. All in all then, it was nearly eleven when they got to his home and as they'd have to be up early to catch a train to London, they went straight up to bed. He would, he'd decided, do his own packing in the morning.

She had been excited and their lovemaking had been quite wild and almost abandoned, then she had fallen asleep almost at once. Lewis had lain awake for a long time, not quite able to rid his mind of all his worries. He fell asleep at last at about three in the morning, and dozed fitfully until he was woken by Beryl at six when she brought him a cup of tea. She looked lovely, he thought, as she stood holding out the cup to him, her hair all awry and wearing only a flimsy dressing gown. He pulled her down into the bed again and this time their lovemaking was slow and very satisfactory. Perhaps everything would be okay, he told himself drowsily, drifting back into sleep before being prodded back to life by Beryl poking him in the ribs.

"Oy, come on. Get up, time for you to pack and for us to get off," she told him firmly.

CHAPTER 25

On Boxing Day, DS Kenneth Rutter came back from his two day Christmas break to find his DI, Tom Fenwick, alone at the police station. Rutter was new to the force, having transferred from Northumberland a short while ago where he had been a detective constable. He was short for a policeman and Fenwick, looking at him as he walked into the room, wondered if he actually was five foot eight as regulations stipulated. Or if perhaps a sympathetic doctor had let him through with a bit of leniency. He was fit and healthy though, the DI acknowledged, and very intelligent. So if he wasn't quite tall enough, Fenwick had no quarrel with his apparent lack of a fraction of an inch.

Fenwick smiled at his sergeant. "Good morning, Ken," he greeted him. "Hope you had a good break."

Rutter nodded his head, which was completely bald despite his age of twenty-six. "Sir," he replied, "And you too, I hope." Getting just a grunt in reply.

"It's been quiet over the holiday, I've been told," his inspector said, "and there's little to do. So I'll leave you on your own after lunch, if that's alright. Everyone else is still on holiday or in the case of DC Hubbert out somewhere. I'm going to see the Boro play, so if you need me you can contact the superintendent on duty at Ayresome Park and he'll find me. But only if you really need me, mind."

Rutter was glad to be on his own. Since joining the team under Fenwick, he had been given the task of trying to find out more about the disappearance of Percy Kerridge and his subsequent murder. He had come to the conclusion that the two bodies buried in the woods near How End House must be linked. Accordingly he'd widened his inquiries and tried to find out the identity of the girl. DC Ted Metcalf had already done a lot of research on this and he wanted to read through all his reports. When he had read them all, he thought the DC had done a thorough job but that the task had been almost impossible. The girl had disappeared in either 1942 or 1943, or at least that's when she'd been killed according to the doctor. Ted Metcalf had looked into every report of a missing thirteen, fourteen or fifteen year old girl from that time. He'd looked at reports from an area stretching from York in the south to the Scottish border in the north. The problem was of course that it had been wartime, and lots of people went missing for all sorts of reasons. Many had been killed by enemy bombs and not all of them were able to be identified. This of course was on top of the normal number of teenagers who just ran away from home. There had also been the problem of many records also having been destroyed in bombing raids. To complicate matters further, the police force at that time was overworked and understaffed. Teesside, Tyneside and Wearside were the mostly likely places where the girl may have come from. These were also where the heaviest bombing had taken place. All of which had made the DC's task almost impossible.

Despite all of the complications, DC Metcalf had come up with a list of ten names, four of which he thought were the most likely. By the time DS Rutter had read all of Metcalf's reports, it was late afternoon and he was tired and so called it a day.

The following morning the office was back to normal and he decided to take Ted Metcalf with him to talk to Elizabeth Waverly, the matron of Blue Doors. She had given Blue Doors as her home address when she was first interviewed and that was where they found her. He had read his DI's comments about the argument between her, the headmaster and Albert McIntyre that a teacher, Lewis Sudbury, had told the DI about.

Miss Waverly was in her flat at Blue Doors and invited them in. "I don't know if I can tell you any more about Robert Dyke than I did when he went missing. He was a nice boy, a bit shy though and also a loner, but always very polite and pleasant."

"It was more Percy Kerridge we wanted to ask you about," DS Rutter said.

"Kerridge? Well, that was a long time ago. I was here of course and knew him," Miss Waverly said. "He was a nice lad too from what I recall. He went home at the end of the year, nineteen forty-four was it? And never came back." She paused and smiled. "It happened quite a bit then, you know. Boys going home and not coming back for all sorts of reasons."

"So I believe," the DC said. He paused, knowing he must tread carefully as he only had a third hand report of the quarrel in the headmaster's study. This had been overheard by a caretaker, passed on to a teacher, who had then told his DI. "I believe," he began, "that you had a falling out with the head over the missing...." Here he paused, as he didn't want to say boy as he believed it may have been the girl they were talking about rather than the boy. So he waited a few seconds and when she just sat staring at him, said, "Mr McIntyre was there as well, I believe."

He got no further as she said loudly, "He shouldn't have said anything. It was a private conversation and there was no evidence just suspicions, but the head told me to say nothing and he, McIntyre, I think he wanted to tell....well, to tell your inspector. But I may have remembered it wrongly."

DC Ted Metcalf was looking perplexed and opened his mouth to say something, but Ken shut him up with a shake of his head then said quietly, "So who do you think she was?"

Miss Waverly was silent for a long time and then said, "Suspected she might be, it was no more than that. But the

136

head said it wasn't possible and didn't want a scandal. Mr McIntyre agreed with him and we all argued about it. Then Mr Sudbury came in and we all shut up. Later we agreed, or at least the head and McIntyre did, that it was all just supposition and I went along with it. So he shouldn't have said anything." She stopped talking and the room was quiet.

"Who did you think she might be, Miss Waverly?" Ken Rutter asked quietly again, breaking the silence.

"He must have said," she said, suddenly on her guard.

"I'd like you to say too, if you would please," the sergeant persisted.

"Yes. Verification, I suppose. Well, I thought she may, only may you understand, have been young Alice," the matron replied.

"Alice?"

"Yes, Alice Bates, the art master's daughter." And it all came out then, once she'd started there was no stopping her. "She was nearly fifteen and a right trollop. Well, he was a bit bohemian you know, her father. He had wild grey hair and a beard and was very excitable. They lived in a caravan, parked it on that bit of land behind the school, near the woodwork classroom. That's that wooden hut beyond the playground. He had his wife and Alice living there with him, that is if she was his wife. But the head would hear no wrong about him, said he was a talented and well known artist. But Alice, she was no better than she should have been, if you know what I mean. Despite this I quite liked her, she was only a kid really and quite lonely I think. Anyway in '42, just after the school broke up for the year, he, Mr Bates that is, had a heart attack and died. Then Alice and her mother left. Well, I say her mother but I have my doubts about that as well. Anyway, they left and later the school had the caravan towed away." And she stopped talking at last.

"So why do you think the girl in the woods is Alice Bates?" the DC asked.

"What?" Elizabeth Waverly sounded distracted now, all the energy drained from her. "Oh. Well, I saw the woman again several times after that. She'd taken up with another man in the town, but when I asked where Alice was she said she didn't know."

They could get nothing else useful out of her and she said she didn't know the man's name, only that she hadn't seen any of them for years now.

As they walked back to the police station, Ted Metcalf said, "She wasn't on my list, Sarge, Alice Bates that is. She were never reported missing but it seems likely, don't it?"

"Yes, I'd say so. But we must try to trace any of the others you identified to be on the safe side. But yes, I'd say Alice is our best bet."

CHAPTER 26

It was mid afternoon when Lewis Sudbury and Beryl Cooper reached the small commercial hotel in Bayswater. It was only a short walk from Queensferry underground station which was on the central line. They went up to the reception desk and signed in, handing over some food coupons as they had been told they'd have to. Waiting for Lewis was a letter from his old SOE boss, General Merton, informing him that he would be picked up at nine thirty in the morning to go to his appointment. Wherever it was he was going to meet the man from the Foreign Office, it seemed that 'not too far away' had to be reached by car. Once they had booked in, Lewis and Beryl went back by tube to Oxford Circus to have a walk around the West End.

Beryl had only been to London twice before, both times in the war on short passes when she had been in the Wrens. Then the streets had been full of people in uniform, there were walls of sandbags outside many of the buildings and rubble piled up everywhere. All the shop windows had been covered in webs of white tape to prevent the glass splintering and flying everywhere if it was shattered by bombs. Walking round that Saturday evening, not only had all the defences and rubble been removed but there was hardly a uniform in sight. People's clothes, though, were no smarter than those in Yorkshire, and most of the passersby looked dowdy. There was much more traffic on the roads than in the north-east, which was she thought was just to be expected in such a large city. However most of it was buses and taxis, with quite a lot of horse drawn vehicles. She had expected to see brewers' drays but not the number of wagons carrying goods.

As they walked through the streets, they passed many gaps between the houses where buildings destroyed by bombs had once stood. Quite a lot of the walls to either side of these vacant plots were shored up with strong timber buttresses. In some of them children were playing on the rough ground.

"It doesn't take long for normality to return after such destruction," Beryl observed.

Later that evening they went to see Ivor Novello in 'Perchance to Dream', which they both liked, and then found a reasonable restaurant not far from Piccadilly Circus to round off the day. As they walked past the bomb sites in the dark, they heard the sound of laughter and smelt cigarette smoke coming from some of them, whilst from others there came more suggestive sounds as courting couples' made use of them.

All in all, though, they both agreed it had been a good start to their few days together in London. The next morning, Lewis was up early leaving Beryl still in bed. She had decided to look round the shops later, whilst he went to meet the man from the FO.

At nine thirty precisely, a large black saloon car drew up outside the hotel and a smartly dressed chauffeur got out as Lewis came through the doors. The man had obviously been given a photo or a good description of him for he said, "Mr Sudbury, please get in," with no question in his tone at all. Obediently, Lewis got into the back of the car and they set off. Lewis didn't know London well, in all his previous visits he had travelled by tube and not above ground. They crossed the Thames and went in a southerly direction. Or at least so Lewis thought, though he was soon in unfamiliar territory. However it wasn't a long drive and somewhere near Guildford, he was sure of that as he saw a signpost, the car pulled up at a set of closed iron gates and the driver sounded his horn. A man in a smart black suit came out, checked the car, and opened the gates. Lewis believed the man was a soldier of some sort.

The house had a high brick wall all round it and was a medium sized property built of yellow London bricks, probably constructed in the 1920's, Lewis reckoned. The front garden was small and formally laid out, consisting of lawns and borders of shrubs. As the car drew up, the front door was opened by another military looking man also in a dark suit. All in all, Lewis decided, the householder must be a man of substantial position in the FO, and he wondered just what he wanted of a Yorkshire schoolteacher.

He was taken across a square hallway, which had patterned floor tiles and half panelled walls with green wallpaper above, into a comfortable lounge. The man waiting there for him came forward with an outstretched hand. "Good morning Mr Sudbury, it's very good of you to come all this way to see me. I'm Wilfred Lawrence, by the way, but most people call me Freddie, so please feel free to do the same."

"Thank you, sir," Lewis answered, instantly on alert, for he knew the name. It was what Tom Fenwick had said the man in the third cottage at How End was called. "It was no trouble at all, to come here I mean." Lewis spoke slowly, giving himself time to think. "And please call me Lewis. You have a lovely house here, I see," he said, looking round. It was a large room furnished with comfortable easy chairs placed around a coffee table. Down one side of the room was a dining table with six chairs set round it. It was almost identical in decoration to the hall but had several rugs scattered over the floor. Wilfred Lawrence himself was suave, confident and well groomed with silver grey hair parted down the middle. He was smartly dressed in a blue pinstriped suit, a white shirt and a dark blue tie. He was, Lewis thought, slightly taller than himself with a thin body that was just beginning to thicken out.

"Well, please sit down Lewis. There's coffee coming shortly, but let me tell you why I asked to see you."

"Thank you, sir." Lewis took a chair on the other side of a coffee table to the one Freddie had already taken. It was a comfortable brown leather one and he sat back, relaxing a little. Outside the window he could see a garden and hear children's voices. After the cold of the morning outside, the room was warm and almost soporific. He came awake and alert as the other man spoke.

"Let me start by telling you a story. Many years ago," Freddie began, "twenty two to be precise, in 1925 when I was just thirty....."

Lewis did some quick sums, so that makes him fifty two then, he calculated. A well kept fifty two at that, he thought.

But Freddie was still talking. "....have much of a position, unlike now. I'm a, well let's just say a section head in the FO now, one that is concerned with Russian affairs. I've always been attached to the Russian desk, as I learned the language at Oxford. In those days it was all about the Czar and revolution and so on, and later about being allies in the war. Now of course.... but never mind that. To get back to my story.

"In about 1925 I met a young woman who was married to an older man, who had, still has for that matter, certain.... preferences shall we call them that have nothing to do with young women." He stopped talking and got up and went to the window and waved at someone in the garden. Then he turned round again, once more smiling. The grim face he'd had at the end of his last sentence had gone.

"Let me go back a bit. You may know that I own a cottage at How End, yes? Good, well Sir Keith bought the property, oh a long time ago when it ceased to be a farm, and I bought mine off him some time later. That was when he'd done up the old farmhouse for himself and modernised the three farm labourers' cottages. I bought one of them as a place I could go to from time to time to get away from London.

"Sir Keith was an up and coming man in those days and is now, as you know, a rich and successful business man. He is also quite ruthless and has fallen out with many people over the years, including his own brother. Well, that's as may be, but he has also always been keen to present a conventional front to the world. This of course is because it's good for both his business affairs and also for his social standing. To this end he married a young girl of about eighteen in '21, even though his preferences, shall we say, are far removed from women. But if his true nature had been known at that time, he wouldn't have succeeded so well in his business affairs and he would have been shunned by society. Especially in the north-east in those days, and that's not to mention the legality of it all."

Listening, Lewis wondered just what DS Voyle's reactions would be if he heard of Sir Keith's peculiarities, given his suspicions of the two cousins. Then Freddie continued.

"Well now, to tie the two stories up." Wilfred Lawrence broke off as the door opened, and a woman came in carrying a tray set out with three cups, a coffee pot, milk, sugar and biscuits. It was real coffee, Lewis realised by the smell. There was little sign of austerity in this house, he decided, eyeing the chocolate biscuits on the tray. He'd not seen them since he'd returned to England after the war. The woman carrying the tray was stylishly dressed in a creamy white blouse and a three quarter length black velvet skirt. She had shiny darkish hair with a few streaks of grey in it and a smooth round face. As she came into the room she said, "Hello, Mr Sudbury," and smiled.

Startled, he looked more closely at her and realised this was Angela Dyke. He hadn't recognised her at all, as the last time he'd seen her she had been haggard with deep lines in her face and dark rings round her eyes and was unkemptly dressed. She had looked at least ten years older than her 42 years and now looked, perhaps, only to be in her mid thirties.

"Lady Dyke," he said, returning her smile. "It's good to see you, and looking so well too."

"Angela, please," she replied. "Now, how do you like your coffee? Milk? Sugar?"

When they were all seated with drinks beside them, Freddie went on. "As I was saying when Angela came in, now to tie up my two stories. Angela and I met shortly after her marriage to Dyke. She had been just eighteen when she married him, as I said. He wanted a wife to present a normal face to the world. However, if Angela doesn't object, I will add that the marriage was never consummated, as I have told you already he had other preferences."

"Please, just tell him all the facts, Freddie," she put in. "I don't mind. We need to sort this out."

"Yes, dear," Freddie said. "So, to cut a long story short, Angela turned to me in her distress and after some time we became close. I can say very close."

"We were in love," she cut in impatiently. "The children are his, not my so-called husband's."

"Yes," Freddie agreed smoothly. "But Dyke didn't mind all that much as it made his marriage look as if it was, shall we say, normal. Neither of us could afford a scandal, him for his standing in society and me for my career, which I'm sorry to say I valued highly. Then came the war and he was even busier, just as I was myself. Now, none of it seems so important anymore. As long as there's no scandal, both he and I can manage a divorce without causing any serious damage to either of us. And Angela, I know, feels the same." He paused then said, "So that just leaves the children."

Lewis, who had been wondering about them, said, "Yes, so what about the children, or should I say your children, do you know where they are?"

"Oh, yes," said Freddie, showing a slight discomfort for the first time. "They're here."

"Here?" Lewis said, with a question in his voice. He had in fact worked that out already, but wasn't willing to admit to it. He wanted to find out as much as he could.

"Yes, here," Freddie replied then hurried on. "They came straight here, were here in fact late that evening. That is, the one on which Kitty went missing. Angela had always told them that if anything happened to her they were to come to me for help. They'd been here several times over the years so knew where I lived and they're both very independent."

"But why did they run off?" Lewis asked.

Angela answered. "It was partly my fault, I think. I'd been getting more and more irritable with them. I wanted to get away from Keith and come to live here with Freddie, but there was always some problem stopping me. So when Kitty started getting bullied at school, she turned to Robert rather than me. And Robert was not happy at his school either. He'd just moved up into the fourth form, and the boys were now growing up, and..." She stopped talking.

"The boys were now well into their teens," Freddie went on for her. "The boys in his dormitory, I mean. And boys of that age away from home er, experiment." He paused, glancing at Angela then continued. "Sexually, I mean, you know what boarding school is like."

145

Lewis, who had never been a boarder, simply nodded. He knew or thought he knew what went on.

"Anyway," Freddie continued. "Robert didn't like it, so between them they decided to come and find me."

"And that's all it was," said Angela. "You can go out into the garden and talk to them yourself if you wish."

"I see," Lewis said. He didn't believe that was all it was about, but didn't think it was his place to press the point. Not if the children were here and safe, and their parents were both united in their story. "But why," he asked, "did you want me to come here?"

"We thought," Freddie said smoothly, once more in control of the situation. "We thought you could let your inspector friend know the children are safe and well and...." He paused in thought, and then went on. "And edit, shall we say, the story I've told you. Take out all the references to Dyke's peculiarities. And certainly omit all references to my work in the FO. You've been in the service, and know that some things have to remain secret."

"Why didn't you just get a D notice issued? Then it would all be hushed up," Lewis said.

"I could have done, of course," Freddie said, confirming Lewis' suspicion that he was a high level MI6 officer. "But with a divorce pending in the near future, and Dyke's predilections, that may not have worked satisfactorily. Especially with the two murdered children found nearby. Both the police and the newspapers may have found a way around it. But if you could explain it to the DI, then he can just get on with his murder investigation, without having to worry about two runaway children."

Before Lewis could answer, Angela said with a smile, "We would be ever so grateful, Lewis. And Dyke won't make any trouble about the children. He doesn't like them and will be glad to get rid of them." Then she added, "I hear you are here with my sister, Beryl. Perhaps you could bring her to tea tomorrow, so she can see Bob and Kitty as well, and me too of course."

It was then that Lewis knew just how much he'd been manipulated by MI6. He had thought he'd taken advantage of them by wangling a holiday for Beryl at their expense, whilst all along they'd been quite happy for her to come with him. They had, in fact, wanted him to bring her. He let none of this show on his face though; years of leading a double life in Germany had taught him how to keep his expression impassive. He simply smiled and said, "Sure, I'll ask her if she wants to come. But if I do all this for you, there is something you could do in return." He thought he could use the secret service's resources to his advantage.

"In what way can we help you?" Freddie asked, frowning.

"Well," Lewis answered. "I've been followed by a German. He's an ex-SS man who I knew in Berlin in the war. He was called Kurt Vogel, but will probably be using another name now. He was injured in an explosion and has a scar on his face and a stiff leg that may be a false one. I'm not sure what he's doing in England or how he got here, but I think he holds me responsible for his injuries. If so, he could be a danger to me."

"I'll see what I can do to clip his wings, if I can find him," Freddie promised.

That afternoon, Lewis gave Beryl an edited version of events and the next day they both returned to the house near Guildford and met the children. The rest of their stay in London passed pleasantly, and they returned to Yorkshire in a good frame of mind.

PART THREE
CHAPTER 27

"My mother came from the south of Spain, from a region called Andalucía." Once again Lewis had allowed himself to be diverted from his teaching by his pupils into talking about memories of his childhood. He didn't really mind, as these were his fourth form students who were well up to the required level. They were also 'his' class as he described them to himself, the first one that he taught that he hadn't taken over from Mr Allen. Added to this, it was the last class on Friday afternoon and there was only about a quarter of an hour to go before the school finished for the weekend. "She came from a small village in the sierras." He stopped speaking and looked at the boys in front of him. "What are 'sierras', Bates?"

"Mountains, sir."

"Yes, mountain ranges. What else can it mean, Jones?"

"Er, a saw I think," replied the boy, not quite sure.

"Good enough, yes," Lewis answered. This was another reason he didn't mind the boys diverting him into reminiscing, he could test their knowledge as well.

"She lived in a small village far inland, which only accessible by footpaths and tracks. There were no roads going all the way to it at all. I went there several times, as I've often told you before, to visit my grandparents, cousins and so on. What's cousin in Spanish?" he asked to be answered by a chorus of "Primo" from the boys.

Smiling he went on. "Now, for your homework this weekend, I want you to find the Spanish words for village, footpath, track, road and grandparents. Then you can say what other meaning the word for village has. Yes, Abbott, as well as your other homework. This is just a little extra task to teach you not to try and sidetrack me."

At this point the bell went, and the boys began to put their books away and stand up, talking as they did so.

"Quiet. Sit down and wait until I tell you to move," Lewis said, banging the lid of his desk. Then, as the class quietened down, he said, "Right, off you go. I'll see you all Monday morning. Don't run, boy." But he was smiling as he said it and the boys streamed out calling, "Goodbye, sir," and "Have a good weekend, sir," as they went.

After the boys had gone Lewis sat at his desk, lost in thought. It was the tenth of January, and a lot had happened since his visit to Wilfred Lawrence and Angela Dyke in Guildford in December. He had returned the next day with Beryl as they had suggested, travelling in the same car that he had been taken in. Beryl had been pleased to see her sister and the children, but afterwards had agreed with him that the story of the children's reasons for running away hadn't really been fully convincing. The rest of their stay had been pleasant, and they'd gone to Piccadilly Circus as Beryl had wished to see the New Year in. Despite austerity the crowds had been large and the lights spectacular. They had also seen a couple more shows and visited London Zoo, which was now almost back to normal after the war. It was towards the end of their stay in London that Lewis proposed to Beryl and she accepted. They decided that Beryl would give up her flat in Redcar and move in with him, and that they would get married sometime in the spring.

Two days after their return, Lewis had met up with DI Fenwick and given him a censored version of the story Wilfred Lawrence had told him. In the light of this, he knew that the search for the two children would be called off, albeit after the DI had received confirmation of their safety following a visit to

Lawrence from the MET. Fenwick had also told him of the progress of the murder enquiry, which was now being led by DS Kenneth Rutter, but that it was bogged down with little chance of movement. Fenwick had also said that DS Voyle was being kept well away from the enquiry because of Dyke's preferences, given his strongly expressed views of the lifestyle of the two cousins in Howdale. The police were now almost certain that the bodies were those of Percy Kerridge and Alice Bates, but that no clue as to what had happened to them had been found. The foster parents of the boy were almost certainly dead, he had told Lewis, and no trace had been found of Matilda, Alice's father's wife, who had been Alice's stepmother in name at least, if not in law.

The two men had remained friends, and on Friday evenings still met up in a local pub to have a drink together. They made it Friday nights as Beryl went to see her parents after work then, before going home to The Laurels in Saltburn where she was now living. Usually on all the other evenings Lewis met up with her after work, and then they both travelled back home together.

Since Lewis had returned from London, Fenwick had questioned him as to his knowledge of the art master, Bates, when he was a pupil at the school. However, he hadn't been able to remember anything of significance.

"I remember him, of course I do," he'd told Tom. "He was very excitable and spittle used to come out of his mouth the more excited he got. He was a big man with long hair and a beard, and I remember he always smelled of oil paints and tobacco. He lived in a caravan near the carpentry workshop as I recall. But really that's it, he was a master and I was a boy, so we didn't mix. I remember he had a reputation as a bit of a womaniser."

"What about his daughter, Alice, did you know her?" Fenwick had asked him.

"No, not really, she was just a little kid, I think, when I was there. I do remember he had a daughter though, or at least I think I do. But this wife of his, Matilda you say she was called? I don't recall her at all. But then I wouldn't, would I?" he had told the DI.

Lewis' thoughts were brought to an abrupt end by the noise of boys in the corridor outside his room and he became aware that he was now alone in the room, all the boys having left some time ago. He stayed at his desk doing some marking, where eventually and inevitably, he was joined by the caretaker, Barry Slingsby, carrying two cups of tea. "Here you are, bonny lad," he said. "Get this down yer." They had become friends since Lewis had joined the teaching staff and it had become a habit for Barry to bring him cups of tea.

As Lewis and Slingsby sat and drank their tea, Lewis took the opportunity to question the caretaker about Bates' wife.

"Nah, lad, she weren't Alice's mam. She were late on the scene, she was. I remembers her well enough, short and well rounded with blonde hair. Quite a looker. No, Alice's mam were different altogether. Taller like, and black hair like Alice herself. She left him and the bairn one day, just upped and left. Well, he was an odd bloke, temperamental, hard to live with I'd say. And quite a one for the ladies, so who could blame her. I didn't anyhow." Barry paused, thinking back, then went on. "I was sorry for the kid though, left alone with him. Not that he was alone for long like. That Matilda moved in sharpish. The head didn't seem to mind, I think he was a bit in awe of Bates, as a painter I mean." Another pause then he finished, "Alice grew up a right little flirt, with the older boys and with some of the masters too. She were only fourteen like, but some of them were smitten. That maths teacher I told you were a bit dodgy, Jones, and McIntyre who's in charge of Blue Doors.

"Anyway, after her dad died and Matilda moved on, Alice just went too. I've not seen her since, poor lass. You say she might be the one in the woods, next to young Percy? Ah, it wouldn't surprise me a bit, poor kid.

"Well, I'll be off then Lewis, finish up me work and head off home. Have a good weekend." And he collected up the cups and left the classroom.

Lewis worked on for a while, and then went off to meet Tom Fenwick for their drink together. He'd tell the inspector what Barry Slingsby had told him about the Bates family, which he believed to be fairly reliable.

CHAPTER 28

On the following Monday morning, a man was standing looking out of a second floor window of the Foreign and Commonwealth Office. From where he stood he could see down Whitehall to the House of Commons a few hundred yards away. Rain was hitting the window in a series of hard bursts driven by a blustery gale. It had been a hard winter so far, with snow on the mountains of the Pennines and Scotland, and it was forecast to get even colder. From his vantage point he could see MPs, arriving in taxis and on foot, streaming into the House. His minister and his boss, the Foreign Secretary, Ernie Bevin, was due to deliver a statement to the House later that day regarding the increasing tensions between the allied forces that were occupying Germany, which would be based in part on information supplied by his department. The main tension was of course between the Western Nations and the Soviet Union.

His thoughts on the weather, his minister and that day's debate were interrupted by the buzzing of his intercom. He crossed to his desk and flipped the switch.

"Yes, Janet?" he said into it.

"The Permanent Secretary, Mr Ellis, is here, sir," said the voice of his secretary from the box on his desk.

"Send him in," said the man who was head of MI6. Then, to the man who entered he continued, "Ah, Ellis, come in. My men will be here soon."

"Thank you, Director." Ellis was a stout comfortable looking man dressed in the almost regulation clothes of a civil servant, consisting of a dark blue pinstriped suit, shining black shoes and white shirt. His tie showed that he had been a pupil at Eton. "Terrible weather again, there'll be snow before nightfall, I'll be bound," the Permanent Secretary said.

"Just so," the director answered. "Now, how do you want to play this?"

The other man frowned. "I'll just observe, I think. I'll only chip in if I think it necessary. And neither my minister nor the Foreign Secretary will want to be told any of the details. That way they cannot be held responsible or be accused of misleading the House in any way."

The director smiled thinly, this new government was no different to any other he'd served under, he thought. Let others get their hands dirty whilst keeping theirs clean. But it was what he was paid for, he supposed, that and safeguarding the security of the realm. Then his buzzer went once more and he depressed the switch again. "Yes, Janet?" he said into it.

"Mr Lawrence and General Merton are here, sir."

"Good. Well, I think we're ready for them." He looked at Mr Ellis who gave a nod. "So send them in if you would, Janet. Then could you rustle up some coffee, and biscuits, I think we'd all like some biscuits."

"Tea for me, please," Mr Ellis said loudly.

"Did you hear that Janet? Good, see to it, will you," he said and flipped up the switch on his intercom as the door opened. "Come in, gentlemen," the director continued. "I think you all know Mr Ellis? Yes? Good, well he's here with a watching brief for the minister. Ah, thank you, Janet," he said as his secretary came in with the drinks. "Now, take a seat and we can begin. No, Janet, we'll not be needing you. There will be no minutes of this gathering. It is just for information. You all understand that, don't you?" He looked at the others, getting a series of nods in return. "Now, Lawrence," the director continued, looking at Wilfred Lawrence. "I'll begin, if I may, with a summary of the situation you outlined to me, which is I believe the main reason we are here today." As Freddie made to answer, he waved him

154

down. "No, let me continue. As I understand it, the situation is that you have had a relationship with the wife of a prominent businessman in North Yorkshire. A man who has several important contracts with the government that are mainly to do with shipping. This liaison, shall we call it, has been going on for many years I believe. You have in fact fathered two children with this woman who you now intend to marry. And all of this with the man's knowledge and even consent. Am I correct so far, Lawrence?"

Freddie nodded. "Yes, Director, but you put it very baldly, if I may say so."

"How else can I put it?" the director asked. "All I want to establish is the facts. Now, to continue, these children ran away from home and caused quite a stir, I read about it in the Times. It could have caused you, and therefore by association HMG, a lot of embarrassment."

"Well, I think that's exaggerating," Freddie began.

"Really?" cut in the director. "Well, that's as may be, but I and Mr Ellis here would take a differing view. Now," he went on, "General Merton here I believe was instrumental in putting a lid on it. He did this by enlisting the help of a local schoolteacher, who was one of his ex-SOE operatives who has friends in the local police force. Am I still right?"

"Yes, Director," said the general. "Mr Sudbury has been a great help, and the story of the children's absence from home has been satisfactorily resolved. To the satisfaction of the local police and the press as well."

"Yes," said the directory drily. "All well and good, and if that were all there was to it, we'd not be here today." He paused and then crossed to the window and gazed out into Whitehall, before coming back and taking up his seat again. "However, there are some loose ends that could prove embarrassing or even dangerous to this department, HMG and even, I believe, this Mr Sudbury." Neither of the two men answered him, whilst Mr Ellis stared thoughtfully at his finger nails. "I refer of course to our approach to Five, our sister service. And to the apparent employment by them of an ex-SS man. And lastly of two murdered children who were found in the vicinity of your house in North Yorkshire, Lawrence." A long silence followed and then the director went on. "I'm concerned none of all this came to my attention until last Friday. But putting that to one side, let's try to sort it all out. First, the problem of your house in Yorkshire, Lawrence, I think that you really should be thinking of selling it. Neither you nor Lady Dyke should go anywhere near Sir Keith anymore and nor should the children."

"I agree, sir," Freddie said. "It's already on the market and none of us will be going there again. Except myself perhaps just briefly, if it is necessary for the sale. As to Lady Dyke, Sir Keith has already agreed to a divorce. Angela, Lady Dyke, will provide evidence of adultery. No, not with me, sir," he went on hastily, as the director made to intervene. "She has employed one of those Private Investigators who will arrange for a man to be photographed with her in, shall we say, incriminating circumstances. A co-respondent I think the man is called, one who does it professionally by arrangement." He gave a grimace, bit into a biscuit then continued. "It will be discreetly handled and I will not be involved at all. Then we will marry after a decent interval and I will formally adopt my own children. I may add that Sir Keith has agreed to all of this."

He stopped speaking and the director nodded. "Good. Now, General, perhaps you will explain why you approached Five."

General Merton nodded then said, "Certainly, Director. But first I should explain that my involvement stems from my previous relationship with the schoolteacher, Lewis Sudbury, who was in the SOE during the war, under my command. I should emphasise that he did an exceptional job as an agent for us inside the higher echelons of the SS. It cost him a lot mentally and emotionally. In the end he had to run and he spent some time in hiding before being rescued by our troops as they captured Berlin. After a considerable period recovering, he was finally discharged and took up a teaching post at St Bede's Grammar School, where Robert Dyke was a pupil. In fact, Lewis was the boy's form master. The headmaster of St Bede's asked Lewis to act as an intermediary between the school and both the police and the boy's parents, after the children went missing. By parents, I mean Sir Keith and Lady Dyke and not Freddie, Mr Lawrence, here. I approached him on behalf of Freddie when the children turned up at his house. We both thought that he could be useful in persuading the police that it had all been overdramatized. That the children hadn't really run away at all, but had come to seek help from their 'uncle', as they knew Freddie to be, and that they were both safe and well.

"It was at this point that things got a bit more complicated, shall I say." He paused and looked at the others, then continued. "In the course of his escape from the clutches of the SS, Lewis contrived an explosion, to fake his own death. This explosion, he believed, also killed a SS officer called Kurt Vogel. To his dismay, he..." Once more, the general hesitated then continued. "He recognised this Vogel following him in Middlesbrough. Fearing that the man meant to do him harm, Lewis came to me asking for help. Now, we all here know that our government, along with other governments, uses ex-Nazi people, scientists, intelligence officers and so on, on their behalf. I assumed this Vogel was either one of them, or a SS man on the run who had managed to get to England somehow.

I approached a colleague in Five, another ex-SOE man, to see if they could help locate him. We owe Lewis Sudbury a great deal for his work in the war, as well as with Freddie's children, and I felt that it would be appropriate to see what I could do on his behalf."

"I see," the director said. "I'll talk to my opposite number in Five to see what can be done about this Vogel chap. Now, it seems to me we have some priorities here. First there is Lawrence here, but that seems to be all on track to be sorted out without any involvement of the section. Then there is Sir Keith Dyke. He is at the moment of great use and value to HMG. His position in the shipping industry, so essential for the economic recovery of the country, must come before all else." Here the Permanent Secretary nodded and spoke for the first time, saying, "Absolutely."

"He has," the director continued, "A certain affinity I believe with a teacher at St Bede's, a certain Mr Fenn-Williams. Now, I don't know the exact nature of their friendship and neither do I want to know it. And I must stress here, that we are not policemen who have to uphold the law, even where we may find it to be unsavoury. We are not here to poke about into private lives, but to protect the state from foreign intervention. Do I make myself clear?" He paused, receiving nods of agreement from all the others.

"Good. So now we can concentrate on this man Vogel, or rather Five can, and doing what we can to protect Sudbury. If he is in any danger, that is.

"The only loose end then is the two bodies found near Sir Keith Dyke's house. Is there any indication that he is involved in these murders?"

"Not as far as I am aware, Director," said General Merton.

"And how close are the police to solving the crime?"

"From what Mr Sudbury has told me, not close at all, Director. It all happened a long time ago, in the war, and I'm not sure they even know who the girl was for certain," the general told him.

"Right, well I believe that concludes our business, gentlemen. I'll get on to Five and try to sort out this German character. Perhaps, General, you'll let me know if there is anything in the future about those two unfortunates in the wood. That is, if you hear about it from Sudbury and also if you think it will affect our interests of course. One last point. In future, General, let me know before you go contacting any other agency. Agreed, yes, good."

Shortly after that the meeting broke up, and once more the director was left alone standing and staring into Whitehall, lost in thought. He turned at last with a sigh. Ernie Bevin would be on his feet now, he thought, dealing with more important matters than those he had been trying to sort out.

Then his thoughts went reluctantly back to the events in North Yorkshire that his two men had got caught up in. He could keep Sir Keith out of it, he knew, if it were just a case of unnatural practices. But if it were a case of child murder, then that would be a different thing. He couldn't smooth something like that over, nor would he even want to. The director was not a religious man but, like many of his age and class, had been brought up in the Anglican Church and knew his Bible. "Suffer little children to come unto me, and forbid them not: for of such is the kingdom of God," he said aloud, as the door opened and his secretary came in, shorthand pad and pencil in her hand

"I'm sorry, sir," she said. "Did you say something?"

He smiled at her. "No, Janet, I was just talking to myself. Shall we get on with my correspondence?"

CHAPTER 29

On Thursday 16th January, DS Rutter decided it was time he tried to move the murder enquiry of the two children forward if he could. His inspector, Tom Fenwick, had left him in sole charge of the investigation for a while now. The DI had told him that the superintendent had instructed him that now the two runaways had been found safe and well, that he didn't want too much time wasted on the two bodies in the wood.

"He said to me that there was quite enough for us to be going on with as it is, without spending too much time on them," Tom had told Ken. "He reckons it's too long ago and, as most of the evidence is missing because of the war, it's just a waste of time. But I don't agree with him, Sergeant. So I'm putting you in charge. You can use either DC Metcalf or DC Lince when you need them. And let me know if you make any progress, ok? But try to do as much as you can on your own, eh?"

So Ken Rutter had gone back over all the case notes, and now he was going to try to move things on. He had read his DI's comments on some of the things his schoolteacher friend Lewis Sudbury had told him. Much of that seemed to be based on gossip and hearsay, and quite a lot of it had originated from a school caretaker.

Ken had a lot of time for both the DI and Lewis Sudbury, both of whom he thought of as being more intelligent than himself. But he also believed that they were a bit too highbrow and up in the air. He put this down to their wartime occupations. They had both been in the intelligence services, he thought, which made their thinking a bit too complex. Whereas he, he had joined the force as a PC when he'd left school. Then, when the war had broken out, became a common soldier in the

Durham Light Infantry. He'd gone ashore on Gold Beach on the second day of the D-day landings, and then walked all the way to Germany. On his return to England, he'd taken up his career once more as a PC in the Northumberland force, been promoted to sergeant and then joined the North Yorkshire service as a detective. He was, in his own opinion, a practical down to earth copper, so he would try to put some hard facts on to his inspector's and Sudbury's theorizing.

After reading all the case notes, he therefore decided that the first person he should interview was Barry Slingsby, the school caretaker. He found Barry in his little cubbyhole on the second floor of St Bede's, having been directed there by the school secretary, Mr Willis.

"Come in, lad," said Barry in his broad Teesside accent. "Fancy a cup of tea, do yer?"

Ken Rutter, who strove to moderate his natural Geordie accent, found himself reverting to it and said, "Aye, ah does an all." This wouldn't do at all, he thought, and added, "Yes, please." When they were both seated on two stools in the cramped space that was Barry's domain, he went on. "Now, I have a few questions for you."

"Carry on, bonny lad," Barry said with a grin.

He knows I'm trying to cover up my accent, Ken thought uncomfortably, but went on. "Well, for a start, you told Mr Sudbury that you thought Mr Fenn-Williams, the science master, was in your words 'a bit dodgy' and 'creepy'. What did you mean by that?"

"Well, man," Barry said. "He's like a bit of a, shall I say a loner, he dinna mix with most of the other masters. He's always watching everyone and stirring things up. His wife and our deputy head are having a fling like, an' he doesna' seem t'mind. And he's allus at Blue Doors where the boarders live, chatting with the lads an' smarming up to that matron. As I say, a bit dodgy."

"How do you know all this? I didn't think your duties took you to Blue Doors," Ken said.

"Well, I'm friendly like with one of the maids who works there. She tells me a lot as goes on there like. But I knows this, he's real chummy with one of our governors. A certain Sir Keith Dyke, if you've heard of him. Close as two peas in a pod those two are."

That certainly fitted in with what he'd heard about them from the DI, Ken thought, but did it really tie in with what the caretaker had told Lewis about what Fenn-Williams was like? He'd used the word sinister about him, the DS seemed to recall. Deciding to give it a miss, he then said to Barry, "And what about those other two masters, the one's you said knew more of the girl and Percy Kerridge than they were letting on. Jones and Partridge, I think their names are."

"I told him that, did ah? Well, mebbe I did. But Sylvester Partridge now, the English master, well he's thick as thieves with Albert McIntyre who's in charge at Blue Doors, so if there's anything to know of young Kerridge then he'll know as likely as not," Barry said. "Ian Jones now, the maths master, he's like having it off with that matron at Blue Doors, I reckons, so he'll know all there is to know about both of those two kids."

The DS was taken aback. "Mr Jones and Miss Waverly are having an affair?"

"Have been for a long time, lad. Well, why not, she's not too bad a lass and he's no married. And they're both only in their forties."

"Really," said Ken, wondering if this was just more of the caretaker's gossip or if he could accept it as being true. "But why should he also know about Alice Bates? That is, if the girl in the wood is really her. We haven't any proof of that yet."

"Ah well, has nobody told you lot yet, when the art master died, Alice's dad, and Matty, Matilda Bates as she liked to call herself went off, young Alice went to stay at Blue Doors for a while. Elizabeth Waverly, who she'd always been friendly with, took her in. She were there for about a week or so as I remembers, but it were a long time ago like."

The DS made a note of all this, and knew he'd have to go back and question the matron once more. If all Barry had said was true then she might know a lot more than she'd let on so far, and he thought that this bit of the caretaker's gossip had a ring of truth about it.

When he got back to the station, he found that he'd had a message to ring a Sergeant Elias Salkeld at Alston police station.

"He asked for the DI," said DC Greg Lince, who gave him the message. "But the inspector's taking a couple of days off, and has said that all messages about Matilda Bates should be passed on to you."

"Thanks, Greg," said the sergeant and picked up his phone. When he got through to Alston police station, he asked to speak to Sergeant Salkeld.

"Speaking. Who's that?"

"Hello Sergeant, I'm DS Kenneth Rutter, ringing from Redcar police station. You wanted to speak to my DI and it got passed on to me."

"Oh, aye," Salkeld answered, his Cumberland accent showing. "You put out a call for a Matilda Bates. We got a note of it here and it was in the newspapers as well, I believe."

"That's right," Ken said.

"Well, Matty Musgrave came in earlier. She as was Matty Finch when I knew her as a lass."

163

"Right," the DS replied, not sure what it was all about. "So what has this to do with Mrs Bates?"

"Well she, Matty Musgrave that is, she reckons she were known as Bates when she lived in Redcar. She's married to a local farmer now, out Nenthead way. That's a village..."

"I know where it is," Ken cut in. "I'm from Shields."

"Ah, a Geordie eh? Well, her husband's a bit proper like, Methodist man, a lay preacher as well. So Matty, she don't want him to know if it can be helped. So I've fixed up for you to meet up with her in the Angel Inn on Alston Front Street. Tomorrow at eleven, if you can make it. Do you know the Angel?"

"Yes to both of those questions. Tell her I'll be in the lounge at eleven tomorrow."

CHAPTER 30

The following morning DS Ken Rutter left Redcar early, driving the old Ford the CID called their 'stock car'. He had decided not to interrupt his inspector's few days' off, as he reckoned that Fenwick wouldn't appreciate it. Not for something that Rutter could easily handle himself. He was on the road early as although it was only about a 75 mile drive, he knew that the old Ford didn't go very fast and that there was snow in the Pennines. Even though the forces' old banger could do the journey in about two hours in normal conditions, he realised that it might well be more like three if the roads were bad. So he set off at seven thirty.

It was a cold frosty morning, and he had to drive slowly and be on the lookout for black ice. Despite this, he reached Darlington quite quickly but once through the town when the road began to climb and driving became much trickier, his speed dropped. Once he was past Middleton-in-Teesdale, there was snow piled up on either side of the road, left there by the local farmers who had obviously been out clearing the roads in their tractors with snow ploughs attached to them. Once he was past High Force and in the top of the dale snow covered hills rose up on both sides of the road, with the odd isolated farmhouse nestling at their feet. He wondered which one was where Lady Dyke's sister lived, Gloria he thought her name was. The one that his DI had visited a few weeks earlier.

By the time he reached the hotel at Langdon Beck, it was snowing and he only just made it to the top of the moor. Here, as he went over Cow Green on the very top, he was exposed to the full force of the north-west wind and the car rocked from side to side. Fortunately, as he began to go down into the South Tyne valley, he met a farmer coming up from Alston in his tractor ploughing the snow off the road, and he had an easier ride down into the town.

He reached the cobbled main street of Alston at a quarter to eleven, and went down it to the Angel Inn which was just below the market building. Cold to the marrow, as the car's heater was extremely inefficient, he parked the Ford outside and went into the lounge, to find a woman already there drinking coffee.

"Mrs Musgrave?" he asked. "Mrs Matilda Musgrave? I'm Detective Sergeant Rutter from Redcar police station. I understand you have some news for us."

"Yes," she said. "Please call me Mattie, everyone else does."

Gratefully he took a seat by the log fire in the room, and ordered coffee from the waitress who came in. Then he said, "So you are Matilda Bates who used to live at St Bede's Grammar School in Redcar?" At her reply of "Yes," he went on. "We've been looking for you for quite a while, you know." She was a good looking woman of about thirty five, he guessed. She must have been a lot younger than the art teacher, he realised, who had died in his sixties some years ago. He noticed that she was fiddling with her gloves and was obviously very nervous.

"Well, how to begin," she said. "Please hear me out, Sergeant. I'm married to a farmer now, Bob Musgrave, and we live up the dale near Nenthead. He's a good man, Bob, but a bit strict like, a Methodist. He's a lay preacher so he's a bit different to the men I used to know when I was younger. Well, anyway, I don't read the papers much and Bob, he'll not have the wireless in the house. So I didn't find out you were looking for me until a few days ago. Until I came into Alston, to go to the doctors," and she gave her stomach a pat. Looking, Ken saw that she was pregnant. "It's my first. Oh, I'm so excited. But you don't want to know about that, do you. Well, I'll put it all down

166

in writing for you, but I'd like for Mr Musgrave not to know, if that's at all possible." She looked at the sergeant, pleading.

"I'll try to keep you out of it if I can, Mattie," Ken said.

"Oh, thank you. Well, it's like this, as a youngster I was a bit wild, Mattie Finch I was then. Elias, that's Sergeant Salkeld, can tell you all about that, as we're old friends. Well, I ran off to Redcar as soon as I could and ended up with Bates. He was much older than me and was quite Bohemian. His wife had just left him and young Alice, their kid. But he was good to me and steadied me up a lot. I looked after his kid for him and then one day a year or two ago, he upped and died of a heart attack."

"I think it was about four or five years ago," Ken put in.

"Yes, you're right, I've been back here for nearly five, and married for over four of them now," she said, biting her lip. "Well, when he died Alice went off and stayed with that Elizabeth Waverly who's the matron at Blue Doors. Her who was close, shall I say, to one of the maths masters. I can't remember his name now, but they'd been carrying on together for years. So anyway Alice went to stay with Miss Waverly, they'd always been friends. And then, after a bit, I came back home and married Mr Musgrave. That was a complete change to my way of life, but he's a good man if a bit strict in his beliefs. And now," she finished with a smile, "I'm expecting a kid of my own. I don't think I can tell you anything else."

"There's just one more thing," the DS said, taking the belt out of the bag he'd brought it in. "Do you recognise this?"

She looked at the belt with its fancy clasp. "Oh yes. That was Alice's, her father made that snake clip, you know. He was a real artist, he worked in all sorts of materials. He wasn't just a painter and sculptor. Where did you find it?"

"I'm sorry, Mattie," Ken said. "We found it on the dead girl buried in the wood."

"Oh no," Mattie said with tears in her eyes. "So you think she's dead then, Alice?"

"I'm afraid so," he answered.

"Oh dear, the poor lass," Mattie said "We didn't really hit it off, me and her, but she didn't deserve that. I hope you'll catch whoever did it."

The sergeant took her to the police station which was up the road, almost at the top of the hill where the road to Nenthead went off to the left. The main road went straight on to Darlington. Once at the police station, he typed out a statement that she signed. "I'll try and keep you out of it if I can," he promised her again, as she left the station to go home.

"She was a right handful as a lass, I can tell you," Sergeant Elias Salkeld told him when Mattie had gone. "But she's settled now, I think. Old Bob Musgrave's a good 'un."

Feeling he was now a bit further on with the case, Rutter set off back to Redcar. He got back without any trouble as the snow had stopped and the roads had been cleared.

He had one more task before returning to his office. He went to Blue Doors and sought out the matron, Miss Waverly. When they were alone, he said, "There are two things, Matron. First, you didn't tell me Alice Bates stayed here with you after her father died. And secondly, you failed to say you are close to Mr Jones."

"As to Ian Jones, well, I don't want it to become common knowledge. Not more than it is anyway. And I didn't think it had anything to do with your enquiry," she said.

"I'll be the judge of that, Matron. This is a murder enquiry, and anything might be important," Rutter told her. "Now, what about Alice?"

"There's not much to tell really," the matron replied. "We'd always been friends. Then her dad died, and I said she could stay with me for a bit, that Mattie having gone off. It was only ever a temporary arrangement, and one day she just upped and left. I came back to my rooms, and she and all her stuff was gone. I never saw her again."

"No note or anything?" Rutter asked.

No, nothing," she shrugged.

"Didn't you think that was odd?" the sergeant asked.

"Not really, I knew it was only temporary, and she was always a law unto herself," Miss Waverly said.

He could get nothing more out of her and went back to the police station. He'd be able to tell his DI, when he came back from his break on Monday morning, that they now knew for certain the identity of the girl's body. When he got back to the police station, he wrote up his report of the day's happenings and left it on the DI's desk, before going home.

CHAPTER 31

On the Sunday morning, Kurt Vogel woke up in his small flat near Liverpool Street station a worried and perplexed man. Yesterday afternoon he had been summoned to the office of his superior officer in the Home Office. The man he knew as Mr Jones, the one who'd met him on his arrival in England, had turned up at his flat with the summons. It was a Saturday and was supposedly his day off. Yet Mr Jones had insisted that he come into the office at once, and stayed with him all the way to ensure that he did. When they had arrived, Mr Jones knocked on the door and announced that Vogel was here, just as he had that first time. Then, also as it had happened before, when they had entered the same three men were waiting for them. Then, as if it was a re-run of that first time, Mr Jones was dismissed and he was invited to sit down.

The man in the middle of the three men on the opposite side of the table did all the talking, just as he had on Vogel's previous visit. The man Vogel only knew as 'D'. He had never heard any of the others utter a word on that first meeting, and neither did they on this one.

"Ah, Vogel," D had begun. "Good afternoon. We have had some worrying news. A while ago we understand you undertook a journey to Middlesbrough." He held up a hand as Vogel opened his mouth to speak. "We also understand that you followed a man, a...." Here D looked down at a paper in front of him on the desk. He had no need to do this, as he knew its contents without needing to look. Then he went on. "A Mr Sudbury, a schoolteacher I believe."

Kurt had opened his mouth in astonishment. How do they know this? he thought, but said nothing.

"This perturbs us in several ways," D continued. "First, you were told not to leave London without permission. It is part of your terms of employment. It is one of the conditions you agreed to, to keep you free from prosecution. Second, you assured us that you didn't know or have any knowledge of anyone living in England. But lastly, and more importantly, you have put us, the organisation you are working for and which is the guarantor of your freedom, in conflict with another government department." Here he glanced sideways at his two colleagues, who both nodded in agreement. Then he said, in a hard voice, "You will not go out of London again without our knowledge. You will not go anywhere near this Mr Sudbury again, at all. Do I make myself clear? If you comply with these arrangements, we may, and I mean may, allow you to stay here working for us. If not, you will be repatriated to Germany and face prosecution. Do you understand me?"

"Yes," muttered Vogel.

"Good. Mr Jones," he called loudly, and the man who must have remained just outside the door came back in. "Take Mr Vogel back to his house. Good day to you, sir."

So Vogel had returned to his flat, wondering just how his journey to Yorkshire had become known to his employers. He decided in the end that Manuel Ortega, or Lewis Sudbury as he now knew him to be, must have been aware of being tailed. But not only that, he must also have been aware of who was following him. Perhaps, he admitted grudgingly to himself, his Gestapo men had been right when they'd told him that tailing people was harder than it looked. The question that he was now faced with was just what he was to do about it. That is, if he still wanted to get his revenge on Ortega, who had been responsible for his injuries. Which, he decided, he still very much did want to do. It had become almost an obsession since he'd discovered Ortega was still alive. Without that motive he could have simply stayed in London, safe from prosecution. Now he must have his revenge and then try to escape to a neutral country, like so many others he knew had done. It took him much of the Sunday to decide what he was going to do about the problem. First, he decided he must assume that D would put some sort of watch on his movements which he must evade. Secondly, he realised that he must act quickly to catch everyone by surprise. He reasoned that 'they', as he thought of D and his companions, would think that he would lie low for a while. Then, when he did manage to get back to Redcar, he would have to find a way to discover where Sudbury lived without tailing him, and to do it quickly before a pursuit could be mounted.

To allay the suspicion of any possible watcher, he therefore spent all of Sunday wondering listlessly around London, trying to appear as if he was downhearted. At ten o'clock he switched off all the lights in his flat, just as if he'd gone to bed. Then he slipped out of the back door, carrying a suitcase packed with all his possessions. He knew he could never return here once he'd disobeyed D's orders. He'd spent the evening working out his plans. He'd go to Redcar and stay at the same B and B that he'd used before, which he was sure his superiors didn't know about. Once settled in the B and B, he'd go to the library as soon as it opened on Monday morning, and look through the electoral register to find out where Sudbury lived. Then he'd go there and wait until the teacher came home from school, kill him and then run. He thought he could get a train from Redcar to Darlington and then to York, or even Edinburgh. From there he could go cross country and on to Liverpool. Once there, he could catch a ferry to southern Ireland and disappear. He would, he decided, go to Argentina where he knew several of his former SS colleagues had fled.

Later that night, Kurt Vogel caught the last train to Darlington from King's Cross on the first stage of his journey. He needn't have been as cautious, as MI5 had not put a watcher on to him 24 hours a day. The three men thought that they'd frightened him enough to keep him in check for quite a while. They had completely underestimated his desire to revenge himself on the man who had first deceived him and then attempted to blow him up.

CHAPTER 32

Wilfred Lawrence had been Deputy Director of MI6 since long before the war. He had been lucky in his career since joining the service after he had left Oxford University. His time as a field officer had been spent mainly in Germany, attached to the British Embassy in Berlin. Because he'd been so successful in this, he had been recalled to London and given charge of the German desk in the FCO. This had all happened whilst he was still a relatively young man. While he was section head, he was in charge of British Agents working in Germany at the time of the rise of fascism, the Nazi party and Hitler becoming Fuhrer. His work was so valued that when the post became vacant he was appointed Deputy DIrector.

Around this time, he bought his holiday home in Howdale off Keith Dyke as somewhere to go at weekends to get out of London. This purchase led to him meeting Angela.

Angela was born in Redcar in 1902 to the wife of James Cooper, who was a bank manager in the town. She had a sister, Gloria, who was four years younger than her. Her parents were regular churchgoers and she was raised in a strict way and not allowed much freedom. As a child she had been quite timid and obedient, unlike Gloria who was more rebellious. This resulted in her becoming a naive teenager. When she was seventeen her mother died and her father married again. Her new stepmother was if anything even stricter than her mother had been. Then, when she was eighteen, she met Keith Dyke at a social function that her father took her to. Her stepmother was pregnant and too ill to accompany him, so he took Angela in her place. The First World War was over by a couple of years by then and Keith was already an up and coming business man, and a quite wealthy and influential man in Middlesbrough. He was also a homosexual at a time when it was not only illegal but frowned upon in polite society. If his proclivities had become common knowledge, it would have hindered his business success considerably. Angela was a good looking young woman, and he proposed to her within a few weeks of that first meeting. She, in her innocence, was completely swept off her feet. He plied her with presents, flowers, took her out to dinner several times and flirted with her outrageously. Her father, a shrewd banker but innocent in the ways of the world, was delighted as was her stepmother. When Keith asked them for her hand in marriage, they couldn't believe how lucky she was to have attracted such a successful and influential man.

The night before the wedding, her stepmother gave Angela a 'talking to' as she called it. She impressed upon her stepdaughter that on her wedding night, and subsequently, she would be called upon to 'do her duty' to her husband. But she shed no light as to what exactly that would entail, thereby filling Angela with trepidation and also a fair degree of dread. The day came and the arrangements were lavish, with over two hundred guests at the wedding breakfast. Keith took her to Venice for their honeymoon and, as the first two nights were spent in transit, she wasn't called upon to do anything at all. On the third night in their separate rooms in the hotel in Venice, Angela laid awake all night waiting for Keith to come to her. Which however he never did. A pattern that was to be repeated for all the time they were there. Two years after the marriage she was still intact, still wondering what exactly her duty to her husband was and when, if ever, it would be demanded of her. Her dilemma was made harder by the comments of such women friends she had, who asked her such things as, "How often does Sir Keith (for he was a Sir now) come to you?" or "Oh, you have separate bedrooms, how fabulous, I wish we did.

I might get some sleep at night". She became adroit at giving vague answers to these and other questions she just didn't understand.

And then Lawrence and Angela met. Sir Keith, who wanted to present a happy family to the world, acquired two dogs. As he couldn't, or wouldn't, provide children as part of this picture of an ideal family, he thought a couple of dogs would help fill in the background. So on weekends when Keith stayed at home with his friend Edgar Fenn-Williams, a local schoolmaster, Angela took the two Old English sheepdogs, Abbott and Costello, for long walks on the moors.

Wilfred Lawrence also went hiking from his holiday home in Howdale when he was there and inevitably one day they met. She was now quite a beauty, and he was tall and dashing. Despite being deskbound and no longer a field agent, he kept himself very fit. He used the agency's gym nearly every day when in London, still trained in unarmed combat with the new recruits and when in Yorkshire went on long hill walks. He also went to the firing range used by the services' agents two or three times a week to practice with a handgun. He'd always been one of the best shots in Six.

One day, some months after their first chance encounter, they met up by arrangement to go for a walk together on the moors. It was a lovely warm day, the heather was scenting the air, a skylark was climbing vertically above them, singing as it rose higher and higher. They were walking across Danby High Moor just to the west of Ralph's Cross when they found a dry grassy spot amid the wet peaty patches and scratchy heather and sat down. From where they sat, the main road that ran past Ralph's Cross was out of sight. The small lane that went from near the cross to Farndale was visible on the ridge in front of them. As usual this was empty of traffic or people, so they were totally alone.

It was there that the inevitable happened, and Angela found out at last what her stepmother had been incoherently talking about all those years ago. She found out just what her duty was, or rather should have been, to her husband. And she found it to be no duty at all but a pleasure. Sir Keith soon realised what was going on, but didn't seem to mind at all, as long as the affair was discrete. In fact he found it rather to his liking as his wife became happier and their relationship improved. Her nature, which had been becoming quite sour, mellowed dramatically. When the two children, Robert and Kitty, came along he happily accepted them as his own. He could at last present a happy family to the world. Angela, who also now understood the relationship between her husband and the schoolteacher, was equally accepting of that.

The war came and both Freddie Lawrence and Sir Keith Dyke became very busy, and the situation remained in limbo. After the war ended, both Angela and Freddie wanted to live together but couldn't work out a way to bring this about without Sir Keith's consent or damaging Freddie's career. The children by now almost ignored their father, just as he did them, and when Freddie was at How End spent most of their time with him. Their mother, who had always before had a good relationship with them, became more and more irritable, snappy and distant. The strain of the situation was taking its toll on her.

This was why, when the crisis blew up, they ran off to London to find Freddie. They had been to his home several times before, and he'd always told them that if anything happened to their mother they were to come to him. They were self reliant kids and Bob was a bit of a schemer, and so they did just that. When they arrived at his home that evening, he'd been working in his study. The guard on duty at his gate, an ex-marine, had rung through to the house. "Sir," he said. "Those two kids, your nephew and niece I think they are. Well, they're here, shall I bring 'em up?"

Bob had also inherited his father's devious ways, his use of subterfuge. He planned the whole affair and conceived a plausible reason. In his father's tradition as a spy, he made the story as close to the truth as possible. He had told Freddie that Kitty was being bullied at school and was unhappy there. That was true, though he laid it on a bit thick. He also said that he himself was unhappy at the sexual experiments the boys in his dormitory were carrying out, which were involving him. Freddie, who knew all about boys at boarding school having been to Eton, accepted this at face value.

He'd rung Angela several times, but had always been answered by Sir Keith or a policeman and hung up. Then, at last, he managed to speak to her and they decided not to say anything of where the children were. They agreed that this might just be the catalyst that could lead to an amicable break-up of Angela's marriage. Angela would go to her sister's in Teesdale, he and the children would join her there and then they would all come back to his home. He and the children had in fact been in the farmhouse when the DI had visited Angela there.

Then, on the same Sunday morning that Kurt Vogel was planning his trip north to find Lewis, Bob told his Uncle Freddie the truth. Whilst Angela and Kitty were out walking, he confessed that it hadn't been the other boys who'd been interfering with him, but two adults. He told Freddie because he trusted him, and knew that his mother was planning to marry him. Added to this, Uncle Freddie had been encouraging the two children to call him 'father'. They were both more than willing to do this, having never really had a true father.

Freddie had simply said, "Leave it to me, Bob, I'll sort things out. But don't whatever you do tell your mother, or let her know you've told me. Swear to it now." His training had kicked in and he was already plotting what he would do. He was also pleased just how he'd been able to disguise his fury. But those two would pay, and pay dearly.

His first step when Angela returned from the walk was to say that he would be away for a few days the following week from Tuesday. This didn't worry her at all, as she was used to his work taking him away from time to time. In the morning, he would go into the FCO and tell them the same thing.

Then he would go to a garage he used in East London, where George the owner kept a flat and stored all sorts of things for him. This was an arrangement he had made with George when he was still a field agent and which was unknown to anyone else. Most agents had a bolt hole and new identity hidden away for emergencies. Despite him now being desk bound, he had maintained this arrangement.

One of the things George kept for him was a 350cc BSA motorbike. He would get George to grease it, check the tyre pressures and the oil level, fill it up with petrol and start it up to see it was running alright. He would indent for petrol coupons from the MI6 stores and find his warm motorbike clothes, as the weather was now very cold and it was a long ride to Redcar. He estimated it was just over two hundred and fifty miles, and would take him at least five hours if the conditions were good. He would leave at 5 am on the Tuesday so should get there by twelve at the latest, even if the threatened snow materialised.

He went into his study and retrieved a gun from a locked drawer. He knew it was no good using the one he had been issued with by the service, as the bullets would be traceable. But this one was an old German Mauser he had acquired when he was an agent. No trace of where these bullets came from would ever be found.

The two abusers were in his eyes as good as dead already.

CHAPTER 33

On Thursday the 16th of January, Detective Inspector Thomas Fenwick started a few days' leave. He'd been working since well before Christmas without a break, except for his two days in Birmingham, and needed a rest. Also, because he'd worked on so many of his rest days, the amount of time owing to him was building up and his superintendent wanted him to take some of them. As he didn't relish going back to his parents' home in Birmingham, his first thought had been to simply stay in his flat in Redcar. There were many reasons why this wouldn't be very sensible, he decided in the end. He knew that if he were so near to the police station, some of his officers would try to involve him in the day to day enquiries they were investigating. He also admitted to himself that if he was so close to the station with time on his hands, he'd not be able to resist popping in to see how things were going. Added to all this of course was that he knew he'd be bored silly just staying cooped up in his flat. Then there was the weather. So far this winter there had been several bouts of very cold temperatures and quite a few falls of snow. His flat was draughty and only heated by a gas fire. It also had an open hearth, but like everyone else he was short of coal to burn in it.

He needed to get right away from Redcar, he decided, but the question was where to? He didn't own a car and, even if he had, going any distance would be difficult because of petrol rationing. And then the letter came from Ruth. It had arrived on the Tuesday morning but, because he'd gone into work early before the postman arrived, he didn't open it until that evening. He had known Ruth Tremayne since his posting to Catterick Camp in 1941. At the time she had been a corporal in the ATS, the Auxiliary Territorial Service, the women's section of the army, whilst he had been a sergeant in the Military Police.

The good looking MP with rust coloured hair and the shapely blonde ATS corporal had been attracted to each other from the start. Their romance, like so many other things in the war, was intense and short. After only a few months from their first meeting, Tom had been posted to Hastings whilst Ruth remained in Catterick. At first they had written to each other quite regularly, but over time their letters had become more and more irregular, without actually stopping altogether.

In 1944, she wrote to say she was about to get married to a US soldier from Texas. Over the years since then by way of spasmodic correspondence, he learned that she had married Todd Blevins because she'd been pregnant and he was due to go to France. After the war she'd become one of the GI brides, and gone with her daughter Glenda to live in Texas. Since then her occasional letters to Tom had told of Todd's growing violence to both Ruth and Glenda, and also of their increasing poverty. The latter was the result of Todd's lack of work and growing drink problem. It was, Tom had thought, a common experience of many of the GI brides, but he had been sorry to hear that Ruth had been one of them.

Then, this week, her latest letter told him of her return to England, with her daughter who was now three years old. She had, she wrote, gone back to her home in Wroxham in Norfolk where her parents lived. On an impulse that Wednesday evening, he decided it would be quite an exciting thing to spend his few days off work going to see Ruth. It would be infinitely better than spending it cooped up in his small, cold and draughty flat. He would also be totally removed from any temptation to drop in to the police station.

Thursday morning early saw him on a train to Darlington, then he changed to another going to King's Cross, then on by tube to Liverpool Street station and yet another train to Norwich. He did the last eight miles to Wroxham by bus, which took half an hour, and he was knocking on her parents' door at six on a frosty evening just eleven and a half hours after leaving Redcar.

The woman who came to the door was in her fifties, he judged, and had a small girl behind her skirt peeping out at him.

"Yes?" she said, eyeing him warily. She looked at the suitcase in his hand and said dismissively, "If you're selling brushes or encyclopaedias, we don't want anything, thanks."

Before she could slam the door in his face, he said quickly, "Mrs Tremayne?"

"Yes," she said again, still suspicious. "What do you want?"

Tom paused, unsure of what to reply. He realised he should have worked out in advance just what to say when he arrived here. For a senior police officer, he told himself, he was acting like an idiot. In desperation, he looked at the child and said, "And are you Glenda?"

Mrs Tremayne's retort of "Just who the hell are you?" was interrupted by the arrival of a woman from inside the house who said, "Tom? Tom Fenwick, what in God's name are you doing here?" The "God's" came out as "Gawd's" and the "doing" as "a'doin". She had got a bit of an American drawl, Tom thought, as he grinned at her a bit nervously and said, "Hello, Ruth. I got your letter."

"Who is this young man, Ruth, do you know him?" said a man from behind the group in the door facing Tom. He looked a few years Mrs Tremayne's senior and had grey receding hair. He was wearing the trousers and waistcoat of a dark blue suit, and his shirt was open at the top with collar and tie removed.

He had a newspaper in one hand and a pipe in another. "Anyway, can you all come in and shut the door? You're letting all the cold in."

It was over half an hour later, with Tom seated in an armchair with a cup of tea, before it was all sorted out.

"You've come all this way to see our Ruth?" Edna Tremayne said at last. "Well I never."

"I had a few days off owing," Tom said, somewhat inadequately. "Now, before it gets too late, is there a reasonable place I can go and book in for the night?"

"No, lad," said Bill, Ruth's father, as his wife started to say, "Well there's the..." "You'll stop here. We've plenty of room, and you and Ruth have a lot to catch up on, I'll be bound."

After that had been agreed there was a frenzy of activity. There was a bed to be made up and hot water bottles filled to air it.

Edna Tremayne said to Tom, "I hope you like mutton. We're having a stew for supper made out of it. It'll stretch to another one, I'll put in more carrots and onions and make more dumplings."

"Mutton stew is fine by me," he said and meant it, his normal cooking for himself was never very elaborate nor, he suspected, nutritious. "I've brought my ration book with me, as I knew I'd need it if I stayed in a hotel."

Supper over, the dishes washed and Glenda in bed, the rest of the evening passed with Tom telling the other three something of his life. Then, in the morning, Ruth went into Wroxham where she worked part time in a shop, whilst Tom helped her mother look after Glenda. After lunch, Ruth and Tom went for a walk down to Wroxham Broad, leaving Edna to look after Glenda. It was a cold frosty day with a thin layer of ice on the water and frost on the bare branches of the trees. Out on the broad a few coots and water hens were splashing about in the parts of the lake which hadn't frozen.

Ruth told Tom of her life since she had last seen him, exhaling clouds of mist as she spoke. "When I met Todd he appeared to be glamorous. He totally captivated me, he had money, charm and seemed easy going. All the GI's were like that. It wasn't until we went to live in Texas after the war that I saw the reality. He was a roughneck, and his family were no better. He was usually unemployed and drank too much. He treated the blacks, who he called neegraws, with contempt and the Latin Americans, Latinos to him, even worse. He was violent to both me and Glenda, and in the end my mum and dad sent me money for our fare and we came back here."

They walked on in silence for a while and she thought, glancing sideways at him, 'How did I let this man go to take up with Todd?'

Tom was silent, thinking how little she'd changed since their brief time together. She was a bit older but more mature and certain of herself and just as attractive. The problem was Glenda, and he was honest enough to admit it to himself. Not because she'd had a baby by another man, but because he wasn't good with kids. He thought of his sister's two and shuddered. He thought they were loud and they squabbled with each other all the time. Added to that, he believed his sister didn't keep them in order. They walked on, and a water vole plopped off the bank into the water, breaking the thin layer of ice, as they approached and swam away with ripples forming a V from its nose on the surface once it reached clear water.

Tentatively he took her hand, reasoning that if they had stayed together they'd probably have had children of their own by now. Glenda after all was well behaved from what he'd seen so far and if he ever did become married, he'd just have to get used to having kids about. They walked on side by side, and he told her of the case of the murdered children and of the two that had run away. By the time they'd got back to her home, they were completely easy in each other's company, just as they'd used to be.

Edna Tremayne looked on them and hoped. When her daughter had got home from America she'd been tired, with deep lines in her face, and had lost a lot of weight. Slowly she'd recovered and outwardly looked almost as she had done before her marriage. But something had been missing. Then, yesterday evening, this serious young policeman had knocked on the door. And within minutes she'd got her daughter back, all the old sparkle, the gleam in her eyes and her bouncy confidence had returned. Almost in a flash. Edna thought it really was a miracle. Now she looked at them, wondered and wished, but said nothing.

That night Tom had just gone to sleep when he was woken by faint sounds in his room. He heard a rustle of cloth, and then a naked body was up against him.

"Shh," came Ruth's voice in his ear. "Don't want to wake up mum and dad. It's cold without my nightie." He felt her nipples hard against his back and turned to face her. "I just want to hold you, I'm not trying to force anything," she went on. "But I want to remember how it used to be."

He was roused as he knew she would know and whispered, "Shh, I think I wanted this from when I got your letter."

In their bedroom Bill was sound asleep, breathing noisily thought his mouth, but Edna was awake. She'd heard her daughter's door open and close, and then her feet padding across the landing. Then she'd heard the other door open and close and the quiet sound of voices. When she heard the creaks

186

of the spare room bed, they should really get a new one she thought, she put her head under the covers. She was no voyeur.

On Saturday morning, Ruth told her mother that Tom had asked her to go back to Redcar with him tomorrow for a few days.

"He's got to go early as he's been invited to a do of some sort in the evening by Lewis, a friend of his. And it'll take all day to get there. Especially as it's a Sunday."

"She can stay in the Park Hotel," Tom added. "I know the assistant manager there, he went to school with Lewis, and I'm sure he'd not object to young Glenda staying there."

"No, Glenda can stop here with me," Edna said. "We're good friends and she won't fret. It's too long a day for her to be in trains and then left with strangers while you go out. No, I'll look after the bairn and you need a good break. I'll see Mr Burrell at the shop knows that you won't be in for a few days."

CHAPTER 34

Sunday evening in Saltburn was cold with a strong wind blowing off the sea. The Alexandra Hotel which stood at the side of the cliff road was taking the full brunt of it. Lewis and Beryl went up the steps at its front and into the haven of the lobby. Once inside they opened their coats and went up the wide staircase to the cocktail lounge on the first floor. It was six thirty, half an hour before the start of their engagement party, but Beryl's parents were already in the lounge waiting for them, nursing two glasses of cider. Beryl's father had always been a strict parent and her mother, like his first wife, had similar attitudes. They were quite old now and their puritanical views had mellowed somewhat over the years. This was due partly to their wartime experiences, but also in response to their daughters' lives. Angela, who had been the most repressed, had entered into an unconsummated marriage and was now living with another man, seeking a divorce. Gloria, who had never accepted their control, had run off and married a sheep farmer, and Beryl was now living with a man she wasn't married to. The announcement of her engagement had come as a relief to both of them, and they had taken an early bus from Redcar to get to the Alex well in time.

After greeting Beryl's parents, Lewis went to the bar to negotiate with the barman. He was expecting thirteen guests which made fifteen in all, counting himself and Beryl, and so wanted to buy three bottles of champagne. In these days of austerity this proved to be very difficult, and in the end the barman had to consult with the Alex's manager before three bottles were found.

The next to arrive were Lewis' two elderly neighbours who he'd known from childhood, and who were now firm friends of

Beryl's. The rest of the party followed soon after. First, Billy Roberts, who Lewis had known at school and who was now the assistant manager at the Park Hotel in Redcar. Lewis had renewed their relationship when he'd gone to the Park for his interview and had been friends with him ever since. He'd also invited John 'Piggy' Black, who'd also been a friend at school along with his wife. Beryl had invited two friends from the library, Fiona Nelson and Daphne Waterson. Fiona was a rather shy plain young woman, whilst Daphne was flirtatious and Lewis thought perhaps the most beautiful woman he'd ever seen. Then there was Mr Willis, Lewis had asked the elderly school secretary because he had got to know him very well since he'd been back at St Bede's. When Barry Slingsby arrived with his wife, neither Beryl nor Lewis recognised him. They had only seen Barry in brown overalls, grubby shoes and with untidy grey hair. The tall elegant man in a smart three piece suit, shiny black shoes and slicked down Brylcreemed hair, beside a short stout tightly corseted lady with blue rinsed and permed hair, was a stranger to them. It wasn't until he smiled and said in his Teesside accent, "Hello, bonny lad," that recognition dawned.

The last to arrive, a bit breathless with a striking woman at his side, was Tom Fenwick. Tom was a rather serious man and had always appeared to Lewis to be confident and well in charge of situations. Tonight, however, the DI was clearly nervous and hesitant and, strangest of all, somewhat excited.

"Hi Lewis," he began. "I'm sorry I'm, well, we're late. This is my friend Ruth, we were, that is we first met at Catterick in the war and.... oh sorry, do you mind if she comes to your party? You too, Beryl, do you mind? We've not long been back from Norfolk."

Lewis thought that Tom Fenwick would never stop to draw a breath, so he cut in. "Good evening, Tom. Hello Ruth, did he say your name was?" and he smiled at the woman who grinned back.

"Yes, that's right, pleasure to meet you, Lewis. Tom's told me a lot about you. Do you and Beryl mind if I gatecrash your party?"

"Not at all," Beryl replied, thinking at the same time, is that an American accent?

Barry Slingsby, not one to be slow to step forward, held out his hand to this attractive companion of the inspector. "How do, miss. Friend of our DI here, are you? Well, you'll need to watch that one, bonny lass."

"Oh, I've known him a long time, er...?" Ruth began.

"Barry. Barry Slingsby and this is me wife, Lily."

Such a pretty name for such a formidable looking woman, Ruth thought, as the woman said, "Call me Lil."

When the disparate group were settled down, the barman brought out the three bottles of champagne and fifteen glasses. He was sent back for another one for the extra guest and then he opened the bottles.

Lewis rapped on the table to get attention from everybody. There were only two other people in the lounge, and they looked on with interest at the crowd gathered around him.

"Beryl's father, James, wants to say a few words," Lewis announced.

"Ladies and gentlemen," he began, as the barman filled the glasses with champagne on the table behind him. "Ladies and gentlemen, we are here tonight to celebrate the engagement of our youngest daughter, Beryl, to Lewis Sudbury." James Cooper may have had rather strict and narrow views, but he was also a banker and used to speaking at various functions. He spoke for several minutes before being stopped by a discreet "Dad," in his ear from Beryl and a prod from his wife. "Yes, well, I give you Lewis and Beryl."

Everyone raised their glasses that the barman had brought round during the speech and echoed "Beryl and Lewis."

The two others in the lounge clapped and everyone else shouted "Speech" at Lewis who, for a schoolmaster, was short and brief. Then the guests broke up into smaller groups chatting together. Beryl and Ruth Tremayne were obviously getting on very well together and John Black was deep in conversation with Mr Willis. At one point in the proceedings, Tom took Lewis aside and told him of the events of the last few days in Wroxham. Lewis had never seen his DI friend so nervous and unsure of himself. "It'll all work out, Tom, just give Ruth and yourself time," he advised him.

"I don't know how anyone could treat a young kid like young Glenda like that American Todd Blevins did," Tom said. "It's made me all the more determined to find out what happened to our two murdered kids."

"Are you any further on with that?" Lewis asked him.

"Well, yes and no," the DI said. "I called the station when I got home, and apparently DS Rutter has made quite a bit of progress. I'll catch up on that in the morning. But I think Sir Keith and that friend of his, Fenn-Williams, may be the ones involved. He's a science teacher at St Bede's, isn't he? He seems almost to have moved in with Dyke at How End now. I'm not like my DS, Voyle, and suspect all homosexuals of being child abusers, but there's something about those two I don't like. And they both go to Blue Doors a lot. Ah well, we'll see tomorrow." Then he changed the subject. "I saw the Boro lost yesterday at home to Manchester United. Did you go?"

"No," said Lewis with a grin. "Too busy arranging this shindig, and buying Beryl her ring. The one she's been waving around in the air all night, and trying not to appear to be showing it to everyone. Yes, they lost four-two, the pitch was frozen with a covering of snow I think. Not a nice one to play on."

"Same for both sides though," said Tom, moving off to talk to Beryl and look at her ring.

Sometime later, Lewis went to the Gents which he found empty except for Billy Roberts who was in floods of tears.

"Titch," he said. "What's wrong?" He had noticed that Daphne Waterson had been flirting with his old school friend all evening.

Billy sniffed and said, "What am I to do, Lewis?"

"What do you mean, Titch," he asked.

"Daphne, about Daphne. She's really nice, you know, and well.... well, she's been flirting with me all night and I really like her but...." Billy broke off.

"But what, Titch?" Lewis pressed.

Reluctantly and hesitantly, Billy said, "You know I said I hated school? Hating living in Blue Doors? Well, there were two....." and he stopped talking yet again.

"Two what, Titch?" Lewis prompted.

"Two people. Adults. They er, well they did things that I've not forgotten since. And I can't, I can't respond like to girls, women like Daphne. I wish I could but...." And he broke off miserably.

"Which two, Billy, who were they?" Lewis asked, but the man only shook his head.

"Take your time. Talk to Miss Waterson, she's a nice woman I think. She'll understand. Help you get over it," Lewis said.

"I can't," Billy said, and rushed out of the toilets. Shortly after that he left to go home.

At half past ten when time was called, there was only Tom and Ruth and Lewis and Beryl left in the lounge, everyone else had gone. They left together and went their respective ways; Tom and Ruth to catch a bus to Redcar, and Lewis and Beryl to walk home to Albion Terrace, which was only a few hundred yards away.

"Well, mum and dad were pleased anyway," said Beryl. "They can't wait to get us married off and me no longer a scarlet woman. Given their beliefs, they've not been lucky in their daughters."

"I think they've been very lucky," replied Lewis. "That is, with the two I know anyway." He'd never yet been to Teesdale and met Gloria.

CHAPTER 35

Kurt Vogel caught the last train from King's Cross to Edinburgh on Sunday night. He had taken very great care to avoid any surveillance on his way to the station. He wasn't to know that in fact the department was not keeping a round the clock watch on him. Unlike his previous journey, this time the train was full and he had to share his carriage with seven other people. He had a window seat, and in the opposite one was a middle-aged woman in a brown overcoat. The other seats were all taken up by a party of six soldiers. He could see from their badges that they were from somewhere called Fife. They were obviously going home on leave and, though he couldn't understand most of what they were saying, deduced that they were Scottish. One of them, a sergeant he thought, was called Tam and another one who was probably a private, Jamie. As for the rest, he couldn't make out their names at all. Their Scottish accents were too broad.

They had come well equipped for the journey, with a bag full of bottles of beer which they started to drink long before the train had left the station. The carriage had been warm from the heating pipes under the bench seats when Kurt had gone into it, but it was now becoming even warmer. A fug was also building up from the smell of beer and the smoke from the cigarettes they were all, except the woman, smoking. By the time the train pulled out of King's Cross, the six soldiers were playing some sort of card game Kurt didn't understand. He took off his overcoat and put it up on the rack, but the woman opposite him kept hers buttoned up to her chin despite the heat.

There was a lull in the card game, and one of the soldiers said something to Kurt that he couldn't follow at all. He smiled and said, "I'm sorry, I don't understand."

The sergeant looked at him and spoke clearly saying, "He said, de ye want a beer?"

Kurt shook his head. "Nein, no thank you." His accent was very pronounced.

The sergeant studied him closely. "Ah ye a Hun, a German?"

Kurt almost said yes without thinking, and then stopped himself just in time. These men were soldiers, and from what he had understood they'd come all the way from Bonn. They were part of the forces occupying Germany, and might be hostile to him if they thought he was from there. So he stopped himself in time and said, "Nein, I am Dutch."

The sergeant nodded and smiled "A Dutchy, eh? Well, come on man, take a beer. We're all friends here."

So Kurt took the offered bottle. It was the easiest thing to do. The beer was a pale ale from a brewery called Perkins and was full of gas.

The first stop was at Peterborough where two of the men got off for a brief leg stretch, letting a welcome but cold blast of fresh air into the carriage. Once underway again, Kurt was given another beer which like the previous one he sipped slowly, not really wanting it but also not wanting to antagonise the soldiers who were now becoming a bit drunk. The one who Vogel had discovered was called Jamie tried to get the woman to take a bottle. When she just shook her head, he persisted. "Come on, hen. Dinna be like that." In the end, the sergeant had to come to her rescue and say sharply, "Away with you, Jamie. Leave the wee woman alone now."

The train stopped at Grantham and then at York, before reaching Darlington in the early hours of Monday morning. The woman had got off at York, tight lipped and frowning at Jamie who lifted her case down off the rack for her. "She dinna even gi' me a smile, never mind a thank you," he complained as she left.

Kurt got off at Darlington overtired from lack of sleep, his leg hurting and his stomach bloated and rumbling as a result of the gassy ale. It was even colder here than it had been in London. There was a hard frost and all the surfaces were coated white. Thankfully the buffet was open and he got himself a coffee. The shuttle to Saltburn was already waiting at the short platform next to the Rocket, the first engine to run on the line. Feeling the need of some fresh air after the fug of the express train and the number of cigarettes he'd smoked, Kurt chose a 'No Smoking' carriage. This train had no corridor so he made use of the toilets on the platform before it started. Just before it left, a young woman with two small children got into his carriage. They had obviously been travelling all night like him, and the children were overtired and fractious. Despite his fatigue, they kept him awake all the way to Redcar where he got off. As it wasn't yet seven, it was far too early to go to Mrs Overton's B and B or the library. So once more he went into the small waiting room to shelter from the cold wind.

He hadn't been sat in the waiting room long before the door opened and a woman in an overall, carrying a bin and a brush and shovel, came in. She was short and overweight, with her grey hair wrapped in a sort of turban, and had a cigarette hanging down from crimson lips.

"Morning, ducky," she said with a grimace. "Cold, ain't it dearie. Do you mind, I've gotta clean up in here. Bit warmer than out on that perishing bloody platform, eh?" She sounded cheerful and easy going, and Kurt smiled at her.

"You must do vat you must," he said.

"Foreign, ain't you ducky," she said. "Still, no 'arm in that. We're all bloody friends now, ain't we?" She spat her cigarette out, stamped on it then picked it up and put it into her bin. "Gotta keep it tidy. Mind if I sit down a bit, out o' the wind like?" She seemed friendly, Vogel thought, and was a local and also worked at the station, so she may be able to help him.

He smiled at her. "No, it is much better in here out of the wind. Perhaps you can help me," he began, as she took a packet of cigarettes out. They were Wills Woodbines, he saw, which he knew was a cheap brand. "Here, have one of mine."

The woman eyed the white packet he held out. "Capstans, eh? Ta, don't mind as I do. So what's your problem?"

"I am going on a journey tomorrow. I need to get from here, cross the country and go to Liverpool. How can I find the right trains, and the times of them?" he asked.

"'S'no problem, darling," she said, drawing heavily on his cigarette. "Good fags these. Just go to the office in the entrance hall. Not the one you get the tickets at, the one next to it. Ol' Len in there has got a book, a sort o' timetable thing. It's full of all the trains, in England that is, and the times. He can get you anywhere you want. Clever bloke, ol' Len is."

"Thank you...." Kurt broke off as the door opened, and a tall man in a blue coat and cap with 'Stationmaster' on its rim came in. "'Ere Elsie, you can't sit in here all day skiving. Get out and do the job you're paid for, woman," he said. "Is she bothering you, sir?"

"No, no, quite the opposite," Kurt said. "She's been very helpful."

"Glad to 'ear it, sir," the stationmaster said, as Elsie left the room winking at the German.

Before Vogel left the station he went up to the Enquiries window, where Len lived up to Elsie's recommendation and found him a route to Liverpool. Kurt decided he'd need time to find his man, but also would have to move fast, so he told Len he wanted to leave the following afternoon. Len not only plotted the route for him, but sold him the tickets. From the station he went to Mrs Overton's to rent a room. She was very pleased to see him back again as he was a nice quiet guest, and there were hardly any visitors in the winter.

From there he went to the library and sat at a table going through the electoral roll and street directories. It was a long and fruitless search, which was made all the harder because his eyes were strained and gritty from his lack of sleep. Despite this, he was thorough but although he found a few Sudbury's none of them was a Lewis.

He was sitting moodily wondering what to do next, when he became aware of the two women behind the counter talking. "Oh, Beryl," one of them was saying. "What a lovely ring. You are so lucky and your Lewis, he's so handsome."

Lewis, he thought, it couldn't be, could it? He knew that Lewis was also a surname, he'd come across lots of them during his search. Shortly after that, he left the library and went into a cafe to have some lunch. He thought the best thing to do was to go back to the library to continue his search; perhaps he'd missed finding Sudbury that morning. He would just have to try again or admit defeat, and leave before MI5 caught up with him.

He was nearly asleep at the table where he was searching for Lewis, when the phone ringing at the desk brought him awake. One of the girls on the desk answered it then called to the other. "It's for you Beryl, Mr Sudbury."

Kurt was waiting outside when Beryl came out of the library. He would follow her to her address. It would be easier than trying to follow Lewis, he knew, as his last attempt to do that had proved. He had heard Beryl's' end of the conversation on the phone, and her subsequent comments to the other assistant. From this, he gathered that Lewis would be late home that evening and that Beryl was taking a friend she had just met home with her for the evening, someone called Ruth.

It was easy to follow the two women from the library to the bus stop, and then get on the number 73 bus behind them. On the bus, he realised why he'd not found Lewis at any address in Redcar as he lived in Saltburn. From the terminal in Saltburn, he followed the women to a house round the corner. It was in a street with a sign saying Albion Terrace. It wasn't far from the bus stop. He hung about on the opposite side of the road for a while to see if Lewis appeared. Because there were no houses on that side of the road and nowhere to hide, Kurt went a short way along the street to the entrance to the Ha'penny Bridge where he could stand hidden at the side of the toll booth. He stood beside this octagonal building for over an hour to no avail, getting colder and colder. He was almost asleep on his feet and his leg was aching badly. But Lewis didn't come home. He did learn from a board next to where he was hiding that it cost a halfpenny for every person on foot to cross the bridge, and one penny for every horse, mule or donkey that was led across. There were also charges ranging from two to four pence for carriages and wagons, and that all these charges were for one way. He kept himself awake by reading the list over and over again, but in the end went back to the bus terminus to return to Redcar. He was tired, really tired, and his leg was more painful than he had ever known it. As he got on the bus he belched loudly as the gas in his stomach from the beer came up. He needed to eat and more importantly to sleep. Reaching Redcar, he bought some fish and chips which he ate on the way to Mrs Overton's and then went straight to bed.

Despite his tiredness, he was disturbed all night by dreams of Scottish soldiers forcing beer on to him and pictures of the tariff board at the Ha'penny Bridge toll house. ½d for every person, 1d for every led horse, mule or donkey, went though his mind over and over again.

On the Tuesday morning he woke up to a silent world, with snow falling outside the window. The only thought in his mind was that today he was going to kill his nemesis, and then catch the early evening train to Edinburgh and on to Glasgow, Liverpool, Ireland and Argentina. He'd chosen to go north to Edinburgh, across Scotland and then south to Liverpool rather than York as he thought that might throw any pursuit off his tail.

CHAPTER 36

Detective Inspector Thomas Fenwick woke on the morning after Lewis and Beryl's engagement party completely disorientated. At first there was a feeling of panic, as his narrow single bed felt even more cramped than usual and he couldn't move. Then the warm body next to him moved and a muffled voice said, "Hey, stop pushing," and it all came back to him. Ruth Tremayne, the woman he'd not seen for years, had returned to Redcar with him yesterday and was here taking up more than her fair share of his bed. Ruth, who had an abusive American husband somewhere in Texas, and a daughter in Norfolk. A daughter, only three years old, who would become his responsibility along with Ruth if they were to stay together. Children, he thought, I'm not good with children. His sister's two came into his mind and how he couldn't relate to them, or them to him. Just at the moment, children were everywhere in his life. The two buried in the wood up near How End House, whose murder he was determined to solve regardless of his superintendent. Sir Keith and Angela's two who, it now transpired, had run away to their real father, so Lewis had told him. A man called Wilfred Lawrence, who was Angela's lover and a member of one of the Security Services, who broke all the rules he strove to maintain. Tom agreed with Lewis' suspicion that there'd been more than bullying and a bit of youthful sexual hanky panky behind their running off. Children, he thought to himself, everywhere I turn, bloody children. He knew he'd have to change his feelings towards them if he were to stay with Ruth.

Then the body in the bed next to him stirred again, and a finger poked him in the back.

"Hey, Inspector, is there any breakfast to be had in this place?" Ruth said from behind him.

"Not a lot," he said. "I've been away for four days, remember. There's porridge and I think I can hear the milkman's horse and cart outside, so there could be milk. I've a packet of tea and some sugar. There's not much else though."

The bed heaved beside him, and a naked body jumped out and quickly pulled on a few clothes.

"God, but it's cold, Tom," Ruth said. "I'll go down and catch your milkman, shall I?" and before he could answer she was gone. Tom wondered what the sight of a half naked woman coming out of his flat would do for his reputation, as he followed her out of bed and slowly dressed. He had acted completely out of character these last few days, he knew. He was normally a serious thoughtful man who acted with caution. But since that first impulsive decision to go to Wroxham, he'd acted instinctively and almost without thought. Now what, he wondered, as he went into the living room.

The flat though, for the first time since he'd moved in last year, felt like a home and welcoming. It even seemed warmer, though that was probably an illusion, with Ruth bustling round making tea and porridge. She had also found the end of a stale loaf of bread and two eggs, and was toasting the bread and boiling the eggs. One thing he did know was that if they stayed together, and young Glenda came to live with them, he'd have to find a larger place to live. *They'd* have to, he thought, not just me. Me, I'll have to overcome this indifference to children.

After breakfast, Ruth waved him off to work saying she would tidy up a bit, get some shopping in and look round the town. Then she'd arranged with Beryl to go to Saltburn with her for tea when she finished in the library. But she would, she assured him, be home in time for them to eat together that night. Before he left, he gave her his ration book and a spare key to the flat. As he kissed her when he left, he thought that that had probably committed him.

He spent much of the morning with DS Rutter going over his reports from the previous week.

"Well done, Ken," he praised his sergeant. "Now, what conclusions have you come to?"

The sergeant, whose bald head made him look older than his years, said, "It's too early yet, I think, sir. We know who the two children were now, and roughly when they were killed, but not much more. We need to dig more deeply, but it may have all happened too long ago. I think that Miss Waverly may know more and I've my suspicions about the McIntyre character. Then several masters, Jones, Partridge and Fenn-Williams, are often at Blue Doors where the boy lived. The girl, Alice Bates, was a friend of the matron, and lived there for a while when her dad died."

"So organise a couple of the DC's to help you dig deeper into them all over the next few days," Tom told him. "I still think Sir Keith Dyke has more to do with it as well, and he's a friend of that Fenn-Williams. I think he's almost moved into How End House since Lady Dyke moved out. So I'll go and have another word with both of them. If we can't find any clue as to how those kids died, we must try to make whoever's responsible make a slip, and admit something.

"Oh, and by the way, I think that those kids were probably taken to where they were buried down the lane from Ralph's Cross. I went there with the local PC, Jacobs is his name. It passes very close to the spot where they were found. It makes much more sense than them being carried up from How End. Which means that whoever did it must have a car, or at least access to one."

DS Rutter nodded. "And know about the lane, it's not on many maps, I've checked, and it's hard to find. So they'd need local knowledge. They must live or have lived up there or perhaps done a lot of hill walking."

"Which could bring us back to Sir Keith again," Tom said. "Right, Sergeant, onwards and upwards."

"Sir," replied the DS, thinking that his chief appeared to be happier and more alive than he'd ever seen him since his arrival here. The holiday must have done him good, he decided.

CHAPTER 37

It was Monday afternoon before the MI5 committee that were employing Kurt Vogel, or Otto Kohistedt as he now called himself, met to consider what to do about his disappearance. When he hadn't turned up that morning, his immediate superior Mr Jones had gone to his flat to find the reason for his absence. Receiving no reply to his hammering on the door of the flat, he'd forced an entry. He found it empty and cleared of all Vogel's possessions. After contacting the department, he carried out a full search of the flat but discovered very little that might reveal where he may have gone. In fact, the only things in the flat were a pile of newspapers and magazines and some charred pieces of paper in the otherwise empty hearth. The German must have been an avid reader of the news, Jones reckoned, as he skimmed through the back copies. He then carefully retrieved the unburnt fragments of paper from the fireplace to see what they'd been before Vogel burned them.

Early that afternoon, he returned to the Home Office to make his report. All he could say to the men gathered there was first that Vogel had disappeared without trace, leaving nothing behind. The second part of his report was an observation that in many of the papers certain adverts were ringed in pencil. These all had to do with travel companies that listed sailings to South American states. The third part concerned the charred paper remnants which may have been, in his reading of them, a compilation of times and prices. These were possibly to do with alternative plans of travel, he went on to say.

What they had to decide was if this was proof that Vogel was fleeing the country, or a bluff to divert their efforts of finding him away from the real reason for his flight. Namely that of travelling to the north east again to try and find Lewis

Sudbury, and then to get revenge for the bomb that had led to his injuries. If that was the case, the chairman said, they must stop it at all costs, as he had promised their sister organisation, Six, that they would protect the schoolteacher. He added that any failure to do this on their part would worsen the relationship between them, which wasn't particularly harmonious as it was. But he added if Vogel had simply done a runner after being warned that he was now under surveillance, he must be stopped and brought back.

In the end, the committee decided that what they must do was alert all their agents near any port from where boats sailed to South America to be on the alert to find and stop him. At the same time, their man on Teesside must also be contacted and given Lewis Sudbury's address and a description of Vogel without delay. They also decided to send two more agents from London to help him in this task, even though they thought they wouldn't get there in time. Whatever happened, Vogel had to be found and either eliminated or brought back to London without fail.

By six that evening, the MI5 agent based in Darlington was in receipt of his instructions, Lewis Sudbury's address and Vogel's description and he set off to Redcar to try and locate the German.

It was also at six that evening that Wilfred Lawrence, his preparations for leaving London early next morning complete, was listening to the BBC news. A large part of the broadcast was filled with reports of the winter conditions that were affecting the country. The fuel shortages were getting worse, and the Ministry of Fuel and Power was beginning to bring in emergency powers. If the extreme conditions persisted, they were proposing to restrict electricity supply to domestic consumers to nineteen hours each day and shut down some companies. Newspapers were already reduced in size and radio broadcasting, which was already limited, would be cut back even further, whilst the new television service was to be suspended completely. The bulletin also contained stories of animals and people dying from the frozen conditions. The item which concerned him most was the forecast of heavy snow storms that were due overnight. He had planned to leave London in the early hours to drive up to Redcar, but now decided that he must leave earlier. His motorbike was ready for him in the garage in East London. George had checked it over for him and made it roadworthy. The luggage rack on the back already had his suitcase and a spare five gallon can of petrol strapped on to it. Even without the petrol shortage, he knew that there would be no garages open overnight even on the A1. He turned off the radio and went to find Angela, who was busy in the kitchen, and told her that his plans had changed, and that he would be leaving that evening and not in the early hours of the morning as he had previously told her.

Eleven o'clock that night saw him setting out on his journey north. He was well wrapped up against the cold, wearing a heavy waterproof coat over his clothes, thigh high boots, fleece lined gloves, goggles and a pilot's fleece lined leather flying helmet which covered his head and ears. Despite this, he knew that the ride would be a cold one and he had a thermos of coffee in a rucksack, together with chocolate bars and Kendal Mint Cake. George, who had stayed up, waved him off as he headed for the Great North Road.

The road was virtually empty of traffic and the first stage went smoothly. Freddie drove through Hatfield and Stevenage without a hitch. Sometime later he stopped just before reaching St Neot's for a cup of coffee and some chocolate. Peterborough and Grantham were both empty and their streets deserted, such streetlights as there were shining through halos of frosty air. The only living things he saw were a couple of policemen walking their night time beats and a couple of dogs. At Newark-on-Trent he stopped again for more coffee and with cold numb hands filled his petrol tank from the can on the back of the bike. A few miles past Newark he ran into the first snowstorm and for a while had to pull off the road as his vision was too obscured to continue. Then he was reduced to a stop start crawl, and he didn't reach Doncaster until about six in the morning. The town was just beginning to stir, as people came out on to the snow covered streets to go to work. Originally he'd thought that he'd be in Redcar by now. He stopped again and sheltered beside the wall of Doncaster racecourse to finish his coffee, but it was lukewarm and it didn't warm him up much. So he found a workman's cafe open and went in to warm up properly and have some breakfast. Then he was back on the road heading north once more. Originally, he had planned to leave the A1 and go via Thirsk to Middlesbrough. But he decided the snow would be too deep on that route as it skirted the moors. So he stayed on the Great North Road until he reached Scotch Corner. By now it was well past nine, and the road through Darlington to Middlesbrough was also heavily snowbound. He went on, slithering and sliding with both feet on the ground on either side of the bike to keep it upright.

When he finally reached Redcar, it was nearly eleven. He stopped the bike outside a cafe and put it on its stand. He was cold, tired and stiff and when he got off the bike he couldn't stand up straight. He went inside to warm up and have a cup of coffee and something to eat. There was no rush, he decided, as he wasn't expected back in London for several days, and he certainly didn't want to travel back straight away. The snow couldn't last for long, he thought. He would thaw out then try to find the two abusers after lunch. After he'd dealt with them, then he could find somewhere to stay overnight and go back tomorrow or even the next day. When he was fully recovered and the weather had had a chance to improve. He sat back gratefully in his seat, feeling his muscles easing and a pleasant warmth spreading through his body.

PART FOUR
CHAPTER 38

The winter of 1946-47 was a harsh one in Great Britain, causing severe hardship economically and in the living conditions of almost everyone in the country. Animals and people suffered from the persistent cold temperatures, with many dying by freezing or starvation. Coal stocks ran low, energy was restricted and food stocks also diminished. Then, on Tuesday the 21st of January, massive snow storms swept the country bringing great disruption with them. There were power cuts, deep drifts of snow and a standstill on many roads and railways.

In Saltburn, Lewis and Beryl woke to an eerie silence on that Tuesday morning. They heard the milkman clanking bottles outside, but there was no sound of footsteps on the path or horses' hooves on the road. Shivering, Lewis got out of bed and went to the window, opened the curtains and looked out. It was only seven o'clock and still night outside. There was no moonlight as the new moon was only one day old, and in any case there was full cloud cover. Yet there was a luminous quality to the morning from the carpet of snow which covered everything. As he peered out, he saw the milk cart going silently along the street, all sound of hooves or wheels muffled by the snow on the ground. Then his vision was impeded as a flurry of snow hit the window. After breakfast they left to catch the twenty past eight bus to Redcar. It was running late due to the weather, and they didn't reach the clock tower there until nearly nine o'clock and after a hasty goodbye they each hurried to their work places, Lewis to St Bede's and Beryl to the library.

Tom Fenwick and Ruth Tremayne woke in Redcar to the same conditions as Lewis and Beryl had in Saltburn. The difference was that whilst Tom got out of bed, Ruth stayed put. Tom made breakfast and brought her hers in bed, before leaving early for the police station. Ruth said she'd get up later, go and visit Beryl in the library and then come back and make a lunch, after calling in at the police station to make sure he would be able to come home to eat it. Tom left the flat at ten to eight, and trudged through an inch or two of snow and a heavy blizzard to the police station. When he got there he found it cold and dark and almost empty. The heating wasn't working properly, the electricity was off and all the PC's on duty were out and about in the town, helping with the various emergencies caused by the sudden and violent blizzard. The desk sergeant told him that the failure of the power supply was due to some electricity cables that were down outside the town. In the CID room there was only DC Greg Lince there, all the rest of the squad were either already out on enquiries or had not yet arrived. He went to his desk and, keeping his overcoat on, started reading the incident log from the previous night by the light of an oil lamp.

In Mrs Overton's B and B, Kurt Vogel didn't wake until gone eight that morning. He was feeling much better than the previous day and refreshed after almost twelve hours sleep. Looking out of the window at the silent white world and the falling snow, he started to plan his day. He had to get everything over and done with before four or five o'clock that evening, as his train left Redcar station at five fifteen. Looking at the weather outside, he thought it might be to his advantage. It would surely delay any pursuit from London sent by MI5 to look for him. That was if the various clues he'd left as to where he was going didn't stop them from thinking he would waste time in his flight by looking for Sudbury. It would also help him get near to St Bede's without being seen. He had decided that the best plan would be to wait outside the school as it finished for the day and shoot Lewis as he left. It would be between half past three and four, he thought. Then he could go to the station to catch his train in good time. If Lewis was later leaving he would still have time, even if it made the time to catch his train a bit tight. If it was still snowing as much then as it was now, this would conceal him from being seen and help his escape. This morning he would pay Mrs Overton, take his luggage to the station to leave it in the left luggage office and then find a good place to hide outside the school. He would have time to go inside to look for Lewis, even if he stayed behind after the school finished. The building would be empty except for a few masters and perhaps some cleaners. All in all, he was feeling very optimistic as he ate his breakfast watching the blizzard outside.

In Darlington, the MI5 agent was cursing the snow that morning. He'd been given his instructions to protect Lewis Sudbury late yesterday afternoon, and travelled to Saltburn sometime later. He'd stood in the cold outside the house in Albion Terrace until ten that night then, deciding nothing would happen after that, came back to his home. He couldn't work twenty four hours a day every day, he decided, if the department wanted that sort of cover then he needed assistance. This morning he would go back and watch first the school at Redcar and then The Laurels in Saltburn, keeping an eye out for this Kurt Vogel character. The snow, he knew, would hinder both his search and his vigil.

◊　◊　◊　◊　◊

Lewis reached St Bede's at five past nine to find the school half empty. The place was cold and dark as the electricity was apparently off and the boiler struggling to cope. The floors were covered with moisture and littered with half melted snow off the shoes of the boys who'd managed to get into school. Barry Slingsby met him after assembly outside his classroom, and told him cheerfully that the coke for the boiler was almost gone and the delivery expected today was stuck somewhere up in Durham. There had been only about half the school at assembly and when he called the register, a lot of the boys were absent. He had hardly begun his first lesson when Slingsby came in to say that the head was closing the school for the day, and that all the boys were to go home. He also said that all the boarders in the class were to go to the hall and wait to be escorted back to Blue Doors. He told Lewis that the head wanted all the masters to go there as well.

Alistair Bartlett was waiting in the hall, and asked the teachers who had managed to get into school that morning to make sure that all the boys had left the school. On their way home they were to keep an eye open for any boys who were loitering in the town and urge them to go home. He asked Lewis and Mr Plinney, the housemaster of School House, to help Mr McIntyre to escort the boarders back to Blue Doors. Mr Plinney, because all the boarders were in School House, and Lewis because he'd had a lot to do with the boarders since Robert Dyke had run away last November. The three masters and the boys left St Bede's at about a quarter to ten.

They were the last to leave, and when Vogel arrived outside at just after eleven o'clock there was only Mr Willis, the headmaster and a few staff left in the building. It didn't take him long to realise the school was empty and his quarry gone. Vogel was glad he'd come to the school to reconnoitre the area, but worried as to where Lewis had gone or what he should do next. In the end he decided that his best bet would be to go to the library and keep a watch on Beryl Cooper. Lewis might, he reasoned, go there to see her.

The man from Darlington missed seeing Vogel by just a couple of minutes. If the day had been clearer, he would have caught sight of him from behind limping away and may have made the connection. As it was, the falling snow obscured his view. He too was unsure where to look for the schoolmaster and decided to go into the school to make sure he wasn't still there. By a quarter to twelve he'd established that Lewis was nowhere on the premises, so he walked into the town centre and went into a pub for a quick whisky to warm up and think of what he should do next. Perhaps Lewis had gone home and he ought to look for him in Saltburn. He was undecided, and in the end thought it would be better to look around the town first before going go to Saltburn. What he really needed was some help, but knew he'd just have to do the best he could. The men Five had told him they were sending to help hadn't arrived yet. They could well be stuck in the snow somewhere, he realised. Finding no trace of Lewis in Redcar, he took the ten to two bus to Saltburn, arriving there at about a quarter past two. Given the amount of snow that had fallen, the road wasn't too bad. It ran parallel to the coast and the salt air melted it almost as fast as it fell. The only difficult bit was just past the railway bridge at Marske where there was a steep hill. However, there were a couple of workmen with shovels scattering grit and the bus slowly climbed up the slope. He went to The Laurels in Albion Terrace which he found to be empty. Undecided on the best course of action, he decided to ring his boss in London from the nearest call box only to find the wires down. It was turning into a frustrating day. He decided his only option was to watch the house and wait for the schoolmaster's return.

◊   ◊   ◊   ◊   ◊

Earlier that morning, after all the boys and McIntyre had left Blue Doors to go to school, the matron Elizabeth Waverly had also gone out as it was her day off. This had left Tina Davis, her young assistant, in charge. Most of the dinner ladies and cleaners had managed to get into work despite the conditions, so her task was fairly straightforward. At about ten o'clock the boys had all returned, along with the three teachers. Once the boys were settled all the masters, including Mr McIntyre, had departed, leaving her in charge. She was quite used to this, as often in the evenings and at weekends she had been alone in charge of the house with only a few of the domestic staff there as well. Most of the boys stayed in their own rooms or in the common room, whilst a few went out into the playground to make snowmen or play snowballs.

Tina's only duties were to keep an eye on the cleaners, and check up on the boys from time to time to make sure none of them were up to any mischief. The kitchen staff were not really her responsibility as the head cook, Mrs Watson, could be relied upon for that.

She was in her office when one of the third form boys came in, looking very worried.

"Please, miss," he said hesitantly. "I think Robin Fry might be in trouble."

Tina looked at the small figure standing nervously beside her, staring at the ground rather than into her face. "You're Lightfoot, aren't you?" she asked. "Oscar, isn't it?"

He muttered, "Yes, miss," and she went on, "So, Oscar, what trouble do you think Robin is in?"

"Don't know, miss," he said in a low voice.

She looked at him and saw that he was nearly crying. She would have to go very gently here, she thought. "Don't be frightened, Oscar, you're not in any trouble. Just tell me what it's all about. That's a good lad."

It came out slowly in hesitant sentences, but at last she had the full story. The boy had seen Robin Fry being led out of Blue Doors by two people. Robin had been reluctant, he thought, and protesting but they had almost dragged him down the path to a car parked on the road outside. He had been pushed inside and the car had then driven off. Despite all her questions, he said that he'd not seen who the two people were because the snow had been too heavy and obscured his view. He could only add that he thought the car was quite big and either dark blue or black.

Tina went to the phone to ring the police station but discovered that it wasn't working. She put on her hat and coat, and Oscar fetched his, and they went off to the station together. It was only a ten minute walk and they got there at about ten forty five. Tom Fenwick was still at his desk and he saw them straight away. After listening to the story, he made several snap decisions. He decided that the boy had been abducted, and probably by the same people who had killed the others a few years ago. He'd been reading the notes of his interviews with Sir Keith Dyke and his suspicions of him were near to the surface of his mind. Sir Keith also owned a big black car and the bodies had been found near his house. It all made sense and he knew he must act, and act quickly, to save the boy. He called for DC Greg Lince, who was still the only other officer in the room, to come with him.

"Right, Miss Davis, leave it to me, I'll get him back for you. Take this youngster here back to Blue Doors and don't worry," he told the assistant matron.

On his way out, he stopped at the desk and told the sergeant all the details of what Tina Davis had told him and where he was going.

"Tell any of my DC's who come in all the facts. They can check out any other possible leads in case I'm wrong," he instructed the sergeant, adding, "If the phones come back on, ring the local PC at Castleton, PC Jacobs, and tell him to get out to How End."

By ten past eleven they were on the road in a large Wolsey, heading out of Redcar with DC Lince at the wheel, as the PC who would usually drive was out in the town dealing with the many crises brought about by the snow.

◊   ◊   ◊   ◊   ◊

Ruth had got out of bed at last some time after the DI had left for work, and true to her promise had gone out to do some shopping. Then at about half past ten she had gone to the library to see Beryl. The two women had discovered last night that they quite liked each other and were becoming friendly. Beryl told her that if the blizzard continued they would probably shut the library later in the morning, especially if the electricity didn't come back on.

"There's no one here and if there was, they wouldn't be able to see to read anyway," she said.

As they chatted Beryl suddenly said, "I'm a bit worried, Ruth. It's probably nothing but see what you think. Just the other day there was a bloke in here, foreign I think he was. Well, he was here all day and then I saw him again on the same bus as me to Saltburn when I went home. That's not all, I'm sure I saw him hanging around outside the house a bit later. It's probably nothing but I'm not sure. He walked with a bit of a limp." Then

217

she laughed. "Sorry, I don't want to make it sound melodramatic."

"Do you think he fancied you?" Ruth asked.

"I hope not. I've got enough on my hands already coping with Lewis," Beryl said raising her eyebrows and grinning.

Sometime later Lewis came in. "School's shut for the day," he said. "I'm not sure what I'll do, probably call in and see Tom for a bit this afternoon. If we miss each other, love, I'll see you at home." After a while, he suggested to Ruth that they could go and get a coffee to warm up, and she agreed.

"It's all right for some," said Beryl, as they left.

It was a quarter past eleven and Kurt Vogel missed them by a couple of minutes when he got to the library.

◊ ◊ ◊ ◊ ◊

The first stage of Fenwick and Lince's drive to Howdale went quite well. The road from Redcar to Marske was fairly easy as the snow was quite slushy and not too deep. Kit Plummer, the hill out of Marske, was still reasonably clear but once they'd turned off the Saltburn road to go to Skelton and then Lingdale their progress became slower. There were more hills and, as they went further inland, the snow got thicker on the ground and wasn't being melted by the sea air. Fortunately for them, there was a lull in the storm and the blizzard eased. They also followed a tractor ploughing the road from Lockwood Beck reservoir all the way to Castleton. They stopped at the police station and PC Jacobs organised a farmer to go in front of them to clear the road all the way to How End House. Their progress was slow but they reached the farm safely at about half past one. Leaving the tractor driver and PC Jacobs in the yard, Fenwick and Lince went to the back door of the house as the path to it had been cleared of snow. The front door had a two foot snowdrift in front of it. There was loud music coming from the house and as the door was not locked they went in.

"We can't waste time, Constable, if the boy's here he may be in danger," Tom said.

"It can't be the wireless, sir," Greg Lince said, "as there's no electricity. It must be a wind-up gramophone."

Tom said nothing in reply, wondering to himself just what that had to do with anything. They reached the door to the lounge from where the music was coming. As they stood outside, the strains of 'Sally, Sally, pride of our alley, you're more than the whole world to me' began to go slower and slower, distorting the voice, as the gramophone ran down, proving the DC's assertion that it was a wind up one.

"Right," said Tom. "In we go," and they burst through the door.

Two startled figures turned to look at them. In front of their eyes the policemen saw a peaceful scene. Seated beside a large log fire was Sir Keith Dyke, cigar in one hand and a glass in the other. Next to him was a coffee table with a chess set on it and a malt whisky bottle on the floor beside it. How does he manage to get hold of malt whisky these days? was the inconsequential thought that came to Tom. Standing beside a large wooden gramophone, turning the handle to wind it up, was Edgar Fenn-Williams with a glass in his free hand. As the vibrant tones of Gracie Field's voice once more filled the room, Tom stammered, "Sorry sir, gentlemen. Sorry to disturb you."

It took quite a while for the DI to explain why they were there. He ended, "I'm sorry, but I thought the boy might have been brought up here and be buried like the others."

"You suspected me?" said Sir Keith.

"Well, not really, but I have to look at all possibilities," Tom said, regaining some composure.

"Ah well, never mind. I hope you find the lad," said Sir Keith, whilst Fenn-Williams looked on sardonically.

"God, yes. Come on, Constable, we'll have to get back and organise the search. Sorry to have troubled you, sir," he said and the two policemen went out of the room.

◊　◊　◊　◊　◊

DS Jack Voyle and DC Hubbert got to the police station in Redcar just over half an hour after the DI had left to drive to Castleton. They'd been out to a break-in in one of the houses near Redcar racecourse. They were cold and were thankfully drinking a cup of tea made for them by the desk sergeant, who then passed on the message that the DI had left.

"It's not Dyke," Jack Voyle said irritably. "It's those two so-called cousins who live up there."

"Have they a car, Sarge?" Hubbert wanted to know.

"How the hell do I know?" Voyle snarled. "I wasn't allowed to talk to them. Come on, Constable, drink up, we'll go up there and nab them."

"Do you think we should?" the constable began.

"Shut up. Just do as you're ordered." And he led the way out of the station to the old Ford car used by CID. "You drive," he told Hubbert. They had less trouble than the DI had in driving up to How End House, as the road was still reasonable where it had been cleared from Castleton to Howdale for the DI. Despite having set out more than half an hour after Fenwick, they arrived at How End House just five minutes after him. Ignoring PC Jacobs and the tractor driver, Voyle led Hubbert to the back door of the cousins' house which had also been cleared of snow. As with How End House, the door to their cottage was also unlocked.

"Who would bother to lock their doors out here?" Hubbert said, as he opened it.

Voyle pushed impatiently past him and went into the entrance lobby. From upstairs they could hear loud noises, banging and shouts.

"See, I told you so," said the sergeant, starting up the stairs. "Come on man, the boy's still alive by the sound of it."

Reaching the top of the stairs, he burst into the bedroom with the constable close on his heels. Inside the room he stopped in his tracks. "Bloody hell," he said.

In the room on the large double bed were four naked figures. There were the two cousins and the widow from next door, and a younger woman he recognised as one of Sir Keith's daily helps. DS Voyle hadn't seen a fully naked woman before. His wife went into the bathroom to put on her nightie before going to bed. Just what the four were doing he couldn't imagine. All his married life his wife had lain under him, her nightdress raised above her waist, allowing him once a week what she referred to as his 'rights' and doing 'her duty'. Whatever these four were up to, he now knew that he'd been entirely wrong in his suspicions of the cousins being homosexuals. His jaw dropped in confusion, and red faced he turned and went out of the room and back down the stairs.

DC Hubbert grinned at the four startled faces staring at him. "Sorry, folks," he said. "Carry on," and he went out of the room, shutting the door behind him, and followed his sergeant down the stairs.

Outside the four policemen met up. "What are you doing here?" Fenwick asked Voyle, receiving no satisfactory explanation from the still confused sergeant. "Well, we need to get back to Redcar, there's still a missing boy and time is passing."

It was now gone two o'clock and they had a long drive back. To make matters worse, the snow had started falling again quite heavily. It would be a slow drive, Tom knew, cursing at himself for having rushed off on a wild goose chase.

CHAPTER 39

The two abusers had lain low ever since the boy had run away from Blue Doors and the two bodies had been discovered near How End House. Since then there had been police everywhere, questioning everyone. Also Lewis Sudbury had been poking his nose into everything, on the behest of both the headmaster of St Bede's and the police.

In the past they had chosen and nurtured their victims with care. They would select a first year boy who was shy and a bit of a loner and also a boarder at Blue Doors. One of them would befriend him, and from time to time touch his arm in a supportive way. Slowly they would progress from arm touching to short hugs and murmured words of support. They took their time over this, and it was usually when the boy was in his second year at school that they progressed to more direct methods. As the boy now fully trusted them, they started giving him small gifts and treats. The final stage, which often didn't happen until the target was in his third year, was to take him for rides in the car and on to their house. By now the boy was usually totally in their control and then the abuse started. More often than not the boy was now too far under their control to object, and too cowed or not confident enough to complain about their activities. They were after all adults and in positions of authority in St Bede's. Who would believe him rather than the two abusers? In this way, they'd been able to procure a steady flow of victims over the years.

There had only been two unfortunate incidents. The first had been when Alice Bates was living in Blue Doors after her father died. She had come across them leading a boy out to their car. The boy was crying and trying to run off, and Alice had come to his aid. In the end they'd had to let the boy go back indoors and had forcibly taken Alice away. She wouldn't listen to them, and threatened to report them to the headmaster. To shut her up, one of them had hit her hard on the back of the head with the car's starting handle. They drove up to the small road from near Ralph's Cross to Farndale and buried her in the woods. One of them knew the area well and they didn't think she would ever be discovered.

The second incident happened two years later. One of their boys, Percy Kerridge, who they had thought they had sufficiently subdued into compliance resisted at the critical time. He was an adopted boy and his foster parents had just been killed in an air raid, which could have explained his sudden resistance, they decided later. Whatever the reason, the outcome was the same as it had been with Alice and he ended up next to her in the wood. Both these events had happened during the war, and the general state of confusion and unrest at that time had resulted in nobody worrying about either of the disappearances.

Since then they had been very cautious, and had taken longer to groom their victims before making a move to take them away in the car. Everything had gone smoothly until young Robert Dyke had run away, bringing an enforced lull in their activities. Today, however, they calculated that the police had given up on the two murder cases and it was safe to restart them. The blizzard would also help them, as it would reduce visibility to almost zero and so prevent anyone from observing them taking the boy away from Blue Doors.

They had not foreseen two things. The first was that it was a few weeks since the last time they'd been in touch with Robin Fry, and in that time he had developed a friendship with Oscar Lightfoot. They had also not observed Lightfoot watching them leading his reluctant friend away, nor could they envisage him going to Tina Davis to tell her what he'd seen.

◊   ◊   ◊   ◊   ◊

It was just after twelve, and a few minutes since DS Voyle had started out on his journey to Howdale, when DS Ken Rutter and DC Teddy Metcalf returned to the police station. This coincided with Lewis Sudbury also coming there to look for Tom Fenwick, to see if he wanted to go for a lunchtime drink with him.

The desk sergeant brought them up to date with what was happening and where the DI and Sergeant Voyle had gone. He then tried to get through to the inspector's car on the radio telephone, but the combined effects of the power shortage and the blizzard made this impossible.

"We need a car, Sergeant," DS Rutter said. "If the two people Oscar Lightfoot saw taking the boy put him in a car, he could be anywhere. Is there a spare one in the garage?"

"Well, Sergeant Voyle has taken the CID Ford but I think there's still one of the Wolsey's left. But I have nobody to spare to drive it," the desk sergeant told him.

"That's ok, we'll drive it ourselves," Rutter said. Then, turning to Lewis, said, "Would you come with us, sir? You know Blue Doors and Miss Davis. It would help us if you would."

"Of course, Sergeant," Lewis said. All three of them left the building to go to the garage to get the car.

They were at Blue Doors by twenty past twelve where they met up with Tina Davis. "As far as I'm aware, Miss Waverly is still out somewhere, it's her day off, and I haven't seen her since breakfast. And I've no idea where Mr McIntyre is."

"I think he might still be at the school," Lewis said.

"Right," the DS said. "We'll check Miss Waverly's flat first, and then decide where to look after that."

Tina Davis led the way to the matron's flat, which was at the top of the house up the back stairs used only by the staff. It was a solid old building built in the 1800's, and they could hear no sounds coming from anywhere in the house. As they neared the entrance to the matron's flat however, they heard sounds coming from inside. It sounded as if someone was crying out in either pain, excitement or pleasure. They all stared at each other.

"I don't like the sound of that," the sergeant said. "Do you think it's young Fry in there? If so, what are they doing to him?"

Another loud scream came from inside the flat. Rutter looked at Metcalf and said, "Right, Ted." At which the constable raised his foot and kicked hard at the lock, and the door swung open. They all rushed in, and then into the room on the left hand side of the entrance lobby from where the sounds were coming. Inside they found the matron and Ian Jones, the maths teacher, in the final stages of coitus. Jones, the DS noted as he surveyed the scene, had been one of the teachers on the police list of suspects.

"What the hell are you all doing in my flat?" Elizabeth Waverly said angrily. She was the first to recover from the shock of the intrusion.

DS Rutter did his best to explain and dissipate her anger, but it was only when the matron and Ian Jones realised that a boy could be in danger that they both calmed down.

The three men and Tina Davis went back downstairs, wondering what to do next. Then Lewis remembered what Titch Roberts had said to him in the Alexander Hotel toilets on Sunday night at the party. "We need to go to the Park Hotel," he said. "I think the assistant manager might be able to give us some vital information."

Wilfred Lawrence was sat looking out of the bar of the Park Hotel, drinking a large gin and tonic, when he saw the Wolsey pull up and Lewis get out and come into the hotel. After his warm up in the cafe, he had decided that he needed to find somewhere to stay. He was cold to the bone still, stiff and very tired. He couldn't face looking for his prey any longer today. There was no rush, he had reasoned, he could do it tomorrow. In any case, the thought of driving back to London on his bike through the snow horrified him. The weather could improve by the weekend and make the return journey if not pleasant much less of a nightmare, he'd thought. So he had come to the Park, and was now relaxing and waiting to have a bath. The assistant manager had told him that with the fuel shortages the water wouldn't be hot enough for him to have one until later in the day. They only heated it once a day at present, due to their low coal stocks, he'd said. One thing this escapade had taught him was that he wasn't fit enough anymore to be a field agent, having spent too much time behind a desk. When he got back to the office next week that was where he'd stay, he decided grimly.

As he sat in the bar, he saw Lewis come into the hotel and go to the assistant manager's office. When Lewis came out of the office some minutes later and go past him on his way back to the car, Freddie turned away so that the teacher wouldn't recognise him. I wonder what he wanted with the assistant manager, he thought. Well, whatever it was, it couldn't be to do with him. As the car drove off he finished his drink and ordered another. Tomorrow, he thought, that's when I'll go after the two abusers.

◊ ◊ ◊ ◊ ◊

Lewis Sudbury was sitting in the assistant manager's office in the Park Hotel. It was one o'clock, and waiting impatiently outside in the Wolsey were DS Rutter, DC Metcalf and Tina Davis. The DS had asked Tina to come along, in case they found young Robin Fry alive but in a distressed state. The matron had come down from her flat and taken charge of Blue Doors in her absence, despite it being her day off.

"Come on, Titch, you must tell me the names. I know you don't want to, but a young boy may be in danger," Lewis urged the assistant manager gently.

At last Billy Roberts gave in and hesitantly, almost whispering, he gave Lewis two names.

"Thanks, Titch," he said quietly, before rushing out of the door to the others. "I know where he lives," he told them. "It's not a long drive, just a short way over the level crossing near the railway station."

Teddy Metcalf who was driving started the car and they were off. They reached the house quickly and were there by a quarter past one, just over three hours after Oscar Lightfoot had witnessed his friend Robin Fry being bundled into a car by two people. The curtains of the house were closed and the place looked as if it was empty. The path to the front door, which had obviously been cleared of snow earlier that day, was now covered by a fresh two inch layer.

The four people got out of the car and went up the path, and DC Metcalf hammered on the door and shouted, "Police. Open up." This brought no response and he said, "Don't look like he's in, Sarge."

Then the door of the next house opened and a middle-aged woman looked out. "I know he's in," she said. "His car's parked in the back lane. Terrible weather, ain't it? It's so cold and me electric fire won't go, or the lights," she complained.

228

"Power lines down, madam," the DS said, then to Metcalf added, "Ok, Ted, do your stuff."

"Right, Sarge," Teddy Metcalf said and charged the door with his shoulder. It took him three goes before the lock gave way and the door opened.

"'Ere, what's he doing?" the woman asked, venturing out into the snow which was only falling lightly at present.

"Police, ma'am," Rutter said, before leading the others into the house.

Upstairs in a bedroom lit only by candles, behind closed curtains, they found two men hastily dressing themselves and a naked boy crouching in the corner.

"Look after him please, Tina," said the DS, then he turned to the two men and said, "Albert McIntyre and Sylvester Partridge, I'm arresting you both on the charge of molesting boys in your care. Get the cuffs on them, Ted." He turned to Lewis with a grimace. "Thanks for your help, Mr Sudbury. Do you think we can get 'em for the murder of those two up in Howdale?"

"I'm not sure," Lewis said. "But I do know Billy Roberts, the assistant manager at the Park, who comes from Farndale, told me that Partridge here is from there as well. So he'll know all about the lane through the woods."

"That's enough for me," the DS said. "I'll get the DI to add that to the charge if I can."

Tina Davis had taken Robin Fry out of the room to the bathroom to clean him up and get him dressed.

"We'll get the lad back to Blue Doors as soon as we can and get a doctor to him. Then, as soon as possible, we'll take these two back to the station. Come on, we'll do a quick search of the house first," the DS said to the constable. Then he turned to Lewis. "Can you go back to the station and ask the sergeant to send a couple of PC's with the Black Maria for these two?

Thanks for all your help, I'll see you back at the station when we bring them in."

Lewis got back to the station and told the desk sergeant what DS Rutter required and then sat down in the lobby to wait for the two men to be brought in.

He had just sat down when Ruth Tremayne came in looking to see if Lewis was there, or failing that if anyone knew where he was. Lewis listened to what she had to say then said to the sergeant, "Sorry, I've got to go. Something urgent just came up. Tell Rutter and Tom when he gets back I'll see them soon." Then he turned and quickly left the police station. The boy might be found, and the abusers of both him and Robert Dyke in jail. The murderer of the two children in Howdale may have been caught but he was worried about the safety of Beryl, given what Ruth had just told him.

◊   ◊   ◊   ◊   ◊

After Lewis had left the hotel, Wilfred Lawrence sat on in the lounge sipping his drink. He decided to go up to bed and have a rest. He was really very tired after the long drive in the cold. He finished his drink and stood up, just as Billy Roberts came in looking pale and distraught.

Freddie said, "Hello, old man, you look in a bit of a state. Can I get you a drink?"

"Thank you, sir," Billy said gratefully. "That's just what I need. I'd like a whisky."

When the drink came Freddie said, "Wasn't that Lewis I saw you with a bit ago?"

"Yes. Do you know him?" Billy asked.

"Oh yes, we're old friends," Freddie answered. He'd seen Lewis get into the black Wolsey which he thought was a police car and was curious. "I think he said he was helping the police with some enquiries the last time I saw him."

"He is," said Billy. "He wanted some help from me."

"Really," Freddie said. "I hope you could help him."

Slowly it all came out. Billy had been emotionally upset telling Lewis all about his abuse as a child whilst at Blue Doors, and now in the anticlimax was glad to have someone to listen to him as he tried to come to terms with it all. Someone who was a friend of Lewis, a stranger and only here for a few days seemed to be ideal. The man was also friendly and sympathetic and was a good listener, and so it all came pouring out.

It all took some time to tell and then Freddie couldn't just rush away. But as soon as he could, he left the hotel and got on to his bike again. He went to the address where Billy had told Lewis that the two men lived to find them. When he got there it was snowing heavily once again, but he could see there was a Black Maria outside the house. He then sat there unseen by the policemen, watching as the two men were led out.

CHAPTER 40

Earlier that morning, Lewis and Ruth had left the library to go for a coffee, just minutes before Kurt Vogel had reached there looking for him. Vogel went into the building, and once more went to the reference section and took down some books. He sat at one of the tables pretending to read them. He saw that the same woman was at the desk, the one he now knew was Sudbury's girlfriend.

Beryl Cooper looked at the German with a frown. Just who was he, this man who'd been here twice recently and who she'd thought was on the same bus to Saltburn last night? She was almost sure that she'd also seen him outside The Laurels in Albion Terrace a bit later that same evening. All she knew about him was that he was a foreigner, she could tell that from his accent. She thought he could be German or Dutch or even perhaps Swiss. She knew he walked with a slight limp, as if he had a stiff leg, and had a scar down one side of his face. He always wore a black glove on his right hand. A hand he never used except to steady things and which she thought must be injured in some way. Beyond that she knew nothing of him, except that was that he wore a greenish hat with a curled up brim that had a feather in the grey band round it. She thought it was called a Tyrolean hat, which probably made him Austrian or Swiss, she decided.

At one o'clock, the senior librarian came out of his office and told the women behind the desk to close the library. The electricity hadn't come back on and they were running short of coke for the central heating boiler. With the cloud cover and falling snow, there was barely any light to read by inside the library. "What's the use of a library where you can't see to read?" he asked them. So the two women went round the few customers, asking them to leave the building as the library was closing. Vogel got up and went outside and hid in a nearby doorway. Then, when Beryl came out a few minutes later, he followed her. She went towards the police station to see if Lewis was there but on the way met Ruth, who was on her way back to the library to find her. Ruth told her that she hadn't seen Lewis and that Tom was on his way to Howdale.

"It's something to do with a missing boy, the sergeant at the police station told me," she said.

"Oh dear," Beryl said. "Not another one." Then, when Ruth asked what she was talking about, said, "My sister's son, Bob, went missing a bit ago. It's a bit difficult to explain but he ran off to London with his sister. But they're both alright now. I hope they find this one soon."

"The police are in a bit of a panic about it," Ruth said. "But I expect that's to be expected if a kid goes missing in this sort of weather."

They walked for a bit and Beryl said, "I think I'll go home, tell Lewis where I am if you see him, will you?"

"Sure," said Ruth. "I'll walk to the bus stop with you." The 'sure' was drawled out and the 'I'll' came out more like 'Arl'. She still hasn't lost all her American accent yet, Beryl thought. She then told Ruth that the strange man that she thought may have been following her had been back in the library that morning.

"You take care of yourself now, Beryl," Ruth said in reply.

Soon after that the bus arrived and Beryl got on and sat downstairs, smiling out at Ruth on the pavement. It was just about to leave when a man jumped on to the platform at the back and went upstairs. As the red double decker with 'Saltburn 73' on the back began to move off, she saw that he had a stiff leg and was wearing a hat which was exactly as Beryl had described. He also had a black glove on his right hand.

"God, that's him, he's following her again," she muttered to herself. She must find Lewis and tell him, but where would she find him? The first place to look, she decided, was the police station. Tom might be back and, failing all else, she could leave a message for one of them.

It was just a quarter to three when she got to the station and Lewis was there. She took him to one side and told him all Beryl had said about being followed and described the man. She then added that she was sure that she'd seen the man get on the ten to two bus after Beryl. Lewis looked at his watch and saw that it was now nearly ten to three. He would have just missed a bus, and there wouldn't be another one until twenty past. There was a train though, which he might just make if he hurried. Running was difficult on the snow covered pavements, and the snow was also now falling more thickly again. Despite this, he caught the train with a couple of minutes to spare. The train only stopped twice between Redcar and Saltburn, at Redcar East Halt and Marske, and he was there at three fifteen, just over an hour after Beryl had arrived. When he left the station, it was already getting dark because of the low cloud and the snow had turned once more into a blizzard. He hurried along the street towards his home.

Beryl's bus had reached Saltburn on time at ten past two, just five minutes before the man from Five got there. The blizzard was beginning again and she hurried home with her head down into it, and with her vision extremely limited. Behind her, Vogel struggled to keep her in sight as his false leg made walking on the snow covered pavements difficult. He wasn't particularly worried as he knew where she was heading. When she was unlocking the front door, he was at the gate keeping himself concealed behind the hedge. The house was in darkness and the door locked, so he knew that Sudbury, or Manuel Ortega as he still thought of him, wasn't at home. Through the windows he saw Beryl lighting candles and then drawing the curtains. He decided he'd go in and wait for his quarry in the house, it would be warmer and dryer than waiting out here in the snow. He looked at his watch and sighed. It was already gone two fifteen and he had to catch the train in Redcar at five fifteen. He thought he could probably get on it in Saltburn but wasn't sure, as he'd no real knowledge of where it went after Redcar. Even if he could, he thought, it would probably go at about half past three. There was another problem with catching it at Saltburn, as he'd left his luggage at Redcar left luggage office. Should he take a chance on that and abandon his luggage, or leave on the twenty past four bus as the next one at ten to five might not give him enough time at Redcar? He was fully aware of the bus times, having used them so much and studied the timetable. Whichever he did, time was still short and he couldn't delay his departure as he knew that MI5 would be looking for him. He only had about an hour to spare, and feared that Lewis might not come back in that time. He decided he would go into the house and wait for half an hour or so, and then leave if Ortega hadn't come back by then. What he'd do in that case would be to kill the girl. He knew that was a way to make Ortega suffer, especially if he thought it was his fault. Vogel, his mind made up, walked up the path and knocked on the door.

Beryl opened the door to find the man she'd been sure was following her outside, hat in hand, smiling at her.

"You are Beryl Cooper, Mr Sudbury's friend, Ja?" he asked. "Can I speak to him please, he knows me."

"He's not in," Beryl said. "He should be home by six at the latest. Can you come back then?"

"Not really," said Vogel. "Can I come in and wait to see if he comes back earlier, please? It's cold and wet out here." Then, without waiting for an answer, he pushed past her. "Thank you, Miss Cooper," he said once he was inside. Beryl wasn't sure what to do. She stood there in indecision until Vogel said, all hint of a smile gone from his face, "Sit down. Now we wait. Ja?" Feeling quite frightened, Beryl sat beside the fire she'd just been reviving.

Outside, unknown to them, the man from Five had just arrived. He could see the candle light behind the curtain and thought, 'I wonder if Sudbury is home or just his girlfriend.' Never mind, he would go some way up the road and find somewhere out of the snow if at all possible to watch the house.

Vogel gave it until nearly twenty to four before he decided it was time to go. He wouldn't take a chance on the train to give more time for Lewis to get back. He would catch the twenty past four bus and so give himself plenty of time to get to the station. Now he knew it was time to go. They'd sat in silence waiting, but now he took out a gun and buttoned up his overcoat.

"Right," he said. "Come on. We're going out."

"Out?" said Beryl. "Why?"

Vogel grabbed her roughly and pulled her to the door. She struggled, but he was far too strong for her and he pushed her outside. On the way, he dropped his hat in the hall but didn't notice. Once outside, he took her over the road and walked them towards the Ha'penny Bridge. The snow was falling so thickly that they couldn't be seen from the pavement on the other side of the road. Beryl was only wearing a skirt and blouse, and was soon wet to the skin and very cold. They reached the gates to the bridge which were locked. Vogel aimed his pistol at the lock and shot it out, then dragged the woman through and into the middle of the bridge. Here he stopped. "Sorry about this," he told the shivering woman insincerely.

"What are you going to do?" she whimpered.

"Throw you over. Lewis will think you've committed suicide. That'll be bad enough, but when I get to Ireland I will send him a letter telling him what I've done. Then he'll blame himself for the rest of his life. But don't worry, I'll knock you out first so you won't feel anything." And he raised the pistol, holding the barrel to bring the butt down on to her head.

Suddenly there was a figure behind him and the barrel of a gun came down on to Vogel's head, splitting it open. In one movement, the man who'd wielded the gun caught the German before he fell and bundled him over the railings. They both watched him fall and disappear into the blizzard.

"Sorry I'm a bit late," said the man from Five. "I missed you at first because of the snow. But better late than never. You'll be Miss Cooper, I take it. Good. Well, let's get you home."

He put his pistol away and bent down to pick up Vogel's which had fallen on to the ground. "Can't leave that here or people will think it wasn't suicide," he said cheerfully.

Lewis had passed Vogel and Beryl on the other side of the road without seeing them because of the snow. He reached The Laurels and saw the door was open. "Beryl?" he shouted, without getting a reply. Then he saw the Tyrolean hat lying in the hall. "Hell," he swore and ran back out. There were tracks in the snow going across the road and, as he followed them across, he heard a loud bang which was muffled by the snow. But he knew the sound of gunfire when he heard it and ran in the direction it had come from. He almost ran past the entrance to the bridge, until he saw that the footsteps went towards the gate and that it was open. The smell of cordite was still in the air and he ran on to the bridge. He came across two figures suddenly in the middle. One was a man, his back towards him, with a gun in one hand and the other Beryl just beyond him.

This was what Lewis was trained for and he raised his arm to chop the man hard on the back of his neck.

"No, Lewis, don't," Beryl screamed out, making him hesitate for a moment. The man turned and Lewis saw it wasn't Vogel. Confused, he said, "Who the hell are you?"

Smiling, the man said, "Lewis? Good, yes, well Miss Cooper will explain. I have to go now. Nice to have met you," and he walked past Lewis and disappeared into the snow.

POSTSCRIPT

Later that year on a Sunday in early September, four people were sitting round a table outside the Ship Inn in Saltburn. The Ship Inn is in old Saltburn, which is at sea level below the newer and larger town on the cliffs above. It is reached by a steep hill with an S bend that runs from Glenville Terrace above down to the promenade below. The day was sunny with a blustery cool light breeze. But here, sheltered from the wind, it was warm and pleasant.

Lewis Sudbury, who was one of the four, said, "They seem to be enjoying themselves and getting on well together, despite them not having the same language." Below them two children were playing on the sands, Glenda, Ruth's daughter, and a swarthy dark haired boy of about the same age.

"Yes," agreed Ruth. "That's good, isn't it Tom? I expect they'll be seeing a lot of each other." Her American accent had almost disappeared after over a year back in England.

Tom Fenwick grunted. He had by now almost overcome his previous ambivalence about children having lived with Ruth and her daughter since February, seven months ago. Looking at Ruth, he knew that he'd have to fully reconcile his feelings about them as it was now very obvious that she was pregnant.

Beryl, the other person in the group, said, "How's the situation now with that husband of yours, Ruth? His name's Todd, isn't it?"

"Yes, Todd Blevins." Ruth herself had gone back to her maiden name of Tremayne when she'd come back to England. "I think the divorce is going through." She looked at her stomach. "It might be in time for Tom and me to get married and make this one legal. Now, tell me more about where you found that boy down there playing with Glenda."

"It's a long story," said Lewis. "He's the son of my mother's sister's granddaughter. We rescued him, I think that's the right word, when his parents were killed when we were on our honeymoon in Spain." Lewis and Beryl had got married in August and then gone off on a four week honeymoon in Spain. Beryl had wanted to go there to see where Lewis' mother had come from, and where he'd gone on holiday as a child. She'd heard a lot about it from Lewis, and he had also been keen to meet up with his mother's family again. All they had told Tom and Ruth about it was that the village Lewis' family lived in was a remote one in the sierras near Málaga, and the last seven or eight kilometres to it could only be reached on a mule track as there was no road. They wouldn't tell the others the name of the village, or exactly what had happened to the boy's family. "It would put them in danger if Franco's police ever got to hear about it," Lewis had told them. "You have no idea just how repressive and vindictive the regime is." Tom had an idea that Fermin, as the boy was called, had been smuggled out of the country, but neither Lewis nor Beryl would say anything about it. "That's another story," was all they would say. "Perhaps one day, when it's safer, we'll tell you about it."

"Do you know it's the seventh of September and that my first visit to St Bede's was the ninth, almost exactly a year ago? Six days after that first visit, term started and all those events occurred," Lewis said, to change the subject.

For a while there was silence, and then Lewis went into the Ship to buy more drinks. The shortages of the past few years were not as bad now and austerity was finally beginning to ease, and he came back with sandwiches as well as drinks and ice creams for the children.

Tom said, "We never did get any further with that German who chucked himself off the Ha'penny Bridge." He wasn't at all

240

convinced about the suicide or Lewis' denial of any knowledge of it. He didn't think Lewis had killed the man, but strongly suspected he knew more about it than he was saying.

"Didn't you?" Lewis said, keeping his gaze away from Beryl. She'd got over the events of that night but they still gave her the heebie jeebies, as she put it. The body hadn't been found for eight days because of the weather. It had been buried under snow and hardly anyone had gone walking in the valley gardens. The suspicions of the DI had been raised when he found two passports in the man's pockets, one in the name of Kurt Vogel and the other of Otto Kohistedt. He'd also had a small silver badge which he'd been told was the symbol of the SS. In another pocket was a scrap of paper on which was written 'The Laurels' and some bus times. Lewis though had always denied any knowledge of the man or how he'd come to fall off the bridge near his home, and Tom had no grounds to doubt him. Only suspicions. He knew Lewis had been in the SOE in the war and suspected it was all to do with that. Probably it was all down to the funny sods, as he called the security services. If so, he'd never know the truth of it.

To take the inspector's mind off Vogel's apparent suicide, which clearly he still wasn't happy about, Lewis said, "And what about the shooting that happened after I'd left DS Rutter at the house with McIntyre and Partridge?"

"If only I'd not been stuck up on the moors in all that snow," Tom said mournfully. It had been a constant complaint of his ever since that day in January. "No. We never found out who did that. I told you that before you went off to Spain, and nothing has changed since. I think that all my enquiries have been thwarted by the brass. They don't seem interested about what happened to those two. But in my book, murder is murder."

"Would you ever have been able to convict them of the murders of the two children?" Lewis asked.

"No, as I told you then, we didn't have any evidence. But they would have got long sentences for the abduction and abuse of Fry. Probably of about twenty years or so. But you knew all this before you went to Spain and nothing has changed."

They sat for a few moments, thinking of the events of that day in January. The blizzard had been at its height when the two men had been led out of the house. As they were nearing the Black Maria, two shots had rung out and both men fell dead on to the snow, shot through the head. All had been confusion, Rutter had said, and they couldn't see anything clearly for the snow. It had been remarkably accurate shooting, given the conditions, from someone who was obviously a skilled marksman. All that Rutter or DC Metcalf could remember was hearing a motorbike being kick started and then driven off.

"But that may not have had anything to do with it," they'd said.

"At least young Robin Fry came through it alright," Lewis said. "His parents took him out of St Bede's as you know, and the last I heard he was doing well in his new school in York. I went there to visit him. I don't think I've ever told you that," he added.

There was a long silence as they all looked at each other. They'd gone over this many times since January. To change the subject, Beryl said, "We called in to see my sister Angela and the children on the way home from our honeymoon. They're all very well. The divorce has come through, and she and Freddie plan to get married next month. They've asked me to be a matron of honour. Oh, and Freddie has legally adopted Bob and Kitty. Apparently Freddie had a very bad bout of flu earlier this year, I think it was in February or perhaps the end of January. Sometime like that, during that awful snowy period. It turned into pneumonia, I think, and it got quite nasty, Angela said. He was lucky, I suppose, a lot of people died during that awful weather. But he's alright again now. He looked quite fit when we saw him last week, didn't he Lewis?"

Beryl sat gazing out towards the horizon. She was pleased they'd stopped talking about the man who'd tried to kill her. She still hadn't fully got over that afternoon when the German has tried to throw her off the Ha'penny Bridge. Shortly after that, the two children finished their ice creams and went back on to the beach with Ruth. Then Lewis asked Tom how Middlesbrough had been doing that season so far and Tom began to tell him. Tom knew he'd get no more out of Lewis now about either the German or his adventures in Spain.

Printed in Great
Britain
by Amazon